CLOSURE

Garrett Addison

ISBN: 978-0-9870591-6-1

1

'It's time', Cliff Stokes told himself after looking at his watch. It was barely light enough to make out the room layout from the hallway, but he'd rehearsed his movements enough to do what was necessary blindfolded or in his sleep, even if it was still his first time in this house. Three more steps forward, turn left down the hall, nine normal steps, then one lunged step over the squeaky board. He marvelled at how quiet he could be and how perfect his instructions had been so far.

The bedroom was directly before him, its door ajar slightly, just enough to expose a potentially noisy hinge. He squeezed an oil sodden sponge he'd brought along for this purpose over the hinges, both of them, just to be sure. Then he worked the door marginally back and forth before coaxing it open wide enough for him to enter with a pre-emptive grimace.

The bastard and his woman were lit brightly by the streetlight glow of the fog outside as they slept, especially after the darkness of the corridor. He watched them sleep for only a moment, ever wary of the time, and didn't allow himself to be distracted when the woman rolled over onto her back to reveal a single breast, the other still hidden under the sheet. That she was naked suggested much of what the bastard had probably done before he fell asleep. The guy looked so peaceful and it didn't suit him, so much so that Cliff initially struggled to accept who the sleeping man was. The collar was gone, but it was definitely the same guy. Even asleep, the cast of his eyes was just as described and exactly as he remembered. It was him.

Cliff pulled the hammer from his belt. It was a dubious choice of weapon, but it would be fine. He readied himself and rehearsed the killing blow necessary to do his part. It only needed a single strike across the throat, now exposed with the guy's head on the pillow. He'd thought long and hard about where to aim and had deliberated at length between the skull and the neck. The skull was described to him as the preferred option, but it was hard and liable to deflect a killing blow into an injuring wake-up call. He had one chance and couldn't risk it on something so prone to failure. He fought the temptation to dwell on why it had to be this tool, not something more appropriate to what had been done to him, but eventually accepted it was simply not a choice he would have made.

What to do with the woman still presented a quandary, though. So focused on his target, he'd all but dismissed the potential for her also being present, and he wrestled with the consideration of whether she needed to share her lover's fate. She more than likely knew little of his history; perhaps she was completely oblivious. God knows what he'd said to her to attract such a pretty young woman, still sleeping, milky white skin translucent in the ambient light. Cliff admired her neck and wondered what her reaction was going to be when she woke and a man standing over her became apparent. She could share his end perhaps, and even if she did, it was a small price to pay. He well understood any stress on the matter was going to be short-lived, given that he would be dead soon after making the call once he completed the deed.

Cliff decided it was time for the final '*dry run*', the thought making him smile at the imminent contrast to what was unlikely to be 'dry'. He positioned himself at the bedside, feet shoulder-width apart, just as he'd practised. He held the hammer in both hands above his head; it gave him less range of movement but more control and power, which seemed a fair trade-off for just one well-positioned blow. Whether he delivered a crushing blow to the windpipe or a cervical fracture, the guy wasn't going anywhere without being shrouded by paramedics. The dry run was going to be followed by a wet stroll to the phone. Now he was ready. He took a deep breath in and held it, anticipating the exertion.

He was about to strike when his target thrashed in some nightmare; maybe it was about him or maybe it wasn't, but he didn't have time to reflect at length. The guy was still asleep, but when he stopped moving, his hand remained on the woman's abdomen. The resultant depressed sheet revealed a previously unseen shape. She was pregnant, no question. Perhaps with carefully selected clothing, underwear and stomach control, she might have kept her secret, but not relaxed and naked as she was.

He didn't baulk too much at the realisation. Now a minor change to his plan was necessary. Two strikes were appropriate, two different targets, each of equal importance, but he had only prepared for the first.

He breathed in, then delivered strike one. His aim was a little off, the head of the hammer striking the far side of the Adam's apple. It didn't rupture any underlying artery, not that it needed to, but it was adequate for purpose. The man floundered with what limited bodily control he had left, reacting to the shock and the immediate need for air with his eyes wide open in terror. His mouth fluttered some fluids, but that would not be enough to save him. Cliff wanted to watch the guy suffer, but as expected, his next target was now alert to the intrusion and required attention. He ignored her screams and leapt onto the bed. Kneeling on the panicked chest of his fading first target, he pushed the woman back onto the pillow with his hand over her mouth and nose until she stopped trying to scream.

Cliff watched her eyes, resigned to her immediate peril. He allowed her to breathe through her nose while he readied the hammer once more, now one-handed. Breathe in, hold, breathe out. He had something to say. *"For the bloodline."* It rolled off the tongue so effortlessly, but as he looked at her, he realised this execution was not to be as straightforward as the last.

He took another long breath, mindful his commitment was starting to waiver. This was to be a challenge; an assault without the gut fuelled anger that had made his first strike so justified. He knew nothing of this woman other than his assumption that she carried the bastard's child, and doubt clouded his earlier clarity. This was not the same as striking against the one who had haunted his waking hours and sullied his life.

He rationalised the simplicity of his looming choice. One more strike and he will have played his part, or had he already done enough? Was his legacy to be one of absolute commitment, or just an incomplete contributor? It pained him, but he readied himself to err on the side of caution.

Mute with fear, the woman could only stare up at him while he deliberated. Beyond her relationship with the bastard, she was someone's daughter, perhaps someone's sibling. It shouldn't matter, but it did. So far, he could live with his actions, but to strike this woman was possibly outside his mandate and beyond his grasp. He struggled with the need to deliver a blow hard across her belly.

2

Tom Willson's phone rang. Only two rings breaking his semi-lucid concentration and then going quiet before he could answer. The caller knew he wouldn't get to it in time, not in his current state. It was just a wake-up call. For many years, he knew this day would come; it was inevitable. His long wait was over.

He thought of the speech he'd prepared for the occasion; something to allow him to stare the guy down and show that despite the threat which had haunted him, he would say what needed to be said. "*You told me you'd get me and yes, I deserved it. No matter how many times I say I'm sorry, nothing can give you back what I took from you, but your hate has denied you just as much of a life as you are to take from me.*" He'd massaged the wording over the years, but he now was confident that what he'd say was perfect; repentant but honest. The impending challenge was to deliver it like he meant it enough to make a difference, if that was at all possible.

In a weird way, he was a little appreciative that tonight was going to be the night, especially in contrast to his oncologist's confidence that he wouldn't die just yet. He felt the life drifting from him such that the pain in his bones was beyond what any drug could subdue, even if he had any inclination to use it. His visitor coming tonight justified his decision to refuse all medications; he couldn't risk being too incoherent to make his speech.

He thought of his children and how he'd never see them again, and that he'd not seen them in years now weighed on him. Not that they had children of their own, but he wondered if they did, would they understand his sacrifice more, or less? Perhaps they'd want to see him if he'd given them a chance, or maybe they'd grown to hate the man who'd sent them off to primary school with the unfortunate but necessary lie that he'd see them later. It was far from the worst lie he'd told or had lived with.

The TV was on; the phone was within reach. All he needed to do was keep alert to receive his visitor. He half expected a knock at the front door. He was bed bound and unable to open it, but it seemed like the kind of fearless act that his impending visitor would enjoy. In any case, his door was unlocked and, for the first time, he'd even disabled all of his security. At last, he heard the unmistakable sound of the door re-closing; no knock, just the loud click preceding the sound of several of the deadbolts being slid home manually. Soon the darkness of the stairwell was illuminated with the sound of the light switch and then hard soles on the stairs; someone ascending one step at a time.

Willson turned off the television and silenced the static of the offline CCTV monitors and waited for his visitor to appear at the door. He didn't need to wait long. There he was, back-lit with a well-placed ceiling down light, leaving his face in shadows, but there was no mistaking who it was. "I knew you'd come," Willson conceded.

"As promised," the visitor said as he gave Willson the once over. No malice or anger, just a calm, well-spoken, level-headed tone. "Guilt eating you up, yet?" he asked.

"It's cancer, actually," Willson replied. "Arguably guilt manifested as cancer." He felt the opportunity for his much-rehearsed speech slipping away and opted for the abbreviated version. "If it's any consolation, I'm very sorry."

"It isn't," the visitor said solemnly. "It wasn't then, and it still isn't."

Willson didn't expect forgiveness, but he meant his apology and he needed to say it. "Please know that I'm sorry." He waited for his visitor to react, to say something or respond, but the guy only shrugged and looked at his watch. "If you're going to kill me, do it before I save you the trouble," frustration shortening his tone.

"If that's all I wanted, I would have done it years ago," the visitor said snidely.

"So, are you simply following through on your threat?".

"I told you to watch your back," the visitor began, "to close your eyes by all means, but to never sleep or let down your guard because I'm going to get you and your bloodline."

"I vaguely recall some kind of veiled wording like that," Willson lied; the promise, the threat, was clear in his memory.

"I think you recall it with perfect clarity."

"I think you're mistaken and deluded." Willson dug deep to present as confident a presence as was possible, but he felt like a fraud.

"Your diaries show otherwise."

Willson tried to reach a surreptitious hand under his mattress as if to confirm the insinuation, but his visitor continued. "Your latest diary's probably still there. I wouldn't take that instalment before it was complete, but the rest of your journals made for a good read."

"There are no others," Willson lied.

"The boxes in your garden shed. Remember them?" the visitor teased. "Presumably there's a note with your will so they get found when you die."

Willson struggled to hide his deflation. His last gift to his children would never happen. "Why would you want them?"

"I wanted to know if there was any remorse in that heartless mass of protein you call a body." The man looked at his watch and breathed a long breath. He reached for the phone on the bedside table and placed it in Willson's hand. "I want you to ring your son, Anthony."

Willson did as asked, as if compliance might help, dialling his son from memory, even though he'd never even called the number. It rang only once before being answered. He could hear noise; a guttural pained sound in the background, but no-one announced themselves. "Anthony?".

"Not any more," replied an unfamiliar male voice. "If *Anthony* was even his name."

"Who is this?" Willson queried, unable to reconcile the voice to the distant memory of his young son.

"Just someone trying to make good of their life," came the reply.

"Where's my son?" he asked, still trying to account for Anthony's whereabouts.

"You'll meet with him soon enough."

Willson rested the phone on his chest and spoke to his visitor. "What have you done with him?"

"I've done nothing," the visitor said. "*I*," he continued, placing his hand on his chest, "have done nothing."

Willson got the message. His own words haunting him again, until he became alert to an insistent but muffled voice from the handset. "Hand the phone over," the voice demanded.

The visitor took the handset and walked a few steps from the bed and listened intently, leaving Willson alone with his stress. Occasionally he spoke at an inaudible volume until, after several long, quiet periods, he ended the call. He made the few paces back take an implausibly long time before stopping and bracing himself on the bed frame. "When I said I'd get you, it wasn't a threat."

"So what happens now? You ransom each of my children and scare me until you get a better apology?" Willson dared. "I can't be more sorry than I already am."

"*Sorry* wasn't enough then, and it certainly isn't enough now. You've got more children and more calls to make."

"What are you hoping to achieve?" Willson asked.

"A lot more than you thought you'd achieve by keeping your mouth shut and locking yourself away for all these years," assured the visitor. "I'm a man of my word."

"Just kill me and get it over with!" Willson demanded, angrily frustrated.

"Your other children are dying to hear from daddy dearest after all these years."

Willson closed his eyes, an instinctive part of a medically advised regime to calm his escalating heart rate. His visitor was still present when he opened them again, but now he held the bed rail securely in both hands and had a gritted determination visible on his face. That face was now older than when he'd last seen it, but it had all the makings of the young man etched into his memory. Mature age resentment and anger now replaced a past youthful pain, but there was no mistaking the man before him was the man in his dreams. Willson endured the burning stares of eyes straining to keep their focus, as if there was too much anguish to be restrained behind eyeballs. He waited for the visitor to say something more, something to confirm his intentions or share anything of what lay next.

The visitor, however, said nothing. He stood silently, seeming to concentrate on his own breathing, his eyes opening and closing rhythmically with each slow breath. His fingers stretched on both hands, easing their grip on the bed rail before casually resuming their grasp, over and over, as if he too was attempting to calm himself. Willson watched, waiting for more, when his visitor appeared to sway. He quickly tensed his grip on the bed and feigned a shoulder roll as a distraction, like a drunk trying to sell a stupor as a benign misstep. Seconds passed, punctuated with slow shallow breaths and progressively less determined facial expressions. Soon, the visitor's neck seemed to relax, unwilling or unable to support his head, which then slumped backward. His torso followed suit once his fingers lost their grip. He tumbled backwards to the floor.

3

Doctor James Malter received the call sometime after midnight. He was sleeping soundly, but any call when it was dark outside was always going to demand his attention. Bleary-eyed, he found his vibrating phone and answered with his professional voice, "Malter here."

"It's detective Nate Kelshaw. Apologies for ringing so late, or early, but there's been an incident involving one of your patients."

Malter mumbled, wiping some early sleep from his eyes. "OK," he replied, without too much commitment.

"You aren't interested in who?"

"Detective, I'm a psychologist specialising in the terminally ill," Malter began, struggling a little with civility while more asleep than awake. "It's been a while since a well-meaning but overzealous individual woke me in the middle of the night, but it's not the first time. That said, yes, I'm interested in who and also why this announcement couldn't wait until the morning."

"Perhaps we need to do this face to face then," the detective declared.

"Whichever patient we're talking about, I don't think their condition will change overnight. So why don't you pass it onto the day-shift people and I'll see them when a slot in my morning opens up."

"It will need to be sooner than that," the detective pressed. "Your patient's actions have involved others."

"Assisted suicide issues can still wait until the morning," Malter yawned. "And for the record, I have never advocated for suicide, privately or professionally, on any grounds."

"Dr Malter, you're missing the point. Your patient has killed one man while he slept next to his pregnant partner."

Now more interested in the exchange, Malter sat up on his bed and turned on his bedside lamp. He mentally cycled through the names on his current patient list for who might be capable of what he was being told. No one came to mind, and most of the current batch were too unwell for anything involving physical activity.

"Dr Malter?" the detective asked after what must have seemed a protracted silence. "Clifford Stokes. Your patient, right?"

"I might need to come in," Malter conceded.

"Indeed," the detective said. "I'm sending a car."

The phone rang again while Malter was shaving. He thought about letting it go straight through to voicemail, but the receipt of a second call when he was ordinarily asleep had his curiosity too piqued to be ignored. He wiped the shaving cream from his right ear and cheek and answered.

An unknown voice, male but more youthful than the last, began without even waiting for an acknowledgement. The guy launched into his name and title that Malter barely registered, aside from the mention of police, while he yawned with his phone away from his face. "Dr Malter, I have some news regarding one of your patients."

"I know," Malter exclaimed, a little annoyed at being rushed. "I'm nearly ready."

"This should be news to you," the voice noted, puzzled.

The realisation was slow to rise in Malter. "Who are we talking about here?"

"Travis Greer."

"Alright, two in one night. I'm assuming he's passed. Not surprising," Malter mumbled, his voice trailing off to a mutter. "Just tell me if there's any evidence of help."

"Travis Greer," the voice repeated, still sounding confused. "Your patient."

"Son," Malter began in a condescendingly intolerant tone reminiscent of his father. "I have many patients, all terminal, and their death is never a complete surprise, only the exact timing. I didn't expect Travis' death so soon, but suicide in circumstances such as his is not unheard of. My interest is whether he's coerced or convinced someone to assist him, in which case I need to know if I'm likely to face some investigation as to my complicity. So, did someone help him?"

"Unless the gun used is yours, I wouldn't think so. Your patient isn't the only party involved, though."

"Oh," Malter began with a renewed interest. "I thought cancer would get him before..."

"Before what?" pressed the voice.

"Before he'd do anything."

4

Dr Malter understood he was not under suspicion despite being left alone in one of the police interview rooms. The door being open was enough to remove any potential for concern that they might have brought him in on a ruse; it wouldn't have been the first time that what was initially a casual chat had turned more formal after they had investigated a suicide. Now he was older and much wiser, and just did his best to distract himself in a way that wouldn't betray him from the other side of the one-way mirror. Reluctant to fidget, he checked his grooming and wondered if his salt and pepper hair would look better a little longer or shorter.

Suicides, while familiar, always sparked a little melancholy in him, particularly when being left alone with his thoughts as he was. He wouldn't be human if they didn't arouse some emotion, and he couldn't perform professionally if he fell to pieces, so he typically settled into a mood midway between ambivalence and cursory interest. This wasn't the first suicide he'd need to account for, and it was unlikely to be the last. There was little upside in the promise of terminal illness and the waiting game was difficult for many, even if there was no physical pain.

The pending discussion would never start as an inquisition, but inevitably the tone would shift to his opinion as to the likelihood of the patient 'X' taking his or her own life. It was a loaded question, of course; if there was a higher than 'average' chance, could or should he have done anything to prevent it? He was really being challenged as to his due diligence and duty of care.

A cheaply suited man, maybe a little greyer than Malter himself, entered the room and leaned back into the door gently. He stopped short of pushing the door home fully, leaving it a little open, as if he too well understood the insinuation of a closed door. "Thanks for coming in, Dr Malter. I'm Nate Kelshaw, detective. We spoke at some ungodly hour this morning. Can I start by asking if you're even a doctor? You're just a psychologist."

"Clinical psychologist. The PhD affords me the title of 'doctor', just not a medical doctor," Malter explained. "No need to get hung up on it."

"Sure," the detective shrugged, disinterested, and moved on. He dumped two manila folders on the table and took up his seat. He opened the topmost folder with 'Stokes, Clifford' and an oversized barcode, the only printed markings on an otherwise plain cover. Inside the file was a short stack of computer-printed pages, devoid of any handwriting. "To be clear, this is just a chat. You're not under caution or anything, but I will take notes." Malter nodded.

"I'll start with what we know. Your patient, Clifford Stokes, appears to have broken into the home of a couple and perpetrated a violent act occasioning death."

"Have they formally identified him?" Malter asked. "Cliff was socially isolated."

"So?"

"So I'm interested in who might have identified them. To my recollection, he had no family, and he was so introverted that even his neighbours might not even recognise him."

"Well, they verified his identity from ID on his person and cross-referenced with medical records from his consulting doctor." Kelshaw expected a retort, quickly adding, "You're just the psych consult, so you're not the only one with medical records."

"So what happened?"

"Stokes, Clifford. He appears to have taken a hammer to a stranger while the guy slept. The victim's girlfriend has sustained some injuries but will live."

"So that's the victim, but what about Cliff?"

"Mr Stokes appears to have called the police himself, from the incident location, but he failed to drop his weapon when uniforms asked him to do so."

"So they shot him? That's hardly suicide."

"I never said it was. He was tasered, but he appears to have had a heart attack. D.O.A."

Malter sighed. "That kind of jolt is a challenge to a healthy body, let alone a dying one."

The detective continued, "there'll be an investigation, but I'm not expecting our members to face any scrutiny given the circumstances. Present yourself to police covered in blood and holding a hammer after admitting to attacking a man and his girlfriend and you're unlikely to get much popular support. The uniforms are more likely to be cited as heroes."

"So, what do you need from me?" Malter asked with a sigh, not wanting to be drawn into any discussion about the police's efforts.

"Does the name 'Anthony Castell' mean anything to you?"

"Should it?" Malter teased. "Confidentiality is what it is."

"You're not a real doctor, Malter, so be careful how you play the doctor/patient thing. I'm not asking you to breach any confidences, but I'm appealing to you to give me something off the record."

"We both know nothing is off the record," Malter corrected, "but the name isn't familiar."

"Personally *and* professionally?"

"I don't recall any colleague or friend by that name. Happy?"

"Help me out please, Doc. Might it have come up in any discussions, privileged or not, with this Castell or any of your other patients?"

Malter paused and stared at the detective. It was a loaded question and needed fair consideration whether he should answer. He decided on a simple, "No." The detective mouthed a silent, disappointed 'nothing' as he wrote in his notebook and made a similar annotation on the paperwork in the folder. "Were you expecting anything different?"

"No," the detective said succinctly.

"So, what's your theory? A hammer implies something."

"Quite," the detective said.

"And you've got nothing?"

"It's only been a few hours, but basic checks, financials, social media, phone and email records suggest no prior relationship."

"So your theory is that he just randomly picked a house and attacked a stranger?"

"That's not my 'theory'," the detective pantomimed air quotes, "but we don't have any leads or other lines of enquiry, for now at least." He stared at what was effectively a blank page in his notebook. "Would you have thought that Mr Stokes would be capable of doing this?"

"Not a good question, detective. I now see only terminally ill people and even once they move past the anger at their situation, there's no real telling what they may or may not be capable of."

"When did you last meet with him?"

"Individually, one-on-one, I'd have to check my diary to be accurate as to timings, but it was certainly in the last week. And he's been a regular at group sessions."

"No friendships, or enemies, evident in the groups?"

"They're hardly dating or friendly circles. No friends or family, just people facing their demons before they met their maker with others in a similar situation. To an outsider, there's a lot of crying, anger and talking, but the sessions are unquestionably beneficial."

"And the last group session was when?"

"Yesterday. Cliff did like everyone else; he took part when expected, listened to others and left when it was over, on his own. He wasn't overly social with anyone. If it's any consolation, I would have described him as being at peace. He's come a long way."

"What about Greer? He's the other patient we need to discuss."

"Travis, what about him? Yes, he's also a patient, but you knew that."

The detective shuffled the bottom manila folder to the top. "He's being, been, implicated in another homicide."

"Who's the victim?"

"Why would that be your first question, doctor?"

"No real reason, other than his being quite an animated participant at yesterday's group. I would have described him as being 'agitated'. He's in much the same position as Cliff, but nowhere near as calm."

"You have some thoughts about who the victim might have been? My colleague said you told him on the phone earlier that you thought he might do something before he died of cancer." The detective re-read his notes, as if expecting a need to recount what Malter had said.

"Not really," Malter replied. "I just saw him talking with another participant."

"Yesterday?"

"Yesterday and most days. What has he said?"

"Who was that patient?" the detective asked, ignoring Malter's question.

"Nigel Newcott. You'd better hurry if you want to talk with him. He's already in a hospice, and yesterday will have been his last group. He more than likely won't see the weekend."

"Back to Greer then," the detective said, moving on. "Unfortunately, he appears to have been the victim. We're just waiting for the details to come to light as to the motive."

"So what happened if it's not suicide."

"There's not a lot I can or will share. He was shot and is now deceased. That's as good a summary as I'm inclined to give."

"Who did it?"

"That shouldn't be your concern unless you'd care to offer some insight," Kelshaw said. "Thoughts?"

"Actually, I feel sorry for the other party," Malter confessed. "Travis probably only had a month at most, so unfortunately, someone's going to be in trouble for taking such a limited life. What's the other party said?"

"The guy's not saying much, beyond what sounded like a flawed recollection of what happened. Regardless, the gun was his and legal, and it happened in his home, so his lawyer would need to be a complete moron to not plead self-defence, regardless of reality. All he'd have to do is claim some measure of threat in his own home, which is what his lawyer will tell him to say. He'll walk. It also means that we'll get no story to the contrary out of him."

"Sad. Still, my patient didn't need to die that way."

"Any family?"

"Travis was much like Cliff; single and estranged from family."

"Is that unusual?"

"Not so much unusual, but often people make efforts to make good when the end is in sight. Sometimes the patient is the one wanting peace or closure, sometimes it's their friends or relatives who offer the olive branch. I would have described both Cliff and Travis as being comfortable in their imminent departure and not burdened with any loose ends. Still, it's a turbulent time."

"Thanks for your time. I'll call you if there's anything else I need or something comes up." Kelshaw made a display of collating and closing his folders.

"That's it?" Malter challenged, incredulous at the abrupt dismissal. "I spent longer waiting than talking."

"The chat was necessary, but I thought you'd have more to offer."

"Not that I'd want to prolong this any more than necessary, but I can't think of anything more." Malter looked at his watch and sighed. "You've denied me a night's sleep for want of a five-minute conversation I could just as easily have had hours ago over the phone."

"I'm the one who needed the face to face. The media will get hold of this and I figured you'd appreciate not being woken by them."

"And the wait? I've been here for hours." Malter suddenly appreciated he might be the subject of police interest, and not just as an information source.

"If you were to be implicated, if, I couldn't have you destroying evidence before having some checks and balances in place."

"You said I wasn't under investigation."

"You're not. Hours ago there were enough potential red flags to warrant some precautions, but since then I'm satisfied those concerns are groundless. Probably."

Malter resented the way 'probably' closed out the comment. "Well, I'm *probably* going to continue with my day, then." He stood and offered his hand to the detective as a parting gesture. "You've got my number if your concerns become warranted. *Probably*."

The detective ignored the taunt and the offer of a handshake, choosing to carry the thin files and his notebook in both hands. "I'm sure we'll be in touch." He pointed his chin to the door. "I'll follow you out and get you a lift to your office." Malter shrugged and made to squeeze past Kelshaw, partially blocking the door. "Peaches," he said.

"I beg your pardon, detective."

"Peaches," Kelshaw repeated. "You don't remember me, clearly, but I wonder if you remember 'Peaches'. Peaches Hall. She was my wife."

Malter considered the request. "Yes, I remember her. She was lovely. Perhaps if you shared the same name, I might have made the association," he lied.

"So she never mentioned me?"

"Even if she did, there's nothing I'll share," Malter asserted. "Sorry for your loss." He slipped past the detective to not be drawn any further.

5

When Melanie came to, her parents were at her bedside in what could only have been a hospital room, their eyes crusty from disturbed sleep, and clothes dishevelled from their vigil. She remembered little of the attack and the aftermath, only glimpses of pain, some fluids and a phone ringing, all amid the sound of screaming, more than likely her own. Groggy after what she assumed was some mild and baby-safe sedation, she immediately recognised that her reformation was complete if concern as to her pharmacology and baby was foremost in her mind. She made to talk, but a wave of fatigue moderated her actions to a simple smile. It was enough to bring tears to her mother's face and a tremor to her father's stoicism.

"Sorry," Melanie began, her eyes closed once more.

"Nonsense," her father replied. "Nothing for you to be sorry for. It's an indictment on our society that the victim of such unwarranted violence should feel sorry." He tempered what could have become a paternal rant only when his wife squeezed his hand.

"What your father means is that we are just overjoyed you're all right. It wasn't your fault." She buzzed for nursing attention, as much to allow a distraction as to complete prior instructions from the doctor.

"You're awake... excellent!" a doctor began, perhaps a little too exuberantly, on entering the room. He walked between the parents and slid a spare chair to the bed. "Mr. and Mrs. Nashman, can I please speak with your daughter alone?" he asked, not expecting any objections. The parents wavered, hopeful their daughter would not expect them to leave, but ultimately, they accepted the need for a little privacy.

The doctor sat smiling noncommittally at his patient until he heard the room door close and strayed a brief look over his shoulder to confirm they were alone. "Melanie, I expect you'll make a good recovery. You're very fortunate. The attack could have resulted in long-term damage." He paused for acknowledgement, but not long enough for any interruption. "You're lucky in that you haven't miscarried either. Your wounds are superficial, really, just a graze and some bruising that the police attribute to your slip and fall as you rushed from the scene. You'll be fine."

Melanie considered what she was being told before summonsing the motivation to move her hands over her abdomen, under the cotton bed linen. She felt the bump even if others could not see it. She sat forward to allow herself to feel down her thighs to her knees, sensing a dressing but no pain.

The doctor prevented a prolonged silence. "I expect your pregnancy will be unaffected. Babies in-utero are amazingly resilient." Again, he sought some kind of acknowledgement, but no real response. "Psychologically and emotionally, I'd expect your recovery might take some time, but try to not let it affect your child."

Melanie heard the words from a distant state, as if they entered her brain-space, bounced around to make themselves known and then vanished. She closed her eyes and relived that night. The intimacy of their post-coital embrace, then falling asleep in each other's arms, contented and sated before a world-shattering wake-up call. Her eyes burst open at the recollection.

"Anthony?" she asked.

The doctor sighed. "I'm not privy to all the details, but I know they pronounced him dead at the scene. The police are keen to speak with you as soon as you're able."

Melanie only blinked in response.

"I'm sure this is a lot to take in, so I'll leave you for a while unless you've got questions." He paused a token moment, but didn't expect to be asked anything. "I'll send your parents in. It's up to you what you tell them."

"Please don't send them in," she pleaded. The doctor nodded and left. With the door closed, she allowed the torrent from behind her eyes to be released.

6

After being dropped back at his office, Malter's morning routine was in complete disarray, but oddly, his schedule was unaffected. His body told him he was long overdue for at least two coffees, but his watch showed he was not yet due his first. He tried to realign his routine to his body clock with a café breakfast and enough coffee to address his caffeine backlog. It was times like these he appreciated a decision many years ago to situate his office next to an average eating establishment with excellent coffee. That they were already open also meant he wasn't even that early, despite the abnormal start.

In case he couldn't get his day back on the rails, he appreciated that at least it was a Wednesday; the day always kept under-committed in his diary. Wednesdays meant he had time to manage an unhurried visit without the stress or obligation of trying to squeeze time between appointments. Depending on his patients' states, some weeks he had many visits to make, others less so, and sometimes Wednesdays would simply come too late. Today, he reasoned, he might exploit those gaps in his day to curl up on the couch in his office for a snooze.

This week, today, he knew he had only one pressing visit to make, that of Nigel Newcott. Based on some messages he'd received, his health had failed overnight, resulting in his return to the hospice by ambulance. He wondered what Nigel would have been doing being out and about, anyway, particularly when he was only admitted yesterday and that he'd taken an outing at all was more than a little surprising. He hoped Nigel would finally defer to his judgement and remain in bed. It made sense to visit him now.

Fed and caffeinated, he sauntered to the hospice, taking the time to appreciate its appeal from the street for possibly the first time. It certainly looked homey enough, not too unlike several of the larger homes in the area except for the small visitor carpark where other homes had either lawns or manicured gardens. Inside, it wasn't so much 'cheery' but definitely 'lived–in', despite a subdued quiet that music struggled to liven, and a smell of sadness that no air freshener or disinfectant could mask. He waved at Cindy, the nurse, casually chatting with the receptionist at the front desk and eyed the board to reconfirm which room Nigel was in. The 'rainbow' room, the room closest to the nurses' station at his recommendation, still. His little adventure last night had not lost him the pick of the rooms. Malter oriented himself, and Cindy, smiling, didn't bother to offer directions.

Another of his patients walked towards him, clearly not yet admitted, but perhaps familiarising himself with where he too might end up soon enough. The guy nodded as he passed by, not interacting any further. 'Bye Billy', Malter muttered in a *sotto voce* as he passed, but didn't dwell on the apparent indifference. The guy probably didn't understand there was no obligation for this place to be as quiet as a library.

The good thing about the rainbow room was that it faced east. Drenched in morning sunshine, it never failed to lift the spirits of patients and their visitors alike. For those passing in the night, the sunlight when the room was vacated spoke of new beginnings and cast a positive light far better than any sunset could do. Malter noted the dancing shadows extending into the corridor, but he didn't acknowledge the source of the shadows until he reached the room.

Nigel had the best bed; between two windows, each framing a magnificent sunrise, albeit partially obscured by a hearty gathering around his bedside. Once the initial surprise of seeing guests around his patient subsided, recognition of many of the guests dawned on Malter, then came the realisation that several were also his patients. With so many familiar faces, it was almost like a typical group session.

Nigel smiled a pained grimace at his newest visitor. "Hi, Doc". He made to raise his arm in greeting, but appeared to lose interest in doing so with the exertion. His guests vacated a place at the foot of the bed, each silently accepting that Malter was welcome.

"I didn't think you'd have so many visitors," Malter said as he instinctively reached for the patient chart. "It's a gift to have visitors in what can otherwise be such a lonely place." He smiled as much to relax the visitors as reward himself for remembering to not use the word 'lucky' or 'fortunate'; this was not the time or place.

Whatever conversation existed before his arrival was now long gone, and Malter felt the discomfort of silence. He allowed himself to be distracted by scanning the chart and then darted a look at Nigel, recognising the disparity between paper and patient. "You shouldn't be in pain, Nigel. It's not brave, it's just silly."

"I don't like needles and I couldn't be bothered taking the tablets."

"The chart says you've only just taken your PRN meds."

Nigel opened a clenched fist over his bed linen, allowing first one and then several capsules to tumble onto the bed. "While I'm alive, I'd like to be coherent."

"That's your choice," Malter assured as he returned the chart to the rack. "You're NFR, not for resuscitation, so there's no need to lie about it. Just say you don't want them and they'll leave you alone."

Nigel breathed out slowly. "Did you just want to say goodbye, Doc?"

"I wanted to say hello because I didn't expect you to have any visitors," Malter explained. "But I didn't realise you had so many friends."

"I make friends and allies easily, Doc. Except, as it seems, in my body."

"On that, I thought your doctor and I had made it clear that your body is simply not up to that kind of physical activity any more."

Nigel shrugged. "My body is used to it. I've been doing it for years."

"No," Malter began patronisingly. "Your long history of wandering the streets when everyone else is asleep precedes your body failing as it is."

"It helps me think."

"It might have given you a distraction from your brooding, but no more." Malter looked to Nigel for some indication of concurrence. "So, are we agreed you've had your last outing? You must have given your friend a scare last night."

"He's not my friend," Nigel objected vehemently, the tone taking Malter by surprise. He made an effort to settle himself, as if aware his outburst was a little confronting, adding, "Perhaps you want to come back and visit me later."

Malter heard the suggestion at something between hint and request. "I'll try for some one-on-one time later today then."

"Expect more from me than to just die, Doc," Nigel quipped.

Malter smiled at Nigel's confidence in his longevity and left without acknowledging the other visitors. Their time to be the centre of attention would come soon enough.

7

Melanie initially fought the temptation to remain in hospital, but eventually accepted the need to leave. Thinking rationally amid a confused flux of hormones, she knew home was the best place to be, despite the potential for flashbacks and lingering bloodstains that her mother insisted she already had 'in hand'. Mindful she couldn't delay the inevitable, she opted to get it over and done with and smile the next time she saw the police poke their nose in the door.

"Are you feeling up to speaking with us now, Miss Nashman?" a man asked respectfully from the corridor.

Melanie considered a silent nod, and the man entered the room. He started talking even before he sat at her bedside. "My name is DC Nate Kelshaw. I don't want to take much of your time, but I would like to get your version of events."

"I can say what happened to me," she began. "But I don't think I could offer anything as to why."

"Fair enough," Kelshaw said, "but I need to start somewhere."

Melanie took a long breath and began. "I was asleep until he struck Anthony. I remember waking to the sound and being wet with what must've been blood. Anthony was struggling to breathe. And then I saw him there, kneeling on the bed about to hit me." She paused long enough for the detective to scribble some notes and look up to show he was ready for more. "He held me down for a long time. Or maybe it wasn't, I don't know." She struggled with her memory, as if the clarity of her recollection was being confused with a dubious timeline. "His hand was on my face, not enough to suffocate, just enough to keep me from moving."

"And where was his other hand?"

"He held a hammer." Melanie provided a commentary to her memory, her eyes clenched closed in focus. "Right until the phone rang."

"You mean when he made a call?" Kelshaw clarified. "When he rang the police?"

Melanie thought hard. "The phone definitely rang. He looked at his wrist a few times while he held me down, and the phone on the bedside table rang. He put down the hammer to answer it."

"You're sure?"

"The phone rang, and he spoke. I can't think what he said. I don't remember."

The detective scribbled an abbreviated transcript of what she said. "That's helpful, Melanie. We'll see who called. Anything else?"

"After the call, he picked up the hammer again. I watched him loom over me and stare. I remember expecting my turn, but he did nothing."

"And then?" he pressed.

"And then nothing. Then he rang from the same bedside landline and asked for the police. I can't remember anything else, other than it sounded final, as if he didn't care who he told."

"Did you move? Try to get away?"

"I don't think so," she replied, a little offended at what seemed an accusation. "I don't know why that's relevant."

"I'm sorry," Kelshaw said. "Perhaps the question came across a little obtuse. It's just that Mr Castell, Anthony, was hit with a single blow to the throat and you weren't touched. It was a deliberate, non-frenzied attack, so it's odd that he didn't harm you, too. I'm just trying to account for the disparity."

"That I lived and Anthony didn't?" she queried, trying to make sense of the detective's line of enquiry. "Sorry to disappoint. It's not like I'm responsible."

Kelshaw sighed. "Your history and your recent false police report meant I needed to consider the possibility of another explanation, but that said, your bloodwork on admission was clean," Kelshaw conceded.

"It wasn't a false report," Melanie said defensively. "Someone was in my home…"

"Moving on," Kelshaw said as he raised his hand to accept he probably didn't need to broach the woman's background under the circumstances, adding, "Now, I just want to validate an alternate story."

"From who?" she asked, choosing not to dwell on the detective's subtle reference to her past.

"His name is Clifford Stokes. He's allegedly the one who attacked both you and your boyfriend. Do you know him, or ever heard the name?"

"No," she said. "So you caught him and he confessed?"

"More like he rang for the police and told them what happened. His account was solid enough, but it still needs to be corroborated."

"So he's mad?"

"Why would you say that?" Kelshaw asked.

"I don't know, a random attack on innocent strangers, his sticking around to confess to the police. It doesn't seem entirely rational, so I just as assumed he's insane."

"That might be difficult to confirm."

"So will they will put him away?", she asked.

"He was apparently terminally ill, verified by his oncologist."

Melanie picked up on one word more than any other. "Was?"

"An incident when the police arrived at the scene left one male dead. Investigations are outstanding, so I can't say much more than that… but it seems your assailant and the deceased are the same."

"So, did he say why he did it?"

"He didn't actually say he did it," Kelshaw continued cautiously. "It's the among the omissions in his account, more like a third party telling what he saw."

"His story is likely to be way more complete than mine," Melanie offered.

"Do you know him? This Stokes?"

"I don't even think I could identify him even if I had the chance."

"Stress will do that," Kelshaw offered. "So you never met him beforehand?"

"No, and I don't remember Anthony ever mentioning him." Melanie thought more about the question. "Did he say different?"

"He only provided a sterile admission when he called the police," the detective began. "So he said nothing to explain why he was there, why he chose your house among all others, why he killed Mr Castell and allowed you to live?"

"No."

"Nothing at all?" Kelshaw pressed. "He never said he spoke to you, but I'd consider it very unlikely he kept his mouth shut throughout the entire incident."

"I don't know," Melanie offered. "I'm not entirely sure he said it myself. Only talking to you now has me trying to separate dream from reality."

"So what did he say?" the detective asked, determined to move the conversation along.

"Something about a 'bloodline'."

"You can't recall exactly?"

"I'm having trouble with the details. I'd just woken and...". She didn't bother finishing or offering an explanation.

The detective scribbled into his notebook and waited for Melanie to say more, but she was silent. "Melanie, we've got five senses, and I'd like you to consider each of them for details to complement what you've told me thus far," he pressed. "You've told me about what you heard and saw, but what else? Did you smell anything on your assailant? Did he smell clean?"

"He didn't smell dirty or homeless or anything, and it's not like he smelled of soap or aftershave, or not that I remember, anyway." Melanie cycled through her other senses. "Only now I think of it do I remember his tears landing on my face. I remember the taste of salt. Of course, they could have been mine, but I remember seeing the look on his face. He was definitely crying."

"And that was after he made his phone call? Remorse wasn't clear in the transcript of his call to the police. Maybe you were an afterthought."

"So why attack us at all? Why didn't he just walk away?"

"I'm hoping to find some answers, Melanie, but my experience tells me we may well never know," Kelshaw offered as he pocketed his notebook and stood. "I haven't got a complete picture of this guy's backstory yet, and that might yield some clues. If nothing else, I'm hoping to gain some insight as to his mental state or if drugs played a part. Expect to never know, and you might be pleasantly surprised. We are following some lines of inquiry, including with his psychologist."

"So he is, was, mad?"

"We don't know, yet. The psychologist, Malter, is liable to hide behind confidentiality. I'm half inclined to get him to visit you to see if that brings him on board. Little consolation amid the loss of your partner, but I know enough to recognise that understanding the '*why*', if we can, will help you."

Melanie remained silent. Talk of Anthony in the past tense was confronting. "I would like to know why."

"Best efforts are all I can promise you, Melanie. I'll mention you to the psychologist. He might become part of the solution." The detective paused, sensing the need to end the chat. "Thanks for your help, Miss Nashman. I'm sure I'll need to speak to you again, but for now, that will do. Incidentally, I think you're very lucky to be alive. Very lucky." He pivoted and left the room.

8

Malter returned to his office. It seemed a quiet day might allow him to catch up on some reports, and perhaps Nigel would be more receptive to productive interaction later. He practised what he preached, embracing positives no matter how seemingly insignificant, and there was little point in thinking any different now.

"You're late, Doc," his secretary, Tash Sykes, began as soon as he entered the office. "Don't stress too much about it, your 9 am is a no-show. It was only an intro session, so she might have just got cold feet. I'll follow up with her."

"Thanks, Tash. Anything else?"

"The police rang and a detective 'Nate' someone wants you to call him. He wanted a list of patients, but he lost interest when I asked for the warrant."

"Good girl," Malter teased. "I thought he might try that."

Tash grimaced at the use of such a condescending title, but banked it to hold against the good doctor at a later time. "He didn't even say why he wanted it. Anything I need to know?"

"You might like to prepare Cliff Stokes' and Travis Greer's files for closure. There's no review necessary, but I might give them a once-over for completeness."

"That's all you're going to tell me?" she questioned like a matriarch. "Really?"

"Fair enough," Malter conceded. "There's a police investigation pending into both their deaths. To say more might complicate matters and unintentionally bias you. So keep your phone on. They will want to talk to you for sure."

"So they didn't just '*pass*', then?"

"No, they did not. Not as we typically expect. Coffee?"

Tash took the hint and moved on. "Of course. Moroccan is the feature blend. You OK to take calls?"

"Just put them through," Malter suggested, already heading for the coffee percolator in the kitchenette. He filled a mug for himself and walked into his workroom. He left the door open; there was no point in even giving the appearance of needing privacy.

Malter sat and opened Cliff's file on his laptop. He skimmed over the preamble of his history and started reading the session transcripts, which Tash had invariably typed within a few hours of each session ending. He skimmed through eleven weeks of transcripts. The usual questions and typical answers. Cliff was at peace and it seemed there was nothing of much consequence. Just a man with regrets, unfulfilled dreams, and unrealised potential. Way too familiar.

Greer's file was next. The expectation of familiarity was thick in his mind as he read his summary notes. Single. Cancer. Lonely. Disappointed. He could have summarised the page with just those four words; the remaining pages didn't even add much granularity. He started reading the session notes, interspersed with Tash's interpretation of the group sessions. She was good, but not good enough to attribute everything spoken to one of between five and fifteen patients. The result was a series of paragraphs, each preceded by 'male voice', 'female voice' or 'Dr Malter', as appropriate. They were useless to anyone else, or in court if it came to that, but they served their purpose as a memory jogger. Armed with the prompts, Malter remembered each session, hearing the words on his screen as vividly as if he was watching video footage with audio. Travis and Cliff were both present in some of the later sessions, but they never interacted.

Yesterday's group session warranted more than a cursory read. Travis' outbursts were out of character and well represented in Tash's notes. She could associate Travis' voice to his name, most probably because of placative comments from Malter and other patients. 'Travis, it's time to let someone else talk' and similar would have given her the cue to tie a name to the voice. Malter recalled he thought Travis was just venting and his interpretation still seemed accurate. If required to comment on whether there were any clues to what would follow, no professional reading them could think any different. The guy was angry. Angry at himself, angry at the world, and angry at the inevitability of his death sooner than what the national average would have him expect.

Tash alerted Malter to a visitor with her almost shouted greeting, "DETECTIVE WHO?". The way she feigned the need to yell with her earphones on was priceless. She would have understood the guy to be police the moment he opened the door.

"Hi Detective," Malter said confidently in greeting as he joined Tash at her desk side. "'*Probably*' has turned into '*definitely*', then."

"We need to talk, doctor Malter."

"About who? And should we do this in my office?"

"Here's fine. Your secretary will need to be questioned, and talking here might save me time later."

"Based on how readily you wasted hours of my sleep last night, I don't care if I save you a minute. Tash, can you bring the detective here a coffee?" He returned to his office desk, expectant the detective would follow.

Kelshaw groaned a little, but still followed. He dumped himself on the patients' chair and craned his neck to see if anything on the Doctor's computer was visible, just as the screen went blank from disuse. "I want a list of your patients. Please."

"Your use of the 'please' has me thinking you haven't got a warrant. So why don't you ask me a question I'm inclined to answer, regardless of whether there's a 'please' in there?"

"Given that I could get a list of your patients from the Department of Health, I just wanted to see if you were at all defensive."

"I'm thinking you've already got a list." Malter ignored the snipe and drank a leisurely sip of his coffee after blowing a long breath over the mug. He knew the detective would recognise his actions as a ploy to obscure his face, but he needed to be cautious. "What else would you like to talk about?"

"Billy Wentworth. He's one of yours?"

"What if he is? You think or know so."

"Was." Kelshaw flipped open his notebook and made a statement of clicking his pen, ready for use.

"I only saw him recently, certainly less than an hour ago," Malter said, surprised and recollectively.

"Are you sure it was him?"

Malter replaced his coffee on his desk and rubbed his eyes. "I passed him in a corridor at a hospice while visiting another patient. What happened?"

"There was a car incident," Kelshaw explained. "How was he when you saw him?"

Tash knocked gently on the open door as a courtesy as she bought in a coffee in a mug with 'Blame my mother' emblazoned on the side. She placed it on a chair-side table and hovered as if awaiting inclusion in the discussion.

"Anything else?" Kelshaw prompted.

"We only passed in the corridor," Malter said, ignoring Tash. "It's not as if he was muttering obscenities to himself."

"Not drunk?"

"Not to my knowledge, and not that I noticed. Plausible though, sure," Malter said. "So what happened?"

"Initial reports suggest suicide via a deliberate effort to drive at high speed into a wall."

"Shit." Malter let his professional air slip. "Anyone else in the car?"

"Why would you ask that?"

"It's a very reasonable question, detective. I would have thought suicide was beyond him, so perhaps it was a simple traffic accident."

"No one else in the car," Kelshaw said dismissively. "Witnesses say it looked deliberate. I drove past on the way here… there's no way it was accidental."

"He only had six months, but I didn't think he had it in him to go sooner," Malter countered.

"There was someone at the wall, though," the detective said. "That person is also deceased, but yet to be identified. That much might take a while."

Malter felt the immediacy of Kelshaw's stare. "I don't know what to say. Clearly, you're thinking something sinister, but as he hasn't driven a car, legally, for perhaps 20 years, a humble but regrettable accident is far more likely." Kelshaw only shrugged. "So what happens now?"

"I'm going to wait here until the warrant arrives," Kelshaw stated, easing back and sprawling himself across the entire chair.

"What good will that do you?"

"You tell me, Malter. Three of your patients have now died in the last twelve hours. I think that gives me good grounds to consider your role as suspicious."

"Doctor-patient confidentiality…" Malter began before being interrupted.

"Is relevant only for living patients, and medical doctors, which you aren't. You're entitled to privacy, but don't get in the habit of confusing that with legislatively sanctioned confidentiality. Regardless, after your patients die, those records will be sealed pending an inquiry."

"So, what good will the warrant serve?"

"Your patient list, for starters. That's not privileged."

"It's little more than a list of terminally ill people, a list you seem to have, anyway."

"Three of whom are now dead, and I'd like to allow your remaining patients to pass as their health demands, not sooner. I want the full list, if only to compare it to mine."

The phone rang, allowing Malter a moment of distraction. Tash stepped forward to answer the call at the nearest phone rather than at her desk. She introduced herself and then listened, periodically glancing at both Malter and the detective before hanging up abruptly.

"TV or print media?" pre-empted Malter in response to her ashen face. "It was going to happen. Under-paid community servants like the detective here are prone to supplement their incomes by tipping them off."

"I resent that," Kelshaw said, writhing in his seat. "Consider it a reminder that your involvement in this seems obvious, and a warrant is little more than a polite formality. Your patient list is in the public domain, and the media could well have come up with your name from running the names of accident and incident victims. Your notoriety works for you and against you, Malter."

The phone rang again, and Tash instinctively pressed a button on the base station. "All calls to voicemail might be a good idea for the day," she suggested.

"But that won't stop them from coming to visit," Malter sighed. "I might make myself scarce if the detective doesn't have any objections."

"I was going to wait here and talk to your secretary," Kelshaw smirked as he toasted his mug to Tash.

"Right you are," Malter muttered. He made for the door, keen to exit before a further snipe, without success.

"One suicide is a tragedy. Several suicides will justify the need for a pattern to be investigated."

"There's no '*pattern*', detective. And there's nothing to even suggest any similarity or link between them."

"No, you're a common link, and from which, a pattern will surface. As of now, I'd even describe you as a suspect."

"In what?" Malter exclaimed, incredulous. "The deaths of my

patients?"

"Did you coerce them to take their own lives?"

"What a ridiculous question."

"Is that a 'yes' or a 'no'?" Kelshaw insisted.

"It's an emphatic 'no' to an absurd and potentially defamatory accusation."

"You'd better hope your records and notes are in order."

"My notes and my conscience are fine."

"You'd hope so," Kelshaw challenged. "If you're implicated in the death of your patient, patients, they'll be subject to investigation and, if warranted, public scrutiny and criminal proceedings. It all begins with getting access to your files, on your terms or otherwise."

"That sounds like a chicken and egg scenario," Malter suggested. "You can only get access once you've got access to justify your access."

"Or I can find any other means to warrant access. Excuse the pun."

"When you do, you'll be my guest. Until then, my files are *my* files."

Kelshaw eased back his assault momentarily. "In the meantime, can you think of any other means of accounting for a sizeable drop in your living patient count?"

"My patients die, detective."

"From terminal disease, yes, which is not the case of late."

"Detective," Malter began condescendingly, "I've been doing this for a long time. My patients are all just ordinary people willing to take part in a free, federally funded program to monitor their mental health in the face of a terminal illness. Sometimes they leave the program, but typically they'll stay until they die."

"Do you get to know them well?"

"It depends," Malter said, feeling the challenge of scrutiny and being drawn into explanation. "I usually get to know each patient reasonably well, albeit over a short period. Terminal illness being what it is, most don't learn of their condition until late or they refuse to accept their situation until death is close. Occasionally I'll come to know a patient over a longer-term. The program definition of 'terminal' is deliberately vague to allow a wide range of patients."

"So no-one ever suicides on your program?" the detective challenged.

"It happens, sadly," Malter replied. "Maybe a 10% suicide rate among my patients over the years, which would be inconceivable in most quarters, but no one else's statistics focus on such a unique population."

"And it's made you famous," the detective sniped.

Malter shrugged. "Not that you care, but that was not how it started. Initially, it wasn't so much a niche as stable employment until I published my first book. It turns out what I learnt from my sessions made for inspirational reading to many, especially those newly diagnosed. Fast forward years and a series of books later and here we are."

"You get rich watching people die and writing about it," the detective teased. "Your sister would be proud."

Malter ignored the taunt. It would be naïve to not expect people to have looked into his background. "Fact is, most of my books focus on the upside of facing death as a date to make good on one's life. That suicide rate I mentioned has been such a point for so many questions that I focussed on it in my last book, '*Facing it like a man, or woman*'".

"Spare me the plug for your bestseller, Malter. Is your next book called '*I make people kill themselves*'?"

Malter sighed. "What exactly are you wanting to accuse me of, detective?"

Kelshaw responded slowly. "If a person suicides and you put them up to it, you are culpable, just as if you put them in an exploding jacket. When others are injured or killed, it's potentially conspiracy to commit murder."

Malter bottled his resentment and grabbed his jacket. "I think this 'chat' is over," he mumbled as he brushed past the detective, shaking his head at Tash as he exited the office.

Malter knew what Kelshaw was doing; planting a seed of doubt to see how he'd react. Did he have records that might implicate him? Did he say anything to any of his patients which might be interpreted as a call to action? He struggled to suppress his doubts, and nothing could stop him from cycling over his patients and his interaction with each. His interest in what was also the detective's suspicion was now of a higher order.

9

Malter took the opportunity to give Nigel another visit. There was nothing to say he wouldn't still have some visitors, but there was also no guarantee he'd be alive if he delayed. The walk to the hospice wouldn't take long, and it offered a welcome reprieve and a chance to think.

He hoped Nigel hadn't succumbed to the relief of meds, though the thought challenged him more than a little. He didn't want him to endure any more pain, but he wanted him to be coherent enough to converse. As one of the few patients who Malter had known for longer than a few months, he owed Nigel that much. After knowing each other in some capacity for many years, and not just because of his protracted illness, dealing with him was a challenge to walk the line between a long-standing friendship, human empathy and professional distance. Malter fought the temptation to reminisce; he couldn't help it. Abstraction was one thing, but needing to deal with someone who was almost family at one time threatened to derail his ability to assume the role of rank outsider entirely. Nigel remained dubiously between patient, friend and confidant.

"If you're here to see me out early, Doc, you might have a wait on your hands," Nigel began on seeing Malter enter his room. "I'm not ready to go just yet."

"It's just like you to hang on," Malter said. "Who are you wanting to outlast now?"

Nigel relaxed his eyelids into an uneasy looking recline on the bed. "You didn't understand then, Doc, so you couldn't possibly want to understand now."

Malter sat himself down in one of the now vacant seats and slid himself closer to the bed. "Do you want to talk? It might pass the time," Malter suggested.

"Did you ever go on trips when you were little?" Nigel asked. "To the beach or a picnic or something?"

"So?" Malter replied.

"So did your anticipation on the way there improve your arrival?"

"Your point being what, Nigel?"

"That my wait isn't that bad." Nigel rolled his shoulders under the covers. "You're welcome to keep me company if you like, though. Just don't feel obligated."

"It's no obligation, just part of the service. If you don't want to talk, that's fine. I need a break from the office, anyway."

"I understand some of your patients died last night," commented Nigel.

"Is that all you heard?" Malter asked.

Nigel shrugged. "Cliff and Travis liked you. You helped them."

"Perhaps, but their actions aren't showing their appreciation," Malter said. He considered whether to ask what was on his mind. "Did Billy say anything to you when he visited this morning?"

"Of course. He's a friend."

"So, what did you talk about?"

"That's stepping over the line, isn't it, Doc? My obligations to you don't extend to disclosure of everything I talk to anyone about."

"True," Malter accepted the snub. "It's just..." he faltered at the prospect of continuing, but soon conceded to himself he had nothing to lose. "Billy had a car accident a little while after he visited you this morning. He crashed into a wall."

"So cirrhosis of the liver didn't get him." Nigel yawned and rested his head back on his pillow.

"Did you talk about anything?" Malter asked.

"Sure. Friends talk."

"I mean, did he say anything? He left here and then drove into a wall. It's not a long bow to think you might have upset him."

"Now you're sounding like the police."

"Speaking of which, they might want to talk to you," Malter hinted. "They confronted me about Billy this morning and that I saw him here came up."

"They'd better hurry. I won't last forever."

"So he didn't suggest what he might do later?" Malter pressed.

"I'm not the professional here, Doc."

"Maybe he said something which, in retrospect, makes sense now," Malter pressed.

"Nothing like that, but everything about him made sense to me," Nigel offered.

"I checked my notes of the last few chats I had with him, individually and in group, and there wasn't anything particularly special."

"Just because you facilitate some discussion doesn't mean you'd hear everything and just because you've got some credentials doesn't mean you'd understand everything."

Malter considered Nigel's response and was about to comment when his phone rang. He answered out of instinct, momentarily oblivious to the prospect of it being the media.

"We need to talk, Malter," Kelshaw barked, devoid of any niceties.

"With or without a warrant?" Malter challenged, raising his hand to Nigel as if to suggest the call wouldn't take long. "I'm busy with another patient."

"Who?" Kelshaw asked.

"That's not your concern, at least until you get a warrant."

"Fair enough," Kelshaw accepted. "Process of elimination should help me know who you're with now, even without a warrant. I know it's not Kelly Flintshire."

"I've got a session with her tomorrow," Malter replied.

"That little window in your schedule tomorrow has just opened up, Doctor. I'm still here at your office, and I'll get Tash to put a fresh pot of coffee on and see if she remembers my Peaches."

10

Detective Kelshaw was sprawled on the couch in the corner next to Tash's desk, which amounted to Malter's waiting area. He sat with a variety of periodicals and books strewn on either side of him while she continued her work, unperturbed and ambivalent to his presence.

"You've got some great reading material here," Kelshaw declared with Malter's arrival. "Do you ever worry your patients could do without your chats if they just sat here and read this crap?". He stood and tapped an envelope on Tash's desk for a few beats before dropping it on her keyboard. "They might live longer too."

"What happened to Kelly?" Malter asked, ignoring the jab.

"That envelope has your precious warrant, limited as it is, for now. So what was her affliction?"

Malter looked at Tash as she opened the envelope and scanned its contents. After flitting over each page, she looked up and shrugged.

"Kidneys. She's got a rare blood type, so she'll never get a transplant and she doesn't want to spend her life in and out of dialysis wards."

"Not a problem now," Kelshaw quipped.

"What happened to her?"

"She jumped from a fifth-floor balcony, not her own. She hint at this in any of her sessions?"

Malter baulked before looking back at Tash, now reading the paperwork more closely. "I'll need to re-read my session notes, but nothing comes to mind. According to the law, I'd need to act if I thought she was likely to cause herself harm. I know she'd come to grips with her decision to stop dialysis. Death thereafter is only a matter of time. That said, I don't recall any suggestion that she was going to do anything to circumvent complete renal failure."

"She didn't mention anyone else?" Kelshaw pressed.

"No one. Perhaps if she had someone else, she might have kept on with dialysis, and maybe she might have reconsidered wanting to take her own life." Malter waited for the detective to comment.

"Of course, what's really unfortunate is the pro-bono lawyer minding her own business walking to work when she gets crushed to death by a terminally ill, suiciding patient just as she's about to enter her office."

"You're right, detective," Malter agreed. "That is especially sad."

"Your concern makes all the difference, Malter. It really does. I'll be sure to pass that sentiment onto the real victim's family." The detective paused as if to allow Malter to comment, but after a while, he continued. "Tell me, Malter, how much do you know of your patients?"

"My role is one of guidance, not direction, so within those bounds, I know what I need to know, or what they tell me," Malter offered. "I get to know them enough for me to engage them in their end of life, that's all. Anything else comes through our time together, and that's privileged."

"So what if I told you something of your patient's history? Is it possible I know more than you?"

"I'm assuming you're focusing on criminal history, and in which case, it's wholly likely you'll know more. What I know will be purely what I'm told, and I don't care if that correlates with court records or a police investigation."

"So I couldn't surprise you?" Kelshaw teased.

"Surprise me in an infantile sense, like you're wanting to prove you know something which I don't? Sure."

"What if I said one of your patients is a murderer? Would that surprise you?"

"It wouldn't change the support I offer," Malter replied. "I'm assuming you're talking about Nigel."

"What if I am?"

"There was a time when everyone knew his name. Not surprising when he was front-page news. Got anything else, detective?"

"What about their religion?" Kelshaw moved on. "Does that interest you?"

"I don't push any faith, so the flip side is that I don't need to know or care about their pre-existing faith. Am I in trouble for that, detective?"

Kelshaw ignored the taunt. "So would you know if any of them are, or were, of any religion? What if they wore burkas?"

"You're crossing a line to the point of profiling now, detective. I've got grounds for a complaint right there."

"It's a reasonable question in the circumstances," Kelshaw commented.

"Reasonable to whom?"

"Simple question, Malter. Any of them know how to drive?"

The question puzzled Malter. "I never thought to ask. Why?"

"At least one of your patients ran over someone, for no reason or whatever reason. What if they went barrelling up a pedestrian mall?"

"You're not seriously expecting me to comment," Malter challenged.

"Comment? I'm just saying. I'm thinking I could get support for anything I want if I positioned the potential for more than just one casualty per patient."

"Do what you like, detective. I'll comply with any and every legal obligation, nothing less and nothing more."

"Any of them know how to fly a plane? Maybe someone who's learning to fly, but not interested in learning how to land."

"Now you're just baiting. If that were the case, of course I'd be obligated to act."

"Great, so you have some sense of right and wrong, Malter. That will help us rule out any cause for a 'clinically insane' defence."

Malter shrugged. "Anything I say is just a waste of time, then, isn't it?"

"But admissible, Malter. When we get more details of the others, you'll be the only person of interest. I'll tell you that now."

"Who else? Who else has died?" Malter asked, flustered and struggling to continue with a rational calm.

"We don't know, yet, Malter," Kelshaw persisted. "Until we get access to your files." He redirected his focus from Malter to Tash. "Brace for some legally necessary inspection."

"But you're expecting more, then?" Malter asked with his eyes closed, digging deep to keep his composure. "Terminal patients, people, die. My patients, those that stay on the program, all die. It hasn't raised alarm bells until now."

"That doesn't exactly help your case, Malter," Kelshaw smirked, scribbling in his notebook. "I'm extending my interest back to the very beginning of your '*program*'".

"This is… a farce," Malter remarked. "You're making it sound like a conspiracy."

"Perhaps," Kelshaw said. "Of course there's some work for me to do before I can prove it, but what's important in the immediate term is that I stop you now."

"There's nothing to stop."

"A jury won't see it that way, Malter. I'm expecting more."

"Let's back it up a little, detective. You can't possibly think I have something to do with this."

"This what? Which of your recently deceased patients do you think I *shouldn't* be interested in?" Kelshaw asked incredulously. "That there's a list makes you questioning my interest sound a little arrogant, wouldn't you say?"

"Not ideal, but I'll comply within the bounds of the law."

"So you're not obstructing my inquiry, then? Not so cocksure about this now, huh?"

"I don't recall ever saying I wouldn't help, but I just resented, resent, the insinuation of my involvement or guilt. Tash here will help you, as will I, but I will not pander to any misappropriated accusations, and I have other patients who I will continue to see."

"That's not happening, Malter. If you were a pilot, I'd call you effectively grounded pending my investigation at the moment. Your patients are going to need to look elsewhere."

"So I'm under arrest or free to continue my work. Which is it?" Malter asked with a heartfelt confidence. "My patients don't deserve to have their care compromised while you carry out some witch-hunt. See yourself out, detective."

Kelshaw stayed seated, unflinching. "You're not seriously expecting me to leave."

"Leave or stay. I don't really care, but I've got patients to see and you're not staying to intimidate them or annoy me. Tash, please tell me I've got someone to see now, so I can wave this gentleman goodbye."

"Your 9 am rescheduled. She's due any minute," Tash feigned, glancing over her screen as if to add authenticity to her claim.

"I've been doing this a long time, Tash, is it?" Kelshaw asked. "You're not a good liar."

Tash struggled a little but tried her best to double down on her comment, emphasising her use of the mouse, and straining to look at her screen. "I'm looking at our booking system. 9 am."

"Name? What's the patient's name?" Kelshaw asked, smiling. "Second thoughts, I don't want to out you for a lie which might later prove to be grounds for complicity in what your employer is doing."

Tash didn't bother continuing, looking instead to Malter for comment. "I'm going out for some fresh air," Malter declared. "Tash, you're free to do as your conscience demands."

"As the law demands, too," Kelshaw added.

Malter sighed and shook his head as he left his office.

11

Melanie was comfortable with her decision to leave the hospital; just as well, because she didn't have any grounds to prolong her stay. Beds were at a premium and doctors' advice was that her wounds were superficial and she could rest at home just as well as in-hospital. Her parents were keen to argue the point, but their efforts required a commitment on her part too, and she just wasn't up to it. Yes, it could have been worse, but for now, instructions to keep a bandaid on her grazes seemed to trivialise her recent trauma.

Her ward bedside phone had barely stopped ringing; mostly sincere well-wishers tiptoeing around the rumour that she might be pregnant. They never mentioned Anthony, which wasn't surprising given that in the weeks since they'd met she had drifted from many friends, something these friends attributed to, or more correctly blamed, on Anthony. There was even a snide suggestion that now he was out of the way, she might return to being the social one. Melanie was noncommittal. It didn't seem right to move on so quickly and she couldn't go back to her fast track to rock bottom. Instead, the comments seeded by her friends festered in her mind until she began to doubt the man and their brief romance.

Love was indeed blind, especially in retrospect. What did she know about this man? She'd allowed herself to be drawn into the immediacy of a loving friendship that blossomed out of a dark place. Only now did it dawn on her she knew next to nothing of his history, his family or his life prior to their meeting. It wasn't a problem then, but now it seemed right to understand the makings of the man who could have been the father to her child.

What remained of Anthony at home was 'limited'; that's how the police described his personal effects, only clothes, every single piece of which she had purchased throughout their relationship. It seemed such a loving gesture he was so willing to run with whatever she offered or suggested, but now, it was perhaps a little odd. What she'd do with them now would be one of the first things she'd need to contend with when she got home. The doctor's decision to expedite her release was only bringing forward the inevitable.

It made little sense to hide away, so she sat on her bed, awaiting the return of her parents to take her home, when the phone rang. She lifted the receiver but didn't answer, not wanting to pre-empt anything. The caller was mute but for the bristling of whiskers on his handset. Eventually, he spoke, "I'm sorry for your loss, Melanie."

"Who's this?" she asked.

"I'm your partner's, ex-partner's, father," replied the voice. "I can only imagine he didn't tell you about me."

"Actually, he said you were dead," Melanie stated.

"Same difference now, I guess."

"So why contact me at all? That he wanted you out of his life is probably as good a sign as any I don't need you in mine, especially now."

"It wasn't like that," the voice continued, unperturbed at Melanie's point. "It's not that he didn't want me in his life. I didn't want him in mine."

"Either way, your chance to win father of the year has passed." The voice was silent and Melanie made to hang up the phone but instinctively added a "Goodbye" as she did so.

Alert to the imminent end of the call, the voice spoke up. "I thought I could save him."

The comment salvaged Melanie's interest. "If you knew something... why are you telling me this now?"

"The police wouldn't have believed me, and neither would you," the voice continued. "And Anthony would probably have hung up on me. That said, this is not about Anthony, and it's nothing I can explain over the phone."

"This is the only avenue you've got," Melanie declared.

Again, the voice was quiet for a time. "Can I ask what your attacker said to you during your attack?"

"Nothing," she lied.

"I don't think that's the case," the voice said. "I think he might have made mention or reference to a '*bloodline*' or something like that. Am I right?"

Melanie pressed the handset closer to her ear, but said nothing.

"I can explain, but not over the phone," the voice teased.

12

Malter walked the long way from his office to the hospice. He half expected the media to appear from behind a tree or leap from a vehicle, so he headed in the complete opposite direction, zig-zagged through backstreets and crossed the road randomly before appearing in the staff carpark from a vacant lot. He only stopped obscuring his face with his hand when he entered the front door.

"Again?" Nigel asked on seeing the doctor enter his room. "I sense special treatment, Doc." He smiled casually and pointed to a chair at his bedside.

"You more comfortable now?" Malter scanned the patient's chart out of habit on his way to the bed. It was unlikely to differ from when he'd last seen it an hour earlier, but he always began with a review.

"Getting there, Doc."

"It's most definitely time to talk about end of life, Nigel." Malter expected more reaction from Nigel than just a yawn, which prompted him to continue. "Beyond what I'd love to see you confront in your remaining time, there's lots to make that time easy."

"I'm not going anywhere just yet," replied Nigel.

"If we had less history, I'd describe that comment as either naïve or wishful, but because I've known you for some time, I get that you're thinking your anger will keep you going forever."

"So you're not expecting me to make a remarkable recovery?" Nigel quipped. The flippancy of the comment took Malter by surprise. "Relax, Doc. I know I'm dying and there's no one else I need or want to talk to."

"Time is not your friend here, Nigel. Your chart tells me you haven't got long and no amount of pent up hate will stop what's coming. Your body is shutting down, and you'll note that I didn't say '*slowly*' there."

"I'm in no great rush."

Malter edged the faux-leather armchair closer to the bed and oriented it to face Nigel instead of the window before slumping himself into it. "So no-one you'd like to talk to?"

"You and I are talking here now, Doc. It will have to do."

"But wouldn't you prefer to speak with F…"

"Family?" Nigel interrupted. "I'll do that when I'm dead."

"I was going to say friends," Malter offered. "Typically, I'd also ask if there was anyone you'd like to make peace with, but I'll spare you that."

"Just as well. I have no intention of wasting any of my remaining time making peace or making good with anyone."

"But…" Malter tried.

"Doc, I get that this approach has sold you a lot of books, but I'm not interested, just as I don't care for friends."

"It's not about selling books, and it's not about what will benefit your friends," Malter settled. "What would help you see some closure?"

"I'll get the closure I need before I die. Or after. It doesn't matter which. Talking with you won't make that come any faster or slower, other than to pass the time."

"Well, I'll give you something to pass the time, and as luck would have it, that's just what I need. I'm being hounded by the Police."

"You can hide here if you like," Nigel suggested. He looked at Malter, adding, "We can overlook the hypocrisy of your not wanting to face the inevitable. I can even put in a friendly word for you with the police too, if it comes to that."

"I hardly think it's the same thing. The police are just an annoyance and regardless, I'd much rather be here with you. It will help."

"You're right. I'm such a nice guy, and why wouldn't you want to spend time with me?" Nigel asked half heartedly.

"That's a start. You're a nice guy and keep that front and centre. Focus on the positives, gloss over the negatives, but be mindful of what you've learned. It helps."

Nigel considered the prompt. "I'll tell you what I've learned and what I know." He wriggled himself up in bed to make it easier to engage with Malter. "The world isn't right for some people."

"How so?"

"A few notable exceptions aside, I've done the right thing and look where I'm at now."

"Death is a part of life, Nigel. Taking stock, you've overcome more than a little adversity and got on with your life better than anyone would have expected, except for when you..." Malter said before being interrupted.

"In the battle between good and evil, I wonder who's winning?" offered Nigel.

"Now we're getting somewhere," Malter remarked, feeling Nigel's communication tapped. "Let it out..."

"Forget it, Doc. I won't rant. I'm comfortable with what's happening around me."

"End of life is challenging, Nigel. It's time for you to confront things."

"Got my house in order, doc? Please don't trivialise my remaining hours with cliches."

"What you're describing as a cliche is also timeless wisdom. You've had your last outing, Nigel. You're not going anywhere now. If ever there was an opportunity to confront your past, it's most definitely now."

"I have confronted it, Doc. Trust me."

"So you're at peace?"

"Being at peace is not the best measure of confronting my past."

"Nigel, I've never been in your exact position, but I know my time will come. I'd like to think that when it does, I'll be comfortable with my time on this planet. In contrast, I look at you and I see anger and I see emotional pain. Clearing that might help your transition."

"By 'transition' I take it you're meaning for me to be pharmaceutically zombified to ease pain. I don't need my last hours to be as a docile, compliant patient, and you're belittling me and demeaning yourself if you want to coerce me."

"No-one's coercing you. I just want to see you comfortable, is all," Malter said. "Trust me, I've seen the merits of a comfortable passing. I've seen family and friends relieved and a restless soul turned ready."

"Look around you, doc. See any family, any friends?"

"No, but..."

"So don't offer platitudes or compare me with others. Angry or not, when I go, my contribution will be done. I don't care if I'm going to be adored, mourned, or vilified."

Malter signed at the familiarity of the exchange. Nigel was not the first to be so resistant to his offer of help. "So, there's nothing you want to share?"

"Actually, Doc, I would love to talk about you if you have the time and inclination."

"Sorry, Nigel. This is a time for you, not me."

"What if I said talking with you might help me recognise what I'm avoiding in myself? These are your words, Doc, so why wouldn't I see merit in doing it?"

"Good try, but I'm not talking about me. There are professional ethics at play."

"I look around this room and see no one who'll challenge your ethics on my behalf, and I sure won't do it on my own. So what harm would comparing your life to mine do? You owe me that much."

"Owe? I don't owe you anything," Malter dismissed.

"Perhaps. Stranger things have happened."

"Stranger things, sure, but it's unlikely that between now and your passing, I'll be indebted to you."

"OK," Nigel conceded, but moved on almost immediately. "Talk to me for our shared history, then. Let's blur that line between sharing of yourself and sharing of our history."

Malter baulked. "Alright..." he began before Nigel embraced the opportunity.

"Did you love your sister? I know I did, but I want to hear what she meant to you."

Malter thought about the question. "I know people reminisce and only think of the good or the bad, but in my case, being younger than her when she died, it was easy for her to always be the faultless, bigger sister."

"Died? That's such a poignant word, Doc. I never think of that word," Nigel challenged angrily. "My memory has me struggling with other, less passive ways to describe her passing."

"Whatever words you use, they haven't helped and won't help you now."

"Spoken like the little brother," Nigel said. "Me, I'm speaking as the one grilled by police for hours while she was still missing. I'm speaking as the one treated like the criminal before and even after they found her body."

"My memories of that period don't even feature you as being implicated or investigated," Malter recalled. "They revolve around my father driving the streets looking for her, periodically returning home to report his progress to my mother and to bring her another calming bottle of spirits. I remember my dad falling from the car with fatigue after what felt like days of wondering where my sister disappeared to."

"It was days. The police only had the right to hold me for eight hours without charge in those days, but hey, I was 'helping with their enquiries'. Those words for the media justified their ability to interrogate me relentlessly. Shift after shift, I put up with accusation after accusation. I remember the sickly sweet scent of their aftershave and deodorant contrasting with my odour of frustrated sweat for hours in the stuffy interrogation, sorry, '*interview*', room. Every 12 hours with me not 'cracking', the old guard would give way to the new."

"Does it help that your time in custody made your eventual exoneration straightforward?"

"It helps a lot," Nigel said, cynically upbeat. "It comforted me that the police would later drop me home with little more than a 'sorry for your loss' when perhaps she'd still be alive if they were more focused on their search for the real perpetrators than the guy they tried to pressure to be guilty."

Malter moved on. "I don't even remember much about the funeral. Only now I think of it do I guess that was the last I saw of you for a while until our paths crossed again. When I saw you later, between my maturing and your incarceration, I recognised how much you'd changed."

"I wouldn't say it 'changed' me so much as hardened my resolve."

"What resolve?" Malter asked, feeling some emotion shifting in Nigel as he spoke. "I guess I could ask what it achieved and if it was worth it?"

"My parole hearing tiptoed around the same question, with perhaps a little more understanding than the police. They couldn't say my actions were justified, of course, but on my release, I knew they recognised my actions were warranted. Statistically, I knew each member of the parole board had a sister, wife or girlfriend, and my actions forced them to confront what they'd do in my situation."

"Most would leave it to the legal system, not take matters into their own hands as you did. Civilisations crumble when people challenge the central tenets of their society."

"The legal system had already failed me. I would not let it fail your sister, too."

"So you think it was worth it?". Malter urged on Nigel's willingness to communicate. "You're on your deathbed, and this is when you get to look back and reappraise, before it's too late."

"I'd do it again in a heartbeat," Nigel proclaimed. "Sure, it cost me years, but it gave me time to think and it yielded opportunities."

"You don't think had you not gone to jail you'd have had even better opportunities? There's no right or wrong answer here. I'm just wanting to hear your perspective."

"Think it would make for a wonderful book, Doc?" Nigel teased.

"If it's any consolation, I couldn't use anything of your story in a book. It's intrinsically tied to my history and it would cross a personal line, if not a professional one. So come on, now that you served your time, do you have any regrets?"

"Not how you'd think, Doc. Several people set upon my girlfriend, your sister, and ultimately killed her… they had their fun and it took them days. I killed only two of them, and I did it quickly."

"The law says the last one was innocent," Malter dismissed with a shrug.

"You know what, Doc?" Nigel asked. "I marvel at you."

"Why so? That I've moved on?"

"Far from it," Nigel said indignantly. "That you can be in such denial."

"I see enough regret to know it serves no one, Nigel, me especially, and actions such as yours have helped no one, especially you. You should take comfort in what time you had with my sister, and what time you have left."

"And that's supposed to comfort me how?"

"Little comfort to be sure, but… I understand your sentiment."

"If we're done, Doc, I've got plans," Nigel said dismissively.

"Nigel, look at you," Malter began. "It's not me who's in denial."

"Glass houses, Doc." Nigel closed his eyes and took a few calming, deep breaths. "It wouldn't hurt for you to expect more from me."

"I look at you and think, hope, the most I can expect from you is that in your remaining time, you'll find some peace." As much as it saddened him, Malter accepted there was little point in saying anything more.

Nigel said nothing, but relaxed into a trance-like state of calm, punctuated with deep breaths in and slow exhales.

13

Detective Kelshaw hovered at the nurses' station to see those entering Nigel's room, but without being seen himself. He hated this place, ever since he'd first needed to consider it as an option for his Peaches, and no amount of professionalism and friendliness from the staff could shift his thinking on the matter. People came here to die and everything reminded him of his wife and the inevitable thoughts of whether this place would have been a better choice than watching her drift away at home. Only seeing Malter already with Nigel lightened his mood marginally.

He had tried to press the hospice staff beyond small-talk, but quickly realised their interest was foremost on their patient's care and secondly on their patient's best interests, so he'd resigned himself to the need to wait for Malter to leave. Eventually, Malter left with only a cursory nod to one nurse as he darted off down the corridor. Now was his chance.

"Mr Newcott. Nigel. I'm detective Nate Kelshaw," he said as he entered the patient's room. "I appreciate your time is finite and precious, but I would like to talk about some of your friends, fellow patients of Dr Malter."

"I've spent more than enough of my life talking to police and I have no intention of wasting a minute with you, now," Nigel declared.

"I can't comment on what happened in the past, but I am most interested in your friends, and you, now," Kelshaw began, unperturbed. "I know of your past, and your current incapacities, which is all the more reason I'd like to talk. It won't take long."

"So why talk to me at all?" Nigel asked, raising his arms above his head in a disinterested yawn-like stretch.

"I intend to speak with all of his patients, his surviving patients. You're as good a place as any to start, and I followed Malter here so I know he's met with you. That he came here just after I spoke with him interests me."

"I'm his patient and I'm admitted here. What's so odd about him visiting? He came here earlier, but I had guests, so he more than likely just came back after they'd left and you pissed him off."

"Too convenient," Kelshaw replied. "I don't do convenience."

"He mentioned you took it upon yourself to drag him in overnight," Nigel said. "So, what are you trying to pin on him?"

"That he's spoken with you tells me a lot. Your loyalties aside, I have concerns he's coercing others to perform acts harming others."

"Unlikely. He's just someone to talk to."

"But he's a common link in several deaths," Kelshaw suggested.

"You're going to need more than that to convince me of any link, and I'm guessing a jury will have the same problem."

"So what did you talk about?" Kelshaw moved on.

"None of your business."

"Excellent. I'll just note your defensiveness and use it to justify my need to bring you in for questioning," the detective teased, making an almost pantomime-like effort to emphasise the use of his pen and notebook. "Were you planning on dying here, or at the station?"

Nigel took in as big a breath as his body would allow. "Detective, I could die right now if I wasn't so interested in staying alive. If you want to take me in, you'd need an ambulance to get me out of here and permanent medical staff to babysit me wherever we go. You and I know that won't happen, so spare me the threats."

"You're not for resuscitation," Kelshaw replied, pointing to the signage above Nigel's bed head. "I'm guessing that might mitigate the need for at least some special care."

Nigel pressed his staff alert buzzer and almost immediately there was a sound of movement from the corridor outside his room. The nurse appeared soon after, slipping between Nigel and Kelshaw as if the patient was the only one in the room. "What can I get you, lovely?"

"I'm withdrawing my consent to be *not for resuscitation,*" Nigel announced.

The nurse slipped the perspex N.F.R. plate from underneath the whiteboard labelled with Nigel's name and embellished with hand-drawn pictures of flowers. "Done," she declared. "I'll be back in a little while with some paperwork, but that you've told me is enough for now."

"You're kidding, right?" Kelshaw exclaimed, expectant of a more arduous process. "He can't just change his mind like that."

"Sure he can," the nurse confirmed. "There's more paperwork to not be resuscitated than to withdraw it. It's the patient's choice and just because this is a hospice doesn't diminish his rights to choose." She smiled and withdrew from the room.

"Detective, you were saying something about my being NFR and that somehow that would make me more capable or inclined to be questioned elsewhere."

"You're just as bad as Malter."

"Being bad is both relative and misunderstood," Nigel said. "In some circles, my history would have me seen as being the bad guy, yet in others, perhaps not so much."

"The circles I'm interested in are the ones sanctioned by the law. Vigilante based actions, no matter how noble you think they are, still earn the perpetrator the title of 'bad'. Your history, what you did, was wrong in the same way as whatever Malter is doing, is wrong."

"Do you think anyone cares?" Nigel asked with almost disinterest. "Malter's patients who died were going to die. Who are you to interfere with how they go? I knew them all, and I'd go on record to state that their passing was not as implausible as you seem to think."

"Suicide is illegal..."

"So, are you going to arrest a body?"

"Let me finish, Mr Newcott. It's not their suicides that interests me, and we aren't talking about two deaths now."

"I don't think Malter would have sold anywhere near as many books if he'd put them up to it, if that's your insinuation."

"If you or anyone else kills themselves, that's a matter for you to take up with your maker," Kelshaw said. "But you take someone with you, some innocent bystander, that changes everything."

"Would you be that interested if the roles were reversed, detective? If someone died and took a terminally ill patient with them?"

"I hardly see why that's relevant," Kelshaw said, puzzled.

"Just gauging your perspective is all. Would you still be looking at Malter if that were the case?"

"Don't be so ridiculous and don't waste my time with irrelevant questions. I have serious concerns as to the wellbeing of all of Malter's remaining patients, including you."

"But it's not us patients that you're interested in. Just the other parties."

"You're not being very helpful, Nigel. The time I waste with you might come at a cost of more lives, maybe even your own."

"I won't be big on your list of concerns, and all of Malter's patients are in varying degrees of decline," Nigel suggested. "So who are they?"

"Who?"

"The people you're interested in," Nigel explained. "The ones who died."

"I'm not at liberty to discuss all the details. Suffice to say, they are people who didn't deserve to die because someone killed themselves, potentially at the direction of someone else."

"Would it matter if they deserved to die?" Nigel teased.

"You've now moved from irrelevant to insensitive questions."

"It seems both sensitive and relevant, to me at least," Nigel said. "You want me to talk with you under the auspices of your impartiality and that your interest is purely about the law. I'm asking if it would matter in your enquiry if these people weren't merely docile, god-fearing innocents."

"It wouldn't matter to me. They're entitled to die as nature demands, and not before."

"Until you want to investigate them for their crimes. You see my point?"

The detective sighed. "So tell me about them," Kelshaw invited. "What were they like?"

"Your use of the past tense is not inspiring, but beyond that, who are we talking about?" Nigel asked.

"Malter's patients. I hear you had quite a crowd of them this morning, so the process of elimination should tell you who I'm most interested in, but by all means, start anywhere."

"What's said in group, stays in group," Nigel proclaimed. "It might not be as binding as the doctor-patient thing, but I think it's a good thing just the same."

"OK... so what will you share?", the detective pressed confidently, holding up his notebook.

"With you? Nothing," Nigel dismissed. "Waste your time all you want, but I'm not talking with you."

"Mind if I wait for you to change your mind?" Kelshaw tried without too much conviction.

"Mind if I call the nurse to have you removed?" Nigel replied, moving the buzzer to his chest. He kept his eyes closed while waiting to hear the detective leave his room.

14

Malter thought to call his office while walking down the corridor, heading for the main exit of the hospice. He needed to distract himself from his current stress, but as with many of his patients, he now realised that his life comprised work and little else. He had no family or friends, and that void was now very apparent when he needed a friendly ear that wasn't Nigel. His mind edged back to the thought of work like it usually did, but that only refocussed his stress on his current predicament. He detoured into a small sitting room and closed the door behind himself for a little privacy while he made the call.

"I need a fresh set of eyes, Tash."

"Why?" she asked.

"The police are going to scrutinise, and I'm at a loss for what they are looking for. Anything looking like a vendetta will spark their interest, but I don't know what else. The detective as good as hinted his interest in biasing his investigation for radical Islamics."

"I'd remember transcribing anything which raised my eyebrows, believe me," she offered. "With that in mind, there's nothing in any file I've seen."

"Swear to it?"

"I'm not bound by the same code of ethics as you, Doc, but I'm still bound by the standards which enable me to sleep at night. Someone threatens action to any extent would have me scanning the news. I love working here, with you, but the reality of what I hear, see and transcribe is little more than what I'd describe as sentimental drivel. No offence."

"None taken," Malter said. "That attitude will help if my files make it to court. I'm not suggesting it will help my case, mind you, only that it's comforting you didn't think there was anything of merit."

"So what are the police looking for?" she enquired. "More to the point, what am I looking for?"

"Start somewhere, look for a pattern, and work from there. That's all I've got."

"My memory isn't that bad, but regardless of where I start, I'm guessing I'll find nothing common in your recent patient list. Second and subsequent passes would reveal the same thing," she said. "Different backgrounds, different lives, different people. The only thing they have in common is that they are, were, your patients."

"I can't help but think the same thing, Tash," Malter accepted. "I was wondering if it was just me."

15

Detective Kelshaw dialled Constable Piper Richards the moment he left the hospice foyer. He had wondered if he should have brought her with him, and if a female presence would have made Newcott any more likely to talk. Experience told him that some people just didn't communicate with police regardless of whether they had a 'Y' chromosome, and Newcott's history had him outside the realm of 'some people'. Still, he thought it was worth a bet, and yet again, Piper was in for a dollar. Kelshaw marvelled at his arrogance at even suggesting the wager after reading Newcott's old interview record.

"I owe you a dollar, Piper."

"I'll add it to what you already owe me," she said. "Nothing of interest?"

"Not a complete waste of time. He suggested the patients get to know at least a little about each other, so it's not all just private sessions. That in mind, we might get lucky with some of the other patients. Regardless, we'll be able to implicate Malter."

"Anything for me then," she asked, "or did you just ring to share your loss in another wager?"

"Aside from that, I think we need to pick up the history of the victims. Newcott teased me about wanting to know who each of the victims are, or were. I'd hate to be blindsided and miss that the victims and perps might know each other."

"That almost sounds like hedging your bets, Nate."

"Saying it out loud, it sounds beyond plausible and well into the realm of likely. Malter tells them to get even with whoever so they can die in peace. That, Piper, is excellent grounds for an extended warrant to get at all his records."

"But it's just an unsubstantiated theory, nothing more. Basic checks gave us nothing special on both Stokes and Greer. They lived across town, they never worked together and from what I saw, before their involvement with Malter, they'd never even met."

"Look deeper," Kelshaw insisted. "If Newcott can hold a grudge for the best part of his life, it's reasonable that Malter could help them see someone from long ago as being worthy to get even with."

16

Melanie arrived at the address provided by the male voice on the call, allegedly Anthony's father. She'd spent the drive debating her instinct to ignore the call and the requested meeting, relative to her curiosity to learn more of her Anthony. She was still undecided, right until she arrived and committed to going inside only because of proximity, not by any actual decision on her part. The prospect of being alone and entering what might be the home of an unknown male didn't seem to represent that great a risk, considering how just sleeping had recently become 'risky' behaviour. She still kept her car unlocked in case she needed speedy departure, and the extra seconds fumbling for keys didn't appeal.

She rang the doorbell with her phone in her hand and the emergency number pre-dialled, just in case. All she needed to do was press the dial button. Too apprehensive about not having a plan and too curious to walk away, it comforted her that if the meeting turned ugly, she could hit that button and have the police on their way. The plan was plausible, at least until her phone rang.

"Hi Melanie, you've found me just fine," Anthony's father said.

"I'm at your doorstep now."

"I know. You're on several cameras," he said. "The door's unlocked and I can't make it downstairs." He hung up before Melanie had any time to object.

Melanie grabbed the doorknob but baulked. She rubbed her hand over her belly while she re-evaluated the risks and locked her car by remote before entering the house.

Inside, the smells of a clean home comforted her. Had the house smelled of detritus or even cigarette smoke, she would have faced another wave of nausea, reluctance, or fear. Instead, her pregnancy enhanced sense of smell met with a clinically sterile ambience. She leant back on the door, forcing it home heavily to produce a loud click that echoed up the hardwood stairs before her and disappeared down the hallway beside her. Around the entry were bare walls decorated only with the crossed shadows of the security screens in the morning sunlight. She brushed aside the thought of the plain walls being a canvas ready for bloody decoration in the hands of a serial killer and waited for some acknowledgement from the occupant to confirm his whereabouts.

"I'm upstairs," he announced, using some unseen intercom. "I appreciate your caution, but it's just us and when you see me, you'll understand I'm no threat."

Melanie left the security of having her back to the door and moved to the base of the stairs. She looked up and gingerly placed her right foot on the first step, paused, and then put her left foot on the second step a little more loudly. Emboldened, she continued with slow, deliberate steps until she reached the top.

"Centre door, on the right," came another announcement on cue. "You're welcome to investigate the other rooms, but I'm in the middle one."

Committed, Melanie walked to the door as fast as her heels and her wounded knee would allow. The door was only slightly open until she pushed it wide, relaxing on seeing what the voice had pre-empted. Before her was an old man reclining on a hospital bed; an unlikely threat given the IV tubes in each arm and solitary nasal tube in his left nostril. The half-filled catheter bag hanging on the foot of the bed proved the final reassurance that the guy was definitely bed bound.

"We spoke on the phone," Melanie said cautiously. It felt a little odd to be introducing herself in the bedroom of an elderly stranger.

"I know, Melanie. I'd offer you a seat, but I don't receive visitors, only carers and those delivering meals, none of whom stay to converse while their meter is running. There's a chair in the corridor, though. Perhaps you could bring it in and we could talk."

Melanie looked over her shoulder and accepted that the request wasn't onerous and the chair was liftable. "I don't even know your name."

"It's Tom. Tom Willson. Two 'L's. Even better would be to talk over a cup of tea," he suggested with a smile. "I prefer green tea, not that it's miraculously cured my cancer. Regardless, I'm sure a cuppa would encourage frank discussion of the elephant in the room."

Melanie accepted the simplicity of the request and headed out of the room in search of the kitchen.

17

Piper intercepted Kelshaw as soon as he entered the corridor from the station's male toilet. "Nate, we need to talk about the next of kin of Anthony Castell." She presented a small stack of manila folders like a street urchin asking for more food.

"What have you got, Piper?" Kelshaw asked as he dried his hands on his thighs.

"Castell had siblings. Two brothers and a sister."

"And what, you can't find any next of kin?" Kelshaw asked.

"Let me finish," she insisted. "They were all each other's next of kin, and uniforms have found one of them dead in his home. Looks like a murder-suicide."

"So, was he the 'murder' or the 'suicide' part of the equation?"

"Not confirmed, yet," she said. "The brother, Chris Morgan, got a shotgun to the face, both barrels before the other party reloaded and then unloaded into his own mouth. That's certainly how it looks."

"So that's one brother," Kelshaw said, prompting continuation.

"Jenny Pisano, Castell's sister, drowned in the back of a car that drove into the river early this morning." Piper paused a beat, waiting for any sign of acknowledgement. She struggled to replace the file at the top of her pile as if Kelshaw would need to see it. "It's not your problem and upstairs has got it. They rescued the driver from the car, but they couldn't resuscitate him. Both of his hands were zip-tied to the steering wheel, which slowed his release from the submerged vehicle."

"Ouch," Kelshaw said. He flitted open the top folder being held by Piper and glanced at the top-most crime scene photo. "Both bodies identified?"

"All four. Pseudo-formally, sure, between neighbours and ID on their person… we still need the next of kin. I'm doing the backgrounds on the perps."

"So, three members of one family?" Kelshaw slowed to a reluctant halt and took the folders. He skimmed over the cover page of each. "All different names, though. You sure they're related?"

"All verified. It gets better," Piper said exuberantly. "The guy who shot in self-defence, the other thing occupying your morning… that was the other brother. David Kingsley." She waited to see the spark of understanding in Kelshaw. "Want more? Ask me about the mother."

"Just tell me, Piper," Kelshaw sighed, a little short. "What about the parents?"

"So glad you asked," she began. "The lawyer who broke the fall of the jumper, Malter's patient…"

"What about her?"

"That's the mother," Piper declared.

"You sure?"

"All confirmed. I'm guessing this doesn't make you inclined to ease up on Doctor Malter?"

"Fat chance," Kelshaw said. "We've got a family with enemies tied to one person, and please tell me no-one upstairs is suggesting some weird coincidence!"

"Obviously not, but the priority is what's going on with the family, and lucky you, you've just taken on all the files."

"The surviving brother won't be just the victim of a random attack, and I'm guessing he won't be out of the woods, yet." Kelshaw knew he wasn't saying anything that both Piper and upstairs wouldn't appreciate, but it was refreshing to see her nod in agreement. "What about the other parent?"

"Tom Willson. I've only got an address for him, but it took a while. He's a blank sheet with no history at this point, like old-school 'off-the-grid' blank."

"OK," Kelshaw accepted. "So someone's checked on the dad and the surviving brother?"

"Uniforms are visiting the brother again. He's not answering his phone. You're checking up on the Dad," she said with delegated authority. "I was told to tell you as much."

"Thanks," Kelshaw replied cynically. "Isn't speaking to a bereaved parent a female thing? So, isn't that your job?"

"Good try," Piper said with a measure of accomplishment. "He's all yours. Family vendettas rarely end with the kids."

"You might want to rush that background on Willson."

"I'm still looking," she said. "Willson's obviously just an assumed name. I'll ping you as soon as I get some kind of grounding. Meanwhile, you get on your way."

18

Melanie oriented herself in the stranger's kitchen. She found the green tea and some oolong for herself without too much difficulty, and used the time waiting for the kettle to boil to explore the rest of the house, initially with some trepidation but with progressively more confidence. The man, Tom Willson, used the intercom to guide and even encourage her inquisitiveness, assisted by some unseen surveillance devices. The entire house was empty and sterile in a way that she couldn't place until the lack of photographs became apparent. No photos, next to no food in the fridge, and only a takeaway food leaflet secured to the outside of the fridge with a magnet. By the time she returned to his bedside with two mugs and a packet of cream biscuits tucked under her arm, she felt as if she'd given the entire house the once over.

"This is a treat, Melanie."

She looked at the biscuits. "I guess. I used to love them as a child."

"Quite, but I meant your company," Willson began. "I never thought I'd get to meet you."

"Anthony only mentioned you once in the past tense. He said it with such finality that I never pressed for more and we never went there again, and he never pushed for more as to my family either."

Willson closed his eyes and breathed a slow breath. "It's the way his mother brought him up." Willson welled up in the eyes a little before pre-emptively wiping away a tear. "She would have encouraged him to keep to himself and not bring me into anything."

"So you weren't a candidate for 'father of the year'?" Melanie tried to make light of the comment. "My dad wasn't great either." She appreciated that she might have been a little forward and tried to correct. "I don't know the details from your side, but I don't even know where mine is. My father, that is."

"It wasn't for a lack of love, Melanie. I loved Anthony and his brothers and sister, and their mother, for that matter."

"My dad said the same line, except he added a footnote about another woman. My mother described it as the lure of a fresh start with a new family."

"It was nothing like that. I never left for another, and I've been single ever since."

"So did you abandon the others as well, or just Anthony?" Melanie said, flaunting the same loaded word her mother had used throughout her upbringing. "I didn't know he had *any* family."

"You likely met them, but perhaps Anthony introduced them as friends, omitting details of their shared history. Jenny, Chris and David. Familiar?"

"I never met any of his friends."

"It doesn't matter now, anyway," Willson said with a little melancholy.

Melanie's temporarily absent abstraction from the events of the night before returned with brutal finality. She dug deep to prevent losing herself in a sadness which her Anthony would only describe as pointless. "You said you knew more about Anthony's death."

"Ah, yes," Willson offered, "'the elephant in the room'." He paused until he had Melanie's full attention. "So Anthony never mentioned any family?" he asked, ignoring Melanie's subtle prompt for information.

"I know it sounds odd, but I don't even know where he worked. It was just too lovely to meet a nice guy so totally unencumbered by work, friends or interfering family..."

"So he never spoke of anyone else?"

"No-one," Melanie said tersely, a little annoyed at being cut short. "I came here under the pretence of learning a little more about Anthony or his death, and I'm still waiting. For someone who's lost a long-estranged son, you don't seem too perturbed."

"Melanie," Willson began. "I appreciate you lost someone close, my son, but I have lost more than you, and far from being sanctimonious, I'm trying to help. Last night, I think I lost my entire family."

"You're not sure?"

"I'm sure enough. The police are liable to call or visit, and when that happens, I'll know for sure. Until then, I can hope."

"You haven't called to check for yourself?" she challenged. She paused to think. "And why wouldn't you call the police if you're so concerned or certain? I've come here expecting to learn something of Anthony, but I'm thinking of leaving appreciative of only the biscuit and the distraction." Willson said nothing to the retort.

The phone on Willson's bedside disturbed silent, bitter acrimony between the pair. He answered the call with his eyes closed but said nothing beyond mono-syllabic responses to questions heard only by him. Only with the return of the phone to the bedside was Melanie aware that the call was over.

"I have three sons, two of whom are dead and one dead daughter." He looked at Melanie and sobbed.

19

Detective Kelshaw received the call en route to see Tom Willson. "Nate, it's Piper. You're in luck. Castell's brother and sister are all confirmed as murder in murder/suicide."

"Not really news. It's hard to kill someone else when you've just shot a few shells into your brain. Whoever dies with the gun on them is the one who suicided."

"But you're in luck if you want to keep going with the Doc."

"Instead of visiting Willson?"

"As well as. It looks like patients of your doc were the ones who attacked Willson's other kids. Three from four. Travis Greer and Cliff Stokes, that you know of, but also Jason Metcalfe, who did the brother. His name isn't on your copy of the patient list, but he's a patient. I'm still looking into the guy who did the sister."

"What about the other two patients, Billy and the blond, Kelly? And have upstairs come onto my way of thinking about the Doc?" Kelshaw asked with snide arrogance.

"Uniforms are on their way to get the Doc while you speak with Willson."

"I'd prefer to deal with the doc now. Based on the ages of his kids, Willson himself must be at least mid-seventies. He'll be in no great rush."

"He isn't just old, he's bed-bound and dying, so he's not going anywhere, but you still need to meet with him."

"Willson isn't a patient of the doctor by chance?" Kelshaw asked. "He says he only deals with the terminally ill."

"I know. I read some of his books when my mother had breast cancer, but to your question, I don't know if he's a patient. As much as the records I've seen, he's not on the patient list."

Kelshaw sighed a little with disappointment. "Get more uniforms to get to Willson, then. Malter's mine."

20

Melanie was not comfortable with her efforts to console Willson. It should have been cathartic, but she didn't know what to say. She couldn't bring herself to offer a stranger a hug, but she sensed his appreciation for her holding his hand. As much as she wanted to leave, it didn't feel right to leave him in this state. In much the same way, she wanted to learn more, but it didn't feel appropriate to pry.

"The police are on their way, Melanie," Willson declared after burying his face in his hands for a long silence.

"I'll stay at least until they arrive, or I can stay longer if you'd prefer," she offered, trying not to tinge her words with any bias to stay or go.

"Of course their arrival won't change anything," Willson said, ignoring the offer.

"Other than to provide some answers," she struggled with what to say. "You must have so many questions, and the police will understand it all, I'm sure."

"The police will do their best to help, but they are in the business of answering the wrong questions. They'll want to know why this would happen to brothers and sisters from the same family. I could tell them, but it won't help."

"The police said the man who attacked my Anthony died at the scene."

"Whoever he is, or was, isn't the problem. He'll be just a tool. The real problem is still out there."

"How can you be so sure?"

"Because he visited me last night," Willson declared with a heavy sigh.

"And the police know this?"

"They might know, or perhaps they'll find out eventually, but that won't help," Willson said, oblivious to Melanie's lack of understanding. "I've denied my children a father and myself a family to stop what is unstoppable."

"So tell the police what you know. You might provide the missing piece of the puzzle..." Melanie insisted, keen to help.

"The police will share their findings when they get here, no doubt. They'll be wanting to find a common history between the people they'll assume are responsible and me, and they won't find one. They'll look wider and maybe they'll get lucky and find someone, but that's liable to make things many times worse."

"Perhaps you've got nothing else to lose," she suggested. "Not trying to put too fine a point on it, but you don't appear to have much time left to bargain with. So just tell them."

"It's not *my* wellbeing I'm interested in. If that was all it was, I'm sure he would have taken it by now."

"Who?"

"He'll be just a name until he finds you, and he will find you, guaranteed," Willson said.

"So? Whoever he is, I've done nothing to him."

"But I did something to him many years ago," Willson replied.

"So, if his quarrel is with you, why are we having this conversation? Tell the police and let them deal with it."

"A long time ago, he swore he'd get back at me. To do so then wouldn't have given him the joy of having me wait for the inevitable, so he's had a lifetime of brooding and I've had a life of waiting."

"If he's killed your children, surely he's settled that score."

"You're looking at this differently to him," Willson said dismissively. "You're lovely and you're young, but you're looking at this like someone who sees a need to fight with gloves on. You see yourself as being above the animals and you see that restraint is the mark of your civility."

"I'm not that young, or innocent," she said.

"Yes, but you probably wouldn't kill someone if they spilt your coffee. That's not necessarily a bad thing, mind you, but my point is, you have boundaries, moral lines which shouldn't be crossed. You have a western, twenty-first century, enlightened perspective and through which you have a sense of measure in any response or retaliation. Someone spills your coffee, you have a sense of what might seem reasonable, what we might see as excessive, and what's inconceivable."

"But this isn't about spilt coffee."

"No, it's not. In some parts of the world, one's perspective implicitly includes history. Not just the last minute or day, or week, or even year. It's not even your lifetime, or anyone living's memory. It's generations' worth of hate, artificially capped periodically, but no amount of time or external interference is going to suppress what lies beneath the surface. Think Balkans or Armenians. Spilling a coffee just provides an excuse."

"Mr Willson, Tom, where's this going?" Melanie asked, her patience waning as the old man's words degraded into a lecture.

Willson was momentarily distracted by the appearance of uniformed figures at what must have been his front door, visible on a security monitor. "When you meet a man named Nigel Newcott, you need to think of hate which transcends your realm of perspective."

"If you don't want to tell the police who he is, I will. I'm sure they'll provide the means of sharing with anonymity."

"Melanie, you're going to need to trust me on this, at least until you understand." The uniforms pressed the door buzzer repeatedly, which Willson ignored. "I need you to trust me."

"Why, Tom? Right now, you're as good as someone harbouring a criminal."

"True, but I think you're pregnant, and if Nigel even thinks you are expecting Anthony's child, you're likely to be the subject of his interest. Thus, your assailant's reference to a 'bloodline'."

Melanie took a deep breath to speak but ended up just exhaling slowly to settle herself as she instinctively pressed her blouse to her belly. "How could you have known? I haven't told a soul, other than Anthony."

Willson watched as the uniforms at the door separated. One stayed to press the buzzer with annoying persistence, the other left the front porch to do a lap of the house. "I can't profess any remarkable insight, Melanie, but the fact is I have tried to keep tabs on each of my children's lives through various agencies," he said. "Sorry to have had you followed, but I did it for harmless and good intentions."

Melanie was quiet for a beat until saying, "I'm struggling with the fact that you saw fit to follow me."

Willson nodded, but moved on unapologetically. "During Nigel's visit last night, he asked me to call Anthony, but someone else answered the phone. I'm assuming it was you screaming in the background," Willson suggested, not waiting for any acknowledgement. "I wasn't privy to what was said, but we need to assume he mentioned your pregnancy, even though I'm still a little surprised you didn't share Anthony's fate."

"So he knows?"

"I don't rightly know." Willson finally acknowledged the buzzer and welcomed the police upstairs, offering the same instructions he'd given to Melanie earlier. "I need to be hopeful the police will help you without unwittingly helping him," he told Melanie just as two young uniformed police entered.

21

As much as the hospice offered a convenient refuge away from potentially waiting media, Malter knew he couldn't stay there forever. He considered using a service door to leave, but decided against it, opting instead for the main entrance; surely the actions of an innocent man, he thought. He recognised his mistake as soon as he left the foyer.

"Hello, detective. What a surprise," Malter mocked on seeing Kelshaw exiting his car in ambush in the carpark.

"You've earned a good old-fashioned discussion at the station."

"If you've got your warrant, there's nothing else we need to discuss."

"That was before we discovered another few of your patients had died in the service against other members of the same family."

"Who?"

"Your look of surprise is refreshingly well-acted and more than a little convincing, Malter."

"I can't control my patients. I don't know who or why."

"All of that will come out in our chat, but in the meantime, you need to be reminded of your rights. You have the right to remain silent…"

This was not the first time Malter had been mirandised and the words quickly descended into white noise until the detective placed a hand on his shoulder. He felt the initial relief as a gesture of comfort, but then his chest tightened when Kelshaw produced the handcuffs. "Are the cuffs necessary? There is a presumption of innocence."

"I have some discretion, sure, and yes, you are legally innocent until I can prove it, but I think you're a prick," Kelshaw said provocatively. "I sincerely hope the cuffs don't scratch your Rolex."

Malter relented and offered his wrists before him in compliance. "I don't wear a Rolex."

"That's ok," Kelshaw conceded. "Truth be told, I don't care about your watch, whatever brand it is. You won't be able to wear one in jail, regardless."

Malter rang his secretary from the back seat of Kelshaw's unmarked vehicle as soon as they were mobile on a main road. He dialled stealthily, mindful that Kelshaw might be alerted to his inattentiveness to take the phone from his pocket as soon as he hit the call button, but certainly once it was answered.

"Tash, it's me. I don't have much time…" Malter said as he engaged the speaker.

"What the fuck are you doing, Malter?" the detective began as he tried to negotiate his way to the side of the road and to a stop. "End that call now…"

"Tash. Ignore the other voice."

"… End the call, Malter…"

"Ring the lawyer. Get her to meet me at detective Kelshaw's office."

"Anything you say is admissible, Malter…."

"Should you be talking, Doc?" Tash asked with the interruption. "Presumably that's the detective with you. He sounds a little upset."

"Listen to her, Malter."

"Don't worry about him, Tash. He should concentrate on his driving." Malter began before the immediacy of a car horn deafened him. "I need you to review my files and note any names mentioned."

"Malter, I'll be smashing that phone."

"Not someone in particular?" Tash asked.

"I don't know who I'm looking for."

"Right, Malter. Give me that phone." The car finally made it to the side of the road, and the irate detective exited, leaving the engine running.

"How far back?" she continued, oblivious to the actions of the detective making his way to the rear door.

"Hang on, Tash," Malter said as he stretched his cuffed hands over the driver's seat to press the central door locking switch. Kelshaw was infuriated, but now locked doors muffled his incoherent tirade. "Start from the most recent and work back for as long as you can."

"It might take a while," she said.

"You more than likely won't get that long, so just do your best. I expect the detective here is liable to want to move things along pretty quickly." Malter teased a wave at Kelshaw.

"What am I looking for?"

"Just names. The detective suggested there's more of my patients involved. We know of Cliff, Travis and Kelly, but there must be more, so maybe start with a cursory check of who's suddenly out of contact."

"So why the rush?"

"I need to know names. If I know them, the police might look at me from another direction."

"What if they do? You've done nothing," she said supportively.

"True, but that's not what I'm worried about. Come to think of it, it would help if, as you did the list, you tried to separate group attendees from 'others'"

"You've read my transcripts," Tash said. "I'm good, but I'm not that good. I'm unlikely to be able to separate references to people there in the room or not. Most of the sessions just go in one ear and out the other."

"Of course," Malter accepted. "I get that I'm asking for a long shot, but I'm losing patients, Tash, and I'm prepared to clutch at straws."

Kelshaw unholstered his sidearm and gently tapped on the window with the barrel. "10 seconds, Malter, then I break the window. I'm undecided whether to use the butt or a round."

"Tash, I've got to go. Keep anything you get separate or on your person," Malter whispered. "Anything and everything in the office might be the subject of a warrant."

"Ten. Nine," Kelshaw began a very vocal countdown. "If I end up shooting the glass, Malter, don't assume I'll try to avoid hitting you."

"Ok. I think I know what I'm doing," Tash replied. "Unlock the door, Doc. I don't want to need to attend your funeral or look elsewhere for a job."

"Depending on what you find, Tash, that might be unavoidable."

"Seven, Six, Five…"

"Open the door for him, please, Doc," she insisted.

"Will do. Thanks, Tash." Malter ended the call and tried to open his door to the waiting detective, only to be thwarted by the childproof lock of the back seat. He stretched himself over the front seat to reach the central lock as before.

Kelshaw immediately opened the door to grab Malter by the cuffs and dragged him from the car onto the curb. Malter accepted the manhandling as being justified. "Sorry, detective. I just felt the need to make a call," he said, struggling to be audible with his mouth in the dirt and a shoe pressed hard into the back of his neck.

"You're a prick, Malter, but I distinctly recall you instructing your secretary to destroy records."

"I did no such thing," Malter said calmly into the ground. "I merely asked her to check through some files, the result of which might aid your investigation."

"Nope," Kelshaw said. "That's not how I remember it. Your word against mine, and I wasn't the one in the back seat of a police vehicle."

"True," Malter accepted. "You weren't even in the car." It was worth the bait. He braced for his face to be pressed harder into the earth.

22

Malter noticed he was in the same interview room this time as last, but now the door was closed; he was being left to stew in his juice. He wondered if Kelshaw was liable to be in a better mood after a little time to calm himself down, but wasn't very hopeful. The thought made him identify another grain of sand in between his teeth and use the one-way mirror to check for bruising on his face.

"This is way more formal than our last chat, Doctor Malter," Kelshaw said on entering the room. He slammed the door behind himself and slapped some files on the desk.

"You're not advising me to have my lawyer present?" Malter tried to coax a little civility.

"Up to you, of course. You've already had your caution as to your rights."

"I've got nothing to hide."

"That's the spirit," Kelshaw said as he slipped into a chair opposite Malter. "Not even the ever-diminishing circle of your surviving patients has you seeking legal representation."

"Nothing to hide there, just as with all of my patients. It's all in my files and that we are having this conversation tells me still don't have grounds to subpoena them for yourself. Pity."

Kelshaw closed his folder and positioned his pen carefully on top, being particular to orient it parallel to the spine of his notebook. "Doc, I don't think you're at all concerned about what's going on."

"You're right," Malter said. "I'm not worried for myself, and there's no point in worrying about the deceased."

"So, no pity for them?"

"It's what I do, detective; my patients die. They are terminal before I meet them and I never offer them any miracle cure."

"Except, Nigel Newcott. You've known him for longer."

"Well, yes. I've known him in a non-professional and occasionally a professional capacity for many years. Fast forward until his diagnosis and then he too became my patient. That I've known him for longer than my other patients is irrelevant."

"You don't care about the families of your patients, their recent loss?" Kelshaw enquired. "There's several of them likely to want a chat… or an investigation as to your culpability."

"I don't do families. I'm only about the terminal patients."

"Even after they die."

"There's no point in trying to bait me, detective. I'll close their files like I've done with the hundreds before them. You didn't knock on my door for any of *them*, and your interest now is equally warranted."

"OK," Kelshaw said. He baulked a moment and then lunged for his pen. He rubbed it on the folder before using it to lift open the cover. "So, what can you tell me about Jack Bernardo?"

"Excuse me?" Malter asked, but he'd heard perfectly.

"Jack Bernardo. Know him?"

"I'm assuming we're talking about the same person. "

"I *know* we're talking about the same person," Kelshaw said snidely.

"His is a name I haven't spoken of for many years."

"Haven't seen him lately?"

"No," Malter replied. "I tried to keep abreast of his whereabouts for maybe the first few years, but not for a long time."

"So not recently?"

"It was my way of moving on, detective. Professionally, it helped me learn what I was later to write about in my books. It's all about closure."

"Your books don't interest me."

"Perhaps I'll do an edition with more pictures for you then, one day."

"Nice one, Doc," Kelshaw said with a feigned laugh. "So if something happened to him, would that interest you?"

Malter considered the question. "There are a lot of things I could say now, but none of them will help you. There are even more things that I won't say… they wouldn't help you either."

"So not one word for the person everyone knows raped and killed your sister?"

"What's the point?" Malter said. "Would it make you feel better if I clarified some words I won't say?"

"Knock yourself out."

"Pity. I won't offer him pity. Regret. I regret nothing unfortunate which has ever happened in his life." He watched Kelshaw for his reaction before adding, "I do hope he met or meets his end with a measure of pain, though."

"That all?"

"I've moved on, detective. Residual emotions like that don't serve me. It's buried like my sister." Malter expected a reaction from Kelshaw but was instead only met with a vacuous, distracting stare. "You haven't said why Bernardo is even relevant."

"I just wanted to see your reaction to the mention of him. For all your books about *'moving on'*," Kelshaw said with pantomimed air quotes, "it seems you've still got issues."

"He killed my sister and got away with it. Moving on doesn't mean I don't have issues, it only means that I've moved past what destroyed my family to not let it destroy me. And I still don't see the relevance of talking about him."

"You're an angry man, Malter. Suppressed under a veneer of professional calm, sure, but it's still there. In my line of work, I see tragedy and violence whenever that kind of anger gets repressed. It will vent eventually. Perhaps I should write a book about it."

Malter only shrugged.

"What if I said your patients' victims were all related to one man, a Mr Tom Willson, two 'L's? Would *that* be of interest?"

"Of course it would, but I would think that's amazingly unlikely," Malter said. "I don't know who that is, and I've never even heard the name mentioned."

"And yet your patients are still implicated. Maybe they are angry, mountains of suppressed anger, just like you. Maybe they are angry at Willson or his kids," Kelshaw said provocatively. "See it from my point of view?"

"Of course, I get your suspicions, but I don't know."

"So, do you vet your patients before taking them on?"

"It's never come up."

"Sure," Kelshaw said, making a display of his note-taking. "So is Tom Willson a patient, or prospect?"

"I've already answered that, and what if he is? I'm under no obligation to say *yay* or *nay*."

"Jesus, Malter. It's a simple, benign question. If he was potentially a patient, could or would you refuse to take him on?"

"Yes, I could, theoretically. I can decide who I see." Malter softened a little, if only to see if it would moderate Kelshaw. "Happy to say this, off the record, that I don't have any patient on my books by that name. Happy?"

"And you're sure about that?" Kelshaw paused with arrogant confidence. "Want a lawyer yet?"

The interview room door opened without a knock or warning. "My client is saying nothing," a red-headed young woman began as soon as the door started moving. "Doctor Malter is a renowned psychologist and author, and civil libertarians are going to be outraged that confidentiality is liable to be subject to procedural back-dooring."

Malter crossed his arms with an air of finality. "Hi, Jess. The detective here has got nothing on me, but he *is* interested in my patients."

"Presumably you're the lawyer," Kelshaw commented as he closed his files. "You ready for a criminal case?"

"Good guess. Jess Young. I don't do criminal law, but this doesn't meet that definition, anyway. I'm guessing you haven't charged my client with anything that might even remotely challenge my acumen."

"Not yet, but it's not a big stretch. Several patients have died, and in their efforts, they've taken members of a single family with them."

"So several *terminal* patients have died," retorted the lawyer. "Beyond that, I'll be keen to meet with my client. Got anything else? Anything substantial *and* substantiated?"

"The patients were all under his care..." Kelshaw said.

"Which is a matter of public record," replied Jess.

Kelshaw paused a beat to present something which might not have such a ready response. "It's direct involvement or conspiracy. I'll take either at this point. I'm set to get access to his records, and when that happens, you and your client are going to need to have showed compliance."

"No one will give you a warrant for unfettered access to medical files. Privilege is like that."

"I said the same thing, Jess," Malter added. "So can I go?"

"Not on your life, Malter. Your stunt on the way here tells me you've got something to hide." Kelshaw looked at the lawyer. "He made a call to his secretary to get her to destroy records. My statement is what will get me the warrant."

"I did no such thing," Malter said, incensed.

"No need to explain, Doctor Malter," Jess said calmly. "I'm guessing this was the call made when you were in the back seat of a vehicle."

"It was probably the wrong thing to do," Malter said. "I admit to making the call, but it was for innocent and even possibly helpful purposes."

"There's no need to worry, James," Jess said calmly. "Video of you being threatened by the detective here is already doing the rounds on social media. Anything you might have said will be inadmissible anyway, even if you effectively admitted direct involvement on that call."

"Which I did not," Malter said.

"And I'd do it again, given the circumstances," Kelshaw said arrogantly. "I'm liable to be cited as a hero when the truth comes out."

"You more than likely won't get the chance. I've already made a submission for you to be removed from the case," said Jess, while handing over a single sheet on letterhead from her briefcase. "I faxed a copy to the media, too. You might not be a hero, but you're liable to earn the title of celebrity amazingly soon. My suggestions to you for the next time you try a stunt like that is to, 'A', not do it where at least five independent witnesses can film it, and 'B', not do it to my client."

"I should have shot him, accidentally, of course, to gain entry to the car."

"Now, now, detective. No need to dwell on what could have been. In the immediate term, my client and I are leaving."

"Like hell you are!" Kelshaw said angrily. "He's not going anywhere," he said, pointing angrily at Malter, "you," he pointed at the lawyer, "I don't care about."

"Well, we are." Jess produced another sheet and handed it to the detective. "Find someone who can read it to you. Outside."

Kelshaw stood, scraping his chair noisily against the polished concrete floor. "5 minutes." He left the room reluctantly.

As soon as they were alone in the room, Jess placed her case on the desk. "First things. If you are in any way involved, I don't want to know. My responsibility is to you as my client, but that doesn't extend to being complicit in anything illegal. I would like to know what's going on, though."

"If I knew, honestly Jess, I'd tell you, but I don't."

"So, what do you know?"

"Not a lot. A few of my patients suicided."

"As your literary lawyer, that doesn't sound that remarkable. Sad obviously, but not new, especially for you. Probably at least a wonderful chapter in it, if not an entire book."

"They took others with them. Apparently related to a Tom Willson. No idea who he is."

"OK. So that's less common and a lot more of interest. You still happy to declare a lack of involvement?"

"No doubt Joe public, or a jury, might struggle with it being a coincidence that my patients involved themselves with a single-family, but it's nothing to do with me. If it comes to it, do you know any good actual criminal lawyer?"

"I do, but let's not get ahead of ourselves or let the detective get the better of you. The submissions to get him removed and the noise of his videoed intimidation will slow him down, and then there's the privilege component. I'd think it's unlikely they'll be brave enough to charge you in the immediate term, at least until they have something concrete."

"Thanks, Jess, but I don't know where that leaves me now."

"It means you'll be right to leave the station to do as you will, but they'll be keeping close tabs on you. A criminal lawyer might well advise you to use that time, perhaps to clean up what they might end up looking for. Just saying."

"I've got nothing to hide, Jess. I don't know what's happening."

"A good criminal lawyer would praise you for that sincerity, James. Keep it up."

"Not funny, Jess," Malter conceded at the taunt.

23

Detective Kelshaw took a moment for some fresh air outside. The sun was shining, the sky was blue, and it had all the makings of a perfect day, except that he was facing some significant scrutiny from the office of professional standards. He was stressed, but too focused on Malter to take the advice offered by his union representative to go home until the dust settled. Not that he'd faced this kind of attention before, but it was moments like these he regretted quitting smoking, just for the distraction, particularly since his Peaches died. She would have grounded him in an instant.

"White and two sugars," Piper began, appearing behind him with a mug of coffee, three-quarters full. "You better take this. I need to get back. There's a bit of a commotion out front."

"Thanks, Piper," he said, taking the coffee. "I'm not the cause of that commotion, am I?"

"No, some old guy pushed a stranger in front of a bus. She died at the scene," she explained. "This happened across the road and he then came straight up to the front counter here, followed by a throng of witnesses keen to share their statements."

"He confessed?"

"Not yet, but there's no shortage of people that saw him do it. He's asking for family and getting a little agitated that they aren't appearing. Best as we can gather, he's got quite advanced dementia. With his confusion, we don't really know if the family he's asking for are living or dead. Fact is, he could be referring to someone from any time in his life. My grandfather had Alzheimers and I remember him blurring memories of me and his other grandchildren with friends from his youth."

"I don't feel so bad hiding out here then," Kelshaw said into his coffee.

"Between that and the need to do more background on Willson's family, it's a little busy."

"So they aren't letting the lawyer railroad a legitimate case?" Kelshaw asked. "We aren't just talking suicides taking passengers, we're talking *bone fide* murders."

"Not at all," she said, taking a seat next to Kelshaw and looking over her shoulder. "They're still trying to work out whether this is drug or gang-related so they can palm it off on the relevant specialist team."

"It's neither," Kelshaw remarked confidently. "Let me do the backgrounds and I'll give the prosecutor Malter on a plate."

"Upstairs won't allow that. You're still off the case. If it's any consolation, they see it as nicer to you to get an external team onto it. They just don't know who."

"Still..." Kelshaw tried to continue before being interrupted.

"Forget it. You've been red-listed for any interest in any of them, tied to Malter or not. And no, I won't let you use my login."

"So what else is there to do?" he asked.

"My suggestion? As I'm guessing you don't want to call it a day, you might like to visit the nursing home where this old guy was a resident, and maybe do some background. The guy was a known wanderer, but that he absconded from the facility is going to be seen as quite a serious breach of their duty of care, and they might be a little reluctant to help until there's some clarity as to their liability," Piper said. "It gets you out of the way, anyway."

"Better than wasting my time here," Kelshaw said, already standing and fidgeting for his car keys. "So, who's he asking for?"

"The old guy, his name is Eric Barnes, is asking for '*Nigel*'. That's all we've got."

Kelshaw's face lit up. "That's not the most common of names, but it's not the rarest either. Is it too coincidental to think of the Nigel I met earlier? Malter's patient?"

"I didn't think you did coincidences, Nate," she teased.

"I don't," he agreed. "I want a word with the old guy."

"Upstairs won't let you, Nate, not with your current notoriety. Just see what you can get from the nursing home."

24

Malter called Tash from the taxi as soon as he was clear of the police environs, still a little bemused that it had taken so long to leave, despite Jess pushing proceedings. He saw detective Kelshaw watch him leave, but couldn't bring himself to tease or taunt. Such was his declining confidence.

"How did you go, Tash?"

"Hi, Doc. I won't ask where you are, but you don't have the same sense of desperation about your voice."

"Well, I'm not in custody, or on the run, but I don't know how long I've got," Malter said, feeling unreasonably hurried. "What did you find?"

"I scanned pretty much all my transcripts. If I was honest, I barely recalled any session, let alone any name mentioned."

"Would you swear to the content of the files, their accuracy or whatever?"

"I'd swear to the fact that they were mine, but not much more, sorry," she said, comfortable enough to not expect any reprimand for her sincerity. "I recognised my turn of phrase, but I'd say they represented a pretty reasonable effort to record what they said, verbatim."

"That's ok. So names?"

"I've gone back a year, focusing on the patients you mentioned, but also Jason Metcalfe. I rang them under the guise of wanting to confirm their next appointment and got crying family in each case. When you rang, I was cross-referencing the names to who said them. I'm still going through it because it takes time. I'll take a pic and forward it to your private email from my phone when I'm done." Tash felt the need to explain, "I figure if they get a full warrant, anything I email from work might get included, but using my phone might get excluded for at least a while."

"Thanks. Anything obvious or odd?"

"Not yet. Lots of people get mentioned in varying degrees by past patients, but not much in the way of talking as if they want to get even, just a lot of 'if I had my time over' kind of stuff."

"That kind of stuff has sold a lot of books." Malter thought while waiting for Tash to continue or elaborate, but she said nothing. "You said 'not much', so was there anything?"

"Well, no," she said cautiously. "But Nigel periodically suggests wanting to do something. He only ever mentions one name. I know he's a friend, but if asked, I'd be 'wary' of him."

"I know the name and I get what you're saying, but I'd just describe him as 'angry', most definitely angrier than most, but nothing to justify a third-party threat assessment. He's venting."

"Doc, if you can get back here, give them another read. Some of what he said was almost soapbox worthy."

"It's how he is, but I get what you're saying. I can't tell you how you should interpret it, but professionally, I'll maintain that there was no direct threat to anyone."

"I'd take another read," she insisted. "Keep your bias on the shelf and just read."

"Getting in there to do that might not be doable," Malter conceded. "But I might go direct to the source. Thanks, Tash. One more thing. Have we had any interest from a potential patient, Tom Willson? Two 'L's."

"Not yet. The name doesn't ring any bells from my file review, either. Why?"

"The detective mentioned his name as if I'd know it is all. Thanks, Tash." Malter drifted off into thought after ending the call.

25

Malter directed the taxi to the hospice but made the driver do a lap of the block before actually pulling into the carpark. He half expected to see a police car or detective Kelshaw waiting and had forewarned the driver to be prepared to drive on, but his apprehension was unnecessary. Still, he gave the driver a tip with instructions to wait.

A hearse waited at the front door, backed into the entrance to receive a gurney. Malter walked past, unfazed, not curious whether any of his patients warranted the transport. Such was his focus on meeting and talking with Nigel, whose name was still on the board in the foyer, still in the rainbow room. The gurney wasn't for him.

It was business as usual inside the building. Time went on, regardless of a patient's passing. No fanfare, no changes to routines, just another vacant bed available for someone preferring or needing to see out their days in a place that wasn't a hospital and wasn't home. His preference was always to encourage his patients to focus on their comfort in their last days. If that meant being at home, surrounded by familiarity, family and friends, great, but if their demands or pain necessitated more medically oriented care, then he had no issue in recommending the hospice as an option. Sure, the hospice was never as comfortable as home, but that it absolved family from the need to also be carers often made it a preferable option.

"He's restless, Doc," Cindy said, as Malter approached Nigel's room. "Some detective was in earlier to have a word, but he left. He's had visitors though, revolving doors."

"Friends or others?" Malter asked.

"Not like work colleagues, but more like he's made friends with people in a similar boat, so I think they were all your patients," she explained. "They certainly didn't look like family gathering around an inheritance."

"He's got no family," Malter said. "How's his deterioration?"

"Not long," she said with a hearty smile. "Nearly there."

"Thanks, Cindy. See if you can keep the hordes away if you can. I'd like a little privacy with him."

"Sure. For you and for Nigel," she replied. "You know he's a favourite."

Malter smiled at the comment and headed into Nigel's room, closing the door behind himself.

"That detective still interested in you?" Nigel asked, eyes closed, but alert. "Don't worry, Doc. I told him nothing."

"I have nothing to hide, Nigel, but to your question, yes, he still thinks I caused a sudden spike in suicide rates amongst my patients."

"You wouldn't know how."

"I'll take that as an endorsement of my professionalism and acumen," Malter said with a measure of satisfaction.

"What do you want? Or more correctly, why are you here?" Nigel asked.

"I'm here because it's what I do, but I'd be lying if I said I didn't want to pick your brains about my other patients." Malter made himself comfortable bedside in the armchair and fished around in the top drawer looking for chocolates or similar often left by guests. "Truth is, I didn't think they were up to committing suicide, and it's rare that I'd miss something like that, let alone a few in one night."

"Maybe you don't know your patients as well as you think. Their last days, the culmination of all their history, it's a melting pot of thoughts and feelings that you don't fully get, no matter how many books you've written on the subject."

"I understand what you're saying, and no, I've never been terminally ill, but I am experienced through talking with many people like yourself."

"Like me?" Nigel asked, weirdly incensed. "I doubt that."

"Well, not completely alike. We are human and so we're very much the result of many factors, including our experiences, relationships, upbringing, even our vocation helps shape us to more than a degree. That we can think also makes us unique, even considering identical life experiences."

"And yet you maintain you can understand your patients so well as to think them unlikely to commit suicide."

Malter conceded the point and shrugged. "Nigel, I'd like your help."

"My capacity is limited, doc, but sure. Moving pianos might be a stretch, but what do you need?"

"The police are of the impression that I'm responsible for the deaths of some of my patients." Nigel said nothing. "You don't want to comment?"

"I was waiting for you to finish. My lucidity is legally dubious, so I wouldn't read too much into anything I do or don't say."

"But we both know I'm not responsible, right?" Malter pressed.

"That's a bit loaded, Doc. What are you wanting to say?"

"Cliff and Travis attacked someone's children, and I think you might know more than I do about it. That's not an accusation, mind you, just a theory."

"Do the police have a similar theory?" Nigel asked innocently.

"They might come up with something similar if they were less interested in me."

"When they speak to me, perhaps I might say something to put them off your scent," Nigel teased. "Would that help?"

"It might," Malter said appreciatively, before recognising the flippancy of the offer. "You mightn't be stressed about police interest, but I am."

"I'll see what I can do, Doc."

Malter noted the smugness on Nigel's face. "You don't want to talk to me about it?"

"Not particularly."

"You're not denying anything, Nigel."

"Are you wired?"

"No, I'm just speaking to you as your counsellor."

"So, confidentiality aside, this is outside your brief."

"The privilege still applies."

"That being the case, I'm sorry their actions have implicated you," Nigel said. "It will pass, though."

"You're sure of that?"

"Most definitely. You might even thank me."

"You sound very confident, Nigel."

"You sound anxious, Doc."

"Police scrutiny is stressful, and I'm more than a little concerned that they might not uncover whatever wisdom that you might offer. Can I tell them something on your behalf?"

"I won't die before I set them straight, if that's your concern," Nigel said. "I told you I'm not going to finish last. Until then, just relax and trust me."

"Trust what, Nigel? My patients are suiciding, and I'm not prepared to wait or hope that you come clean to police enough to absolve me."

"Calm your farm, Doc. I don't need to come clean to anyone, you included. Consider it a gift. And if what we're doing is a gift, I'd hate to ruin the surprise."

"That's not funny, Nigel." Malter settled himself into his more usual bedside manner. "So why are you doing it, this gift?"

"I'm not doing anything," Nigel said insolently. "I'm just dying in this bed."

"So you have no part to play in this?"

"No more than you have. Perhaps some of your royalties should go to my estate."

"What's that supposed to mean?" Malter asked, a little angrily. "How's what you're doing like what I'm doing?"

"You're encouraging people to make good of their lives and make peace before they go."

"And?" Malter pressed.

"So am I."

26

Kelshaw arrived at the nursing home and parked in the ambulance bay directly in front. He could have parked anywhere but in an otherwise empty carpark there seemed little point to extend himself for any more exercise than was necessary.

He buzzed the door and waved at the front desk. A middle-aged woman rolled her eyes at him and spoke into a phone while holding up her other hand in a universal 'stop' gesture. "We're in lockdown," came an authoritative voice over the intercom. "No visitors and no exceptions."

"Police," he announced, standing arrogantly waiting for the door to open, until the woman relented to leave her seat and come to the door. He held up his ID as she approached, but the woman kept her distance.

She spoke loudly, mindful that the door would dull her ordinary volume. "Sorry, but you'll need to come back later."

"Have you heard the term 'shutting the gate after the horse has bolted'?" Kelshaw teased. "Open the door before I call it obstruction."

The woman huffed but ultimately agreed to unlock the door, first with a security swipe card and then manually releasing bolts at the top and bottom of the door. "Sorry, but we're in lockdown to account for all our residents," she said politely, speaking through a slight opening of the door.

"Bad day?" Kelshaw taunted. "You know they found him, right?"

"Small mercies. I've been asked to meet your colleagues for an interview and to retrieve him if possible. They're making a big deal about it this time, but I don't know why. I'm just hoping the media won't interfere. Anyone who says there's no such thing as bad publicity has never worked in this industry," the woman began. "I just thought I'd organise some things while I wait for the lawyer. She's due any minute."

"I'm sure they'll look after you," Kelshaw said provocatively. He knew she could equally interpret his words as menacing or calming. "About that. Do you have a resident named Nigel?"

"No," she replied.

"You don't want to check your records?" he pressed. "You could pretend to be compliant."

"No need," she insisted. "I'm the director of nursing here and I know every resident, and their families, on a first name basis." She waited to gauge Kelshaw's attention before adding, "can I ask as to your interest?"

"Your escapee asked for him is all."

"Can't help, sorry," she said. "The lawyer said to say nothing until she got here. You understand my position, happy to help but…". She shrugged.

"Is that also why you're in breach of fire regulations by locking doors so that patients can't get out?" Kelshaw pushed. "The door is labelled as an emergency exit and I just saw you need to use a card. You might want to brief your lawyer to have an explanation for that, too."

The woman's mouth was agape. "You're serious?"

"Or you could help me out, maybe just a little," Kelshaw continued. "Open the door and tell me a little about your escapee."

The woman held the door open just wide enough for Kelshaw to squeeze through to enter. She made to re-bolt the door but thought better of it, opting instead to just lean back against it to press it securely home. "Can we please start again?" she asked. "My name is Margaret Nix. Of course I'll help, as much as I can. It's just the lawyer told me to say nothing to anyone, police and media especially."

"Sure. I just want to know about Eric Barnes."

Margaret shook her head with a smile. "He's a sweetheart, but he is quite a handful. He's normally contained in the secure wing, here, but if he sees a chance he'll be off. We just got some new trainee staff and, notwithstanding that it's my responsibility, perhaps someone gave him a fleeting opportunity. That's all it would have taken."

"And no relative Eric might ask for that you know of?"

She shook her head. "If he had anyone, I'd know about them, whether or not they visit, but Eric hasn't got any family and I don't recall him ever getting any visitors. Sad story really. Even if someone was to track down a relative on his behalf, the fact is he's been here since before my time, and that's a while." She offered a smile to Kelshaw briefly. "In anticipation of that kind of discussion, I just re-read his history. He came here before our records were computerised and before I started here. That's well over twenty years, and as good as I can tell, he moved here after a long stay at another institution."

"Not much of a life," Kelshaw offered insincerely. "And no mention of Nigel in those notes?"

"The point is, he's had early onset dementia and while his decline has been slow, it's been happening for a long time," said Margaret. "I'd be thinking Nigel's more than likely someone on some TV soap or that he heard on the news, not that he sits and watches, but maybe he overheard some show."

"And no other residents named Nigel?" Kelshaw pressed. "Or something sounding like 'Nigel'?"

"Nothing and no-one like that," she stressed. "Eric spends his days pacing the corridors, up and down, up and down. He's not social enough to have engaged with anyone."

"So he doesn't wander the corridors talking to anyone on the phone?"

"Detective," she rolled her eyes condescendingly. "He doesn't have a mobile phone. Our residents are welcome to them, of course, but our policy is that the devices are not a staff problem and they can't spend their days looking for their iPhones when the dears misplace them perpetually." The comment made her think before she set off back to her desk while talking. "That said, we recently started logging calls coming through the switchboard as a measure of protection from telemarketers and scammers." She typed and clicked at her computer, and an adjacent printer whirred into action. "There you go. He has at least one friend. A 'Nigel'." She grabbed a printed sheet and handed it to Kelshaw with some accomplishment as she returned to her lean against the door. "Twelve calls over the last few months."

Kelshaw scanned a list of dates and times and flitted the sheet to see a blank page. "He's got a weekly call from Nigel. Is that all you have? So nothing about who he is?"

"We're under no obligation to even do this much, detective," she replied. "Our residents are entitled to have a life and their privacy, and we have no right to parent them as if they're toddlers. I actually thought you'd be happy that the mystery of who this 'Nigel' is has been solved!"

"Well, not quite," Kelshaw disagreed. "All we've done is confirm that your resident knows someone by that name. That's not the same as knowing who he is."

A furious thumping on the front door alerted Margaret to the presence of a smart suited woman mouthing something through the glass. "This is the lawyer. Now especially I need to keep my mouth shut, apparently," Margaret told Kelshaw quietly. "I hope that helps, though."

Margaret eased her back off the door and opened it for the lawyer. "Before you say anything," she began, "Nate here was just asking about this facility for a family member." She winked at Kelshaw, inviting him to take part in the ruse. "Please let me know if there's anything else you'd like to know."

Kelshaw ignored the once-over by the lawyer and returned Margaret's smile. He slid past the women and out the door, listening for the sound of locks being secured behind him.

27

There was a minor throng of people waiting for Malter at his office door. Assuming they were media, he directed the taxi several streets away and returned cautiously on foot until reaching the property of a friend with an open offer to borrow his car as necessary in exchange for a bottle of wine. Anonymous in the car as he later drove past, he pondered what Nigel had said when his phone rang.

"Doc," Tash began, continuing without acknowledgement, "Nigel called and wants to talk with you, or more correctly, Cindy called on his behalf. Regardless, you need to make tracks there."

"I was only just there," Malter sighed. "He's in a bit of a mood."

"And," Tash baulked. "But that's not why I'm calling."

Malter sensed her apprehension. "The detective looking for me? Is he there?"

"No idea. He's not here, but the Tom Willson, two 'L's, you asked me about is on the department of health list as a candidate for your program. He also used to be known as Jack Bernardo. That's the name Nigel incessantly mentions. You know him, right?"

Malter recognised the challenge in simply hearing his name. First from the detective, and now from Tash. All those years of getting his patients to confront their respective pasts to move on with what remained of their lives was suddenly focused inwards, like an exercise for him to do himself. "Yes, I know him, Tash, but you knew I would."

"Sorry. I thought it might help if I did some digging. There was nothing on him, absolutely nothing, so I got a geek friend to help me uncover his history and his real name. It's not like he changed it legally, it's as if he just upped and became this Tom Willson. I had to find out more."

"So, what else do you know about him?"

"Enough. His history with your sister, and with Nigel. And his address. And then he rang the office here wanting to speak to you."

Malter thought for long seconds. "What's his address?"

28

While his visit to the nursing home got Kelshaw away from the potential for disciplinary attention, he couldn't escape the thought that it was a complete waste of time. Now his shift was up and he was liable to head to bed, hoping tomorrow would be better, but he knew he'd never be able to sleep with thoughts of Malter. While he deliberated between pressing for overtime and sleep, Piper called.

"Before you ask, Piper," Kelshaw began before she could speak, "there's no Nigel at the nursing home, but someone by the name of 'Nigel' has been ringing the old guy. Maybe a *bone fide* coincidence, but you'll need to do more digging into his history. "

"Is it too late to put a dollar on it, Nate?" she chirped. "In any case, you need to come back."

"Upstairs change their mind? Or is the wrath of the media raining down?"

"They found David Kingsley. More correctly, they only just identified him as the one squished between a car and the wall by Billy, Malter's patient. So that's all Willson's children accounted for. And dead."

"I'm heading straight for Malter now," Kelshaw said confidently. "Upstairs might want to meet me there if they have a problem."

"No-one's going to argue with your re-engagement on Malter. Backgrounds have ruled out gang involvement and drug interests, but they also found that each of the kids could have known of their attackers. Maybe not well, but certainly enough for Malter to claim zero involvement... with the children, at least."

"I'm waiting for the 'but', Piper," Kelshaw enquired. "If the children are just miraculously co-incidental, I'm wondering why they're happy for me to continue on Malter."

"Willson's history is why," she said decisively.

"I thought as much. Malter must have known him, and I would have got that out of him, but the lawyer arrived and truncated our chat."

"Malter might not have been lying, he just mightn't know Willson by that name. It took some time to work out who he is, but Malter will certainly know him by his birth name, though. Jack Bernardo. Yes, they have *some* history," Piper revealed smugly.

"I know who Bernardo is," Kelshaw said thoughtfully. "Memories aplenty when that name came up in my scan of Malter's background this morning. I mentioned his name to Malter to see his reaction when I wanted to get a rise out of him. I was only a rookie when the whole Bernardo debacle happened. What a fiasco that was—"

"In my time, they used it as a teaching case for adherence to procedure," Piper noted.

"That also potentially implicates Newcott, of course," Kelshaw said, thinking out loud. "Whatever you learned from that case, you mightn't know that Newcott was in a relationship with Malter's sister at the time of her death and they initially investigated him as the perp'. He was also the one who later took it upon himself to kill two of Bernardo's friends, for which he did time, but those actions are probably what gave Bernardo the acquittal."

"Was Bernardo involved?" she asked.

"No question," Kelshaw said, adding, "but with his accomplices dead, it was too easy to plead passenger status and to not even get done as an accessory. A different time, of course, and it might have worked out differently nowadays. My money's still on Malter, though. Nigel's not got long. He looked like death warmed up in a hospice this morning."

"So what? You want to let Nigel pass?" Piper asked, incredulous.

"I never said that," Kelshaw said jovially.

"Just so you know… Willson, A.K.A. Bernardo, called an ambulance to his home last night. It wasn't for him, though. It was for Newcott. No idea what he was doing there, but he got taken back to the hospice."

"I'll put a dollar on the fact that Nigel's getting in on the act at the behest of the good doctor, Piper. I guess I'd better see him again before he expires."

"And…" Piper sought to prevent Kelshaw from terminating the call.

"Melanie Nashman. You met with her this morning. She was also at Willson's place when uniforms got there just now."

Kelshaw was slow to rationalise the new information. "Nigel's definitely worth another visit before I visit Willson, then."

29

Detective Kelshaw was quick to re-orient himself to head back to the hospice. Driving time was thinking time, away from the noise of the station, and it occurred to him that Melanie had mentioned that her partner Anthony was estranged from his family. Not that big a deal ordinarily, but it was odd to go from estrangement to a home visit, even under the circumstances, but particularly when his father was one Jack Bernardo. He pulled over and called her.

"Twice in one day is never a good sign, Melanie. It's detective Nate Kelshaw. We met this morning," he began, not allowing Melanie to acknowledge their earlier meeting. "Can I ask what you were doing with Mr Willson or whatever he gave his name as?"

"He's Anthony's father," Melanie said. "It felt right to meet."

"But you hadn't met him previously? So why now?"

"He called. What was I going to say?"

"How did he take the prospect of being a grandfather?"

"It didn't come up," Melanie said erringly, as if immediately recognising the implausibility of the comment. "We were still talking when we were interrupted and the police arrived."

"A pregnancy is the kind of thing I thought would have led in conversation in such a meeting. So what else did you talk about?"

"Family stuff," she replied. "His children."

Years of investigations had Kelshaw interpret the subtleties of what Melanie had said, and what she hadn't. She wasn't lying, but she was feeling the challenge of implied persecution. She was on the back foot. It was time to press. "That all of his children have died in the last 12 hours. Did that come up?"

"Of course it did."

"How do you think he took the news?" Kelshaw rolled his shoulders to prevent a crick in his neck as he squeezed the phone between his ear and shoulder and readied himself with his pen again. "Was it even news?"

"It was the first thing the uniformed police broached as they entered Tom's room, like it was their reason for being there."

"But you said you were talking about his children with him before the uniforms arrived. You said it was amongst the things discussed such that you never got to talk about your pregnancy."

"Maybe we discussed it then," she conceded.

Kelshaw kept the pressure up. "Which? The pregnancy or that Willson's children were all killed on the same night?"

"I don't know where the tone's coming from, detective. Several hours ago, our discussion had me as the victim, but now I can't help but feel I'm being interrogated or intimidated. So which is it?"

Kelshaw was happy with himself. Melanie was flustered, and easing it back a little would relax her and subconsciously encourage her to yield more. It always did. "If you're 100% victim, I'm sorry. If you're not, I'm not." He left the comment hanging and waited for what response might follow, but none came. "It now seems unlikely that Anthony was the subject of an entirely random attack. Anything you can tell me, no matter how inconsequential, might make all the difference."

"I can't think of anything more to add," Melanie said, adding, "you might try Tom."

Kelshaw thought to press about the familiarity of using Willson's first name, but didn't want to lose momentum. The guy obviously was there with her. "I intend to, but first, perhaps you can tell me about the other *'family stuff'* you spoke about. Did he explain why his family might have been singled out?"

"Tom told me he deliberately stayed away from his family," she said.

"Just like Anthony told you. He didn't say why?"

"No, he didn't. We were still talking when the police arrived, and I'm still here."

"You might like to take *that* up with him." Kelshaw truncated the call without a goodbye. It was as good as steering the conversation between her and Willson.

30

"If you're looking for the Doc, he's not here," Nigel said as soon as the detective re-entered his room. He watched as the detective wandered around the room, touching everything like a toddler in a toy store.

"I'd like to speak to you about Tom Willson. I believe you know him."

There was no mistaking the smirk on Nigel's face. "How's he doing?"

"You tell me. I'm gathering you've heard about what's happened with his children, and I know you met with him last night, which amounts to a convenient alibi, whatever you were doing there with him. He'll probably die after you, though. I don't know if that's any consolation."

"The legal system you uphold acquitted him. Who am I to judge?"

"Nigel, I'm going to be on the level here," Kelshaw offered sincerely. "I'm not interested in you, just Malter. Whatever he's put you up to do, I don't care about, but he needs to be stopped."

"So what about Willson?" Nigel asked. "What happens to him?"

"They acquitted him. There's nothing more that can to be done. You need to accept that and not waste your remaining hours thinking about it," Kelshaw said. "Malter is different, though. Was he the one to suggest you meet with Willson?"

"No," Nigel scoffed. "He wants his patients to make good of their remaining time, sure, but he never suggested visiting the guy who got away with rape and murder."

"So you went to see him of your own volition?" Kelshaw asked earnestly. "Bullshit."

"You believe what you want, detective. I wanted to see him. I saw him."

"So why visit him at all, then?"

"None of your business, detective."

"Did you go there to finish what you started years ago?"

"No," Nigel answered, yawning with his hand in front of his face. "Incidentally, what would you do if I'd said 'yes'?"

Kelshaw ignored the question. "Was Malter with you when you visited Willson?"

"Nope." Nigel pressed the buzzer for the nurse and as soon as he saw her enter the room said, "I'm getting a little tired, and this talk about Willson with you, detective, is exhausting."

Cindy took the cue. "Let's let him sleep, detective. Perhaps you can come back later."

"Nigel's helping me with my enquiry. I won't be too much longer, and more to the point, I'm not leaving until I get answers."

"Any answers you get are coming from a pharmaceutically degraded, dying man," began Cindy. "He's in pain and he's entitled to some peace."

"He'll get that when he's dead," Kelshaw said as he settled back, deeper into his chair. "I'm going to get answers, even if I need to massage them from his dying soul."

"That would make excellent viewing, especially after the footage I just saw of you," Cindy said. "Nigel, did you know you're in the midst of a celebrity? I'll just get my iPhone." She feigned a step towards the nurse's station.

Kelshaw sighed indignantly. "Before I go then," he conceded, "will you at least leave Willson alone? Let him get acquainted with his son's partner. He mightn't live to see the birth of his grandchild, but there's joy to be had in getting to know the woman who could have been his daughter-in-law."

Nigel smiled. "Pass on my best, and to Melanie."

"I'll be back later, Nigel," Kelshaw said. "Don't die before I nail Malter to a tree."

Nigel looked at the nurse as soon as the detective left the room. "It's time."

31

Kelshaw was waiting for Malter on his entry to the hospice. The detective didn't leap to his feet or even stand. He just started speaking to alert Malter to his presence from a trendy armchair tucked away in the foyer's corner. "You're not out of the woods yet, Malter."

"Nice to see you too, detective," Malter said. He considered just continuing on past to the corridor, but he decided against it. "I won't break confidence, but I would like to offer some suggestions."

"A guilty change of heart?"

"No guilt, just a renewed interest in what's right is all."

"You say what you've got, Doc. I'll be the judge of what happens next."

"I have many patients and I could tell you about any of them, if that helps."

"You or me?"

"They are the same thing, detective. Provided you're focused on the truth and not just persecuting me, anything I tell you is more likely to exonerate me than give you my head on a plate." Malter glanced instinctively at his watch but immediately recognised how the detective would interpret what was obviously a nervous action. "So what happens now?"

Kelshaw looked to his front and pointed at another armchair, just like his own. "Maybe we just need to talk," he said, careful to not lace his words with menace or condescension. "Perhaps I just don't see it the way you do. Peaches certainly liked you, no idea why, so maybe I need to hear you out."

"I'm thinking I probably should have my lawyer here before I say anything."

Kelshaw winced and scratched the back of his ear. "Probably, but it's just you and me." He took his phone and offered it to Malter. "Just you and me. It's not like I'm recording anything. See for yourself."

Malter ignored the offer. He looked down the corridor and then back to Kelshaw, and fought the temptation to check his watch again. With a little reluctance, he marched to the chair and slumped himself down and settled. "Detective, I don't know what I could possibly say to convince you."

"So tell me something, then. Make me trust you, at least."

For the first time, Malter looked at Kelshaw and saw a man perhaps a few years his senior, not a detective. He was just a man; liable to failings and merit, trust and deceit, just like anyone else. "I have no idea how to make you trust me, detective," he said, shaking his head.

"You made Peaches trust you," replied Kelshaw. "Why not just consider me a patient like you did with her?"

Malter bit his lip and grimaced. "I remember Peaches," he began. "It was a long time ago, but I remember her as a spiritual woman. I didn't need to do anything to make her trust me. She just knew." He looked at the detective and smiled. "The opposite of you."

Kelshaw grinned to concede the point. "Indeed, she was both spiritual and trusting. Generally speaking, she was an excellent judge of character. I knew you'd have to remember her."

"Can I be honest and say that having her on my program was largely a waste. A joy, but a waste." He accepted how provocatively Kelshaw might receive his words, adding, "I mean, she didn't need my support. She understood the beauty of her own passing, and the part she'd played in the lives of those around her. She was at peace, and I was just a spectator, whereas with others I'd need to be the coach or offer wisdom for their guidance."

Kelshaw was silent while he stared at Malter. "Not hard is it, to say something honest." He reached for his phone and held up a placative hand to allay Malter's immediate concern. He flitted with the device and ultimately presented a picture to Malter; a scanned image with 1970's washed out, vivid colours, a young man with neatly cropped hair seeming to recoil at a lunged embrace from a similarly aged young woman. "Together forever, or so I thought."

"Death gets everyone eventually," Malter said philosophically after leaning forward to inspect the photograph, recognising a beautiful Peaches and stern uniformed Kelshaw from long ago. "The nice ones and the not so nice ones. In my role, I get to see both kinds."

"And which category does Jack Bernardo fit into?" Kelshaw asked.

"I don't know why that's even a question," Malter said with a minor frustration. "Without compromising what I'm hoping is the basis of some trust, you know what he did."

"Indeed, I do," replied Kelshaw. "So what about Nigel?"

"What about him?" Malter teased.

"How would you categorise him?"

"He's a patient," Malter replied. "I can't talk about him."

"It's a simple and benign question, Malter," Kelshaw pressed. "Nigel. Good or bad?"

The question tormented Malter. "He's a good man."

"Who's done bad things," Kelshaw added. "And one of you is doing bad things now."

"What would make you say that, detective?" Malter knew his attempt at ignorance was not very convincing.

Kelshaw smiled. "I don't know, doctor Malter. My experience tells me it's not a stretch. The man who killed your sister, Nigel's girlfriend, is suddenly the victim of a spate of violence. Time passing doesn't wipe history. You must really think very little of everyone to assume they won't make the association. That said, I'm surprised at you on the basis you have a lot to lose, and the measure of arrogance required to think you could really get away with it is rare. Nigel, on the other hand, has a lot less to lose."

Malter considered what to share without betraying his friend or his ideals. The thought amounted to many seconds.

"One of you will go down for this," Kelshaw prompted. "Truth is, I could be happy with either of you. A more ambitious man would want you both."

"Whatever is happening is not by me, and I certainly haven't put anyone up to do anything," Malter said, hopeful it would be enough, but the detective's vacant stare told him he needed to say more. He understood he wasn't helping himself, his patients, Nigel, or anyone else with his reluctance to share. He had nothing to lose. "I think Nigel's using his remaining time to get even with Jack Bernardo."

"Old news, Malter," Kelshaw replied, a lot less interested than Malter expected. "He was there with Bernardo last night."

"If it's old news, why are you still treating me as the bad guy?"

Kelshaw ignored the question and just slunk himself deeper into the chair to enjoy the look of concern on Malter's face; the look of someone so stressed they were liable to help without realising it. "One question for you, then. What's a 'seeder'?" He continued on seeing a puzzled look on Malter's face. "Nigel's employment history lists time as a 'seeder' just prior to joining your program or becoming your patient or whatever you call it."

"I never read the paperwork. I just hand it over to Tash for data entry and program metrics, so I don't allow any history to taint or sway my service delivery. You should try it, detective."

"So you don't know what he did?"

"I do, but I just don't know or care how he listed it on his paperwork. He worked with some evangelical church."

"So he got religion?"

"Not at all. I'll bet he's one of very few who worked with an organisation like that and walked in, and out even, without faith."

"So he lied to them?"

"No idea. I think it speaks volumes as to his intelligence and just how likeable Nigel can be."

"I don't see it, but continue," Kelshaw prompted.

"Anyway, his role, as he described it, was like a comedian warming up a crowd before some live filmed TV show. The guy primes the audience to be receptive to anything even remotely funny to *'seed'* spontaneous laughter," Malter explained.

"I didn't think he was that funny a guy."

"Well, no. The church needed someone, or people, in the crowd to be the first to participate, so the rest of the crowd wouldn't be so shy. Nigel would be the one offering the first vocal 'Amen' or hands in the air, sometimes even a possessed by the devil or the Holy Spirit performance. I remember he laughed about his being the stunt lemming to lead the others off the cliff."

The detective thought for a time. "So his last job required him to influence others?"

Malter struggled to keep his face expressionless. "I need to see my patient, detective. He's asked for me."

32

Malter made his way directly to Nigel's room and leaned back on the door until eventually Nigel smiled, even though his eyes were still closed. He watched as Nigel breathed, noting that it was possibly the calmest he'd ever seen him.

"We need to talk, Doc," Nigel said. "And now is as good a time as any."

"Finally," Malter replied as he launched himself off the door to Nigel's bedside. "It's not common for people to spend their last hours completely alone as you are now. Where are your friends? Earlier today, your bedside was standing room only."

"I'd like to think they've got better things to do than waste it with me. I hope they commit to better things in their last hours."

"So, what would you rather be doing in your final hours, then?" Malter asked.

"Who's to say I'm not doing it?"

"Unlikely," Malter said bravely. "Alone except for me and some old movie on the TV for background noise. Everyone deserves more."

"So how would you spend your last hours, Doc? You're single, your sister can't sit with you, and you've outlived your parents. How are you going to spend *your* last hours?"

"Better than yours, I'd hope."

"Can I offer you a fresh perspective?" Nigel asked with a struggled smile. "What if I'm doing just as I'd dreamed? I'm looking to end my time on a high."

The comment surprised Malter. "This," he panned his arms animatedly about the room, "*this* is not ending your time on a high."

Nigel wriggled restlessly in his bed before settling semi-reclined.

"All those regrets in your life that you think you move past, Doc. What if you can't?"

"I can help, Nigel," Malter said, appreciative he might finally be making headway. "I can help to accept and forgive."

"That's where I have issues, Doc. Acceptance is one thing, but forgiveness? I can't."

"But it's not serving you. It hasn't served you, so isn't it time?"

"What if it was serving me? I could easily rationalise that it's kept me alive until now. Giving up would let him win."

"Nigel, there's a good body of evidence showing repressed anger and resentment is a cause of a variety of conditions, cancer included," Malter said. "I look at you, your history and your health. It's not a stretch at all. Your efforts to 'win' are killing you."

"And moving on now wouldn't change that," Nigel said.

"But perhaps you'd get to die with some comfort," Malter pressed.

"The way I look at it, I'm going to get the same comfort when I watch him burn. On earth or in hell, I don't care which. That will be the closure I need."

Malter couldn't help but sigh at the prospect of rehashing familiar ground. "Professionally, I know that's not what you need to be focussing on right now."

"And there you go, proof that you're not looking at this the way I am. The way any of your patients do," Nigel said with a measure of satisfaction. "In the hours or days or months before your time is up, you can't help but reappraise. You think closure is about finding peace, but it's more than that, and peace won't make amends for what happened to your sister," he said angrily.

"But dwelling on it doesn't help you, my sister or anyone else, either," Malter replied, keen to not escalate Nigel any further. "Surely you see that."

"What if it did, Doc? A lifetime of regret channelled into making amends," Nigel said, drifting off into silent thought.

"It won't bring her back. That's done."

"No, it won't bring her back," Nigel conceded with acceptance.

Malter sensed the need to leave it there. He recognised the fatigue and strain in Nigel and didn't want his best intentions to further tarnish his remaining time. "I need to go," he announced quietly. "I'll be back later, but call me if you need or want me."

Nigel raised an arm to give a subtle wave with his eyes still closed, adding, "expect more from me, Doc." Malter left him to rest.

Once in the corridor, Malter anticipated another looming confrontation with the detective, surely waiting at the main entrance, and opted for one of several alternate exit points he'd noted over the years. In his head, this was wise, not cowardly, while he pondered his next course of action.

A different visit seemed necessary, not just to kill time. He knew the address. He didn't know if he could do it.

33

Malter arrived at the doorsteps of Tom Willson's home. It was an uneasy feeling. In being there, he was close to the man, or one of them, responsible for tearing his childhood and his family apart, yet he'd never been so physically close to him. Rightly or wrongly, his parents had kept him from the courtroom during Willson's, Bernardo's, hearing because he was too young, and it was counterproductive to have him there when it was Nigel's turn. Afterwards, his parents had distanced themselves from Nigel, probably because he was never their choice for their daughter, and thereafter he represented a perpetual reminder.

"Come on up, James," came an announcement from the door security system. "There's someone here I'd like you to meet." The door buzzed, and Malter pushed it open as soon as he heard the click of deadbolts being released remotely. He didn't know what to expect, but a doorstep confrontation never seemed a possibility. The voice added directions across the intercom as soon as he was inside, and he followed them cautiously.

Malter braced himself at the bedroom door as he saw the man he knew as Jack Bernardo reclining on a hospital bed. The man was older and more wrinkled, but there was no mistaking who it was. While he'd never met the man in person, he knew him from the newspaper clipping collection he'd kept for many months until some child psychologist kyboshed it as being unhelpful in his dealing with his family's trauma. His unkempt seventies hair was now a sedate short-crop, now grey, and a t-shirt pyjama replaced the large lapelled collar of his courtroom suit, but it was unquestioningly the same man. He made to talk, to say something, but no words came to mind.

"James," Willson began. "I'm sorry." He paused, as if expecting some retort, but on seeing that Malter was silent, he continued. "I'm sorry for what happened, and for what I did. Time hasn't reduced my guilt and my regret. Before I die, I'd like you to know how much I wish that night and afterwards had never happened."

Malter struggled to compose his thoughts into something coherent and audible. He felt long-suppressed anger coupled with professional abstraction, like two waves so perfectly out of phase that they resulted in calm. "I never wanted to meet you," Malter said. "I saw little point."

"I won't beg for forgiveness any more," Willson remarked. "I don't want to distract my last days with such things."

Malter habitually reached for the patient chart. It seemed appropriate despite the guy not being on his program. Only then did he notice the woman seated at Willson's bedside on what looked to be an out-of-place kitchen chair. She sat, heavy-eyed, as if she'd spent time crying. "Family? Someone to mourn *you*?" he asked, ambiguously directed to both the woman and Willson.

"Not family. Not really," Willson said cryptically, reaching for Melanie's shoulder. "This is Melanie. She was my son's partner. He was one of the many apparently killed at the hands of your patients, according to what the police told me."

Malter grimaced. "Allegations. Their investigations are continuing."

"Their investigations are arguably more interested in me," Willson commented. "They seemed to be keen to warn Melanie about me."

"With good reason," Malter replied. He looked at the woman. "I hope you listened to them."

"Based on what Tom has told me, I wasn't sure how this meeting would go," she said. "He's told me about your sister, and about Nigel. I wasn't expecting you to be so reserved."

"I'm digging deep, Melanie," Malter said, finding a voice. "It's not every day you meet with a rapist and murderer, much less one who turned *my* world upside down. If I was a woman, damned if I'd be here without a police presence or here at all."

"He's trying to help me…" she offered.

"If he's offering help, there will be self-interest. He '*helped*' my sister and offered her a lift when she was hitchhiking, and did he tell you about what he and his friends did next?"

"I told her everything, James," Willson said, taking Malter's attention away from Melanie. "I left nothing out and she recorded my guilt for posterity on her iPhone. If the legal system could process my confession quickly, you could even get to see me behind bars. For what that's worth."

Malter took a moment to process. "That's not worth as much as my sister."

"I'm sorry, and I could spend the rest of my life saying it, but that's not why I called you."

"I won't take you on as a patient, Willson. Consider this me delivering that message in person."

"James, I don't need or want you in any professional capacity," Willson said. "But I have concern for what Nigel is doing."

"Tom, Jack, or whatever you're calling yourself, I don't care about your concern. Your interest in Nigel is sure to be just as self-serving as you seeking me out."

"It's not, I can assure you. I have no more self-interest left." Willson squeezed a tear from long fatigued eyes. "My children are dead. All four in the last day."

"It must be so hard to lose someone you love," Malter said sarcastically.

"I don't expect you to understand, despite all your books, James," Willson accepted. "But yes, I realise the contradiction in sharing my grief, and that you have every reason not to care… even though my children did nothing to you."

"Just as my sister did nothing to you…"

Melanie found her voice to settle the escalating exchange between Malter and Willson. "James," she began, "Tom isn't asking for anything from you for himself. Not pity, forgiveness or anything."

"I'm not offering, Melanie," Malter said. "The longer I'm here, the more I'm considering the feasibility of smothering him with a pillow… except I don't rightly know whether you'll stop me."

"Please, James, Doctor Malter. Please, just listen." Melanie looked to Willson for some encouragement, but on receiving nothing, she continued regardless. "Nigel Newcott, you know who I'm talking about, is responsible, more than likely, for the deaths of Tom's children. And he's now liable to be after me."

"Nigel's not long for this world, anyway," Malter replied.

"James," Willson interrupted to contribute to Melanie's point. "Nigel isn't doing anything himself, so that he's now in the hospice is irrelevant. In any case, my four children are gone, which might not interest you, but he's not finished."

"The police already think I'm responsible," Malter said. "So when they hear this from you, their interest in me should dissipate."

"But that won't help, James," Willson insisted.

"Sure it will. And they won't waste their time on Nigel. He may even be dead already."

"And if he dies, who do you think the police will return their attention to, James?" Willson felt he was getting some traction in making his point. "I'll bet their heart isn't really in it, and you'll do nicely as a scalp."

Malter felt his confidence start to waiver. "I think Nigel will set them straight."

"If he's still alive and willing to assist," Willson continued. "That said, do you think he may be likely to help or antagonise the police?"

Malter couldn't bear to concede the point. "In any case, Willson, surely it's you who's liable to be most at risk, and frankly, I won't lift a finger to save you."

"But would you save me?" Melanie interrupted to ask.

Malter looked at the young woman and noted the stress on her face. "Melanie, I'll bet you're a lovely girl, but this guy is taking you for a ride," Malter pointed angrily at Willson. "If Nigel was to fly from his deathbed to kill Tom here, my suggestion would be to stand clear or go home, whatever, just let it happen. I'm sure you'll be just fine. I wouldn't put it past Tom here to have told you this story purely so you can be a willing participant as a human shield. The guy doesn't deserve protection."

"My children didn't deserve to be brought up without a father, just as my wife didn't deserve to be abandoned. Nigel made that necessary when he was released from jail."

"I'm with Nigel there," Malter said, struggling to control the vitriol which welled up inside him. "You're still not getting sympathy from me."

"From that day forward, I have needed to live every day looking over my shoulder, because I always knew Nigel would come for me."

"It's sad that he didn't get you then, isn't it?"

"James, Nigel visited me last night."

"And you're still alive," Malter said mockingly. "You see, Melanie, Tom's terrified of Nigel exacting some payback, but he's still alive despite a visit. Forgive me for looking for an ulterior motive."

"Please let Tom finish, James," Melanie asserted.

"Nigel wants to make me pay, and it's cost me everything," Willson said.

"Well, perhaps you're all paid up now, so sit back and wait to die," Malter said with venom. "I hope the wait is more painful than you can imagine."

"My problem is that I'm not paid up," Willson said with heartfelt sobriety. "Melanie is pregnant." She stood and pulled her dress taught against her belly to emphasise her limited bump. "She has committed no crime other than to love a son that I never knew and doesn't deserve this."

Before Malter could respond to Willson, his phone rang. On seeing the call was from the hospice, he assumed it would relate to Nigel and he answered with the phone speaker.

"Doctor Malter, James, it's Cindy at the Rainbow Room. I'm just ringing about Nigel."

"He still NFR?"

"He withdrew it in front of a detective Kelshaw today," Cindy replied. "Of course, it doesn't change much in terms of his care. There's not much more to do in the immediate term but keep him comfortable and pain-free, but he's still refusing meds."

"I'll be there shortly if he's coherent."

"He's in and out, but I won't vouch for how much longer. He's given me a gift to pass onto you if you don't get here in time."

"I'll be there as quick as I can," Malter said. He ended the call and looked at Willson. "My immediate interest is in my patient."

"Whoever that was on the call," Melanie began, "she mentioned a detective Kelshaw. I met him myself this morning."

Malter shrugged. "As much as it pains me, I know he's doing his job." He stood, looking at his watch. "And my job requires me to be there for my patients. Nigel arguably more than most."

He nodded to Melanie, scowled at Willson, and left.

34

Cindy handed Malter the gift as he passed by the nurses' station from the fire stairs. He didn't break stride, just smiling to the nurse, mindful that she wouldn't need or expect anything more. He didn’t dwell on what she might have thought of his obviously using an atypical route.

Malter tapped the little bowed box on Nigel’s bedside table noisily. “I got your gift, Nigel, but it’s unnecessary.”

Nigel woke casually, slowly opening his eyes to acquaint himself with his visitor, and then closed his eyes once more. “We’re not finished giving.”

“So what’s this?” Malter asked as he tapped on the box.

“Open it and see.”

Malter sighed as if to emphasise its banality, but his happiness at the offer. He pulled the bow surrounding a small tissue wrapped red felt-covered jewellery box, allowing the wrapping to fall onto the bed, then tentatively opened it to reveal a folded, faded handwritten receipt and an engagement ring. Malter couldn't help but inspect the receipt and recognised its significance. The purchase date was that of his sister's disappearance.

“It’s beautiful, Nigel, but this needs to stay with your estate.”

“You’re the first one I’ve shown it to.”

“But the date?” Malter enquired.

“I was at the jewellery store while Jenny was hitch-hiking. That I wouldn’t share where I was when she first went missing is what made the police think I was responsible. In a way, I know I am responsible, but a differently culpable to what they thought.”

“You can't think like that, Nigel.”

“Easy for you to say, Doc. You lost a sister. I lost my everything.”

Malter suppressed his want to respond. Nigel deserved the same professional abstraction as he offered other patients, even if it was hard. "It's never too late to make good, Nigel."

"I know," Nigel said in reply. "Never too late." He reached for the switch on his medication pump and hovered his thumb without actually pressing.

"I'll take that as my cue to leave." Malter stood, wondering if this might be the last time he'd see Nigel. He couldn't help but think of their shared history. By any measure, he had failed him. He knew it, and the persistent thought weighed on him. That the police wanted to sully his remaining hours was the icing on a lacklustre cake.

"What's your rush, Doc?" Nigel asked, suddenly alert that Malter was liable to slip out of the room if he upped his dose.

"I'm just disappointed that I haven't been able to support you."

"Nothing to worry your head about, Doc. I'm good. Dying, of course, but good."

Malter smiled. "The police are onto you."

"So? What can they do?"

"You're not denying anything, then?"

"No need. I might even say the same thing to them, but of course, anything I say to you is privileged."

"Unless I recognise a plausible threat to someone."

"Which I haven't given you."

"The way you're talking makes me believe you are threatening…"

Nigel produced an iPad from under the covers. He fumbled with the device before replaying a sample of the audio of his current conversation, muffled a little from being under the covers. At its conclusion, he said, "my recollection of this chat might be flawed or even pharmaceutically impaired, but no-one will challenge a recording."

Malter relented a little to sit.

"Relax, Doc. This will all be over soon."

"What will?"

"It will be over soon," Nigel repeated. "What is it you seem to think we should all pursue?" he asked, feigning an exaggerated, thoughtful expression. "That's it. Closure. I might even die with a warm and fuzzy, Doc. Wouldn't that be nice?"

"What if you don't live that long?"

"In that case, maybe you'll get the warm feeling that you assure us comes with closure, instead of me."

"We both lost my sister, Nigel. Nothing can bring her back, and nothing can change what happened. I get your anger, but it's not serving you, just as it didn't serve me."

"Didn't, not wouldn't," Nigel said decisively. "You've met with him, haven't you?"

"Who?"

"The guy who raped and murdered your sister."

Malter paused before saying anything. "Yes, I met with him, and I can't say it was a comfortable meeting, but it wouldn't serve me to do anything to him. I said my piece. He said he was sorry… enough."

"Big of you, Doc."

"He's dying anyway, as are you."

"Of course, if I could have given him his cancer, I would have," Nigel said. He laboured a smile, "but I didn't need to."

"This is pointless, Nigel. You're hell-bound to spend your final hours dwelling on him. Surely, you have something better to do."

"Better than honouring the memory of your sister? As much as it might pain you, Doc, I have nothing I'd rather be doing. In fact, I'm doing just what you've recommended we, all of your patients, do. Your sister would be so disappointed."

Malter made to say something in reply, but the personal aspect of the comment was too confronting. He stood to leave. "Goodbye, Nigel."

35

Malter expected the detective would lurk somewhere nearby as soon as he left Nigel's room, but this time, he didn't feel anxious about the inevitability of another meeting. Sure enough, Kelshaw was hovering in the small waiting room next to the main hospice doors. He watched Kelshaw acknowledge his approach and move to ensure their paths would meet.

"I think we've got a problem, detective," Malter began. "Nigel gave me this and as good as told me he's up to something with Willson." He flashed open the jewellery box and placed the ring on his finger to show it off.

"Your concern is enough for me, Malter," Kelshaw said. "I'll bring him in, or as good as I can manage in his current state."

Malter eased up a little and took a moment to breathe, and only then did he notice the smirk on Kelshaw's face. "You still think I've got something to do with this, don't you?"

"Of course I do. Nigel will give me all I need, hopefully, before he dies. Even if he doesn't," Kelshaw shrugged, "your attempted deflexion onto him is what I need on you."

"Where's the trust I thought we'd started to build?" Malter asked with a sigh. "When we were talking before, I thought we'd put that air of suspicion behind us."

"I heard you out," said Kelshaw. "I see why Peaches thought so highly of you, but I can't let that blur what's so obvious. I just haven't worked out whether you or your friend are on your own or working together."

"I'm tired of arguing with an idiot, detective. If you don't shift your focus, you're going to have blood on your hands."

"Rich from you, Malter," Kelshaw dismissed.

Malter shook his head. "Are you in any way interested in preventing further deaths, detective? I can't put it any more simply than that."

"Who are we saving and from whom, Malter?"

"Willson, Nigel, possibly others, including other patients."

"So we might help an acquitted criminal responsible for the rape and death of your sister, Nigel, who's as good as dead now, and perhaps some other dying patients. Not much to motivate me there."

"What about the innocents?" Malter pleaded. "While I can't believe you're so blasé about my patients, particularly given your history, what about everyone else who might be at risk of being collateral damage or used as a tool?"

"Conjecture, Malter, until it happens and then whoever is responsible will get caught."

"So that means at least one more person is going to have to die, detective. Just because you have no-one in *your* world doesn't mean that's a good plan. Any one person is liable to be important to someone, and I can't believe you're prepared to accept even one more death." Malter hoped he was making a point until the detective shrugged. "What about Melanie, detective? I understand you met her this morning."

"What about her?"

"She's pregnant, and she's with Willson right now."

"I know," Kelshaw said. "So does Nigel."

"So, is she something to motivate you?" Malter asked. "Is she worth it?"

"Just because she's with Willson now doesn't necessarily mean she's at any risk of harm."

"If she was your Peaches, would you be so comfortable to let her stay there?" Malter felt his argument get traction. "What if Peaches was that one person you're expecting to sacrifice to unravel what's going on?"

Kelshaw thought while fossicking in his pocket, eventually producing his car keys. "I'll drive."

36

Kelshaw waved at the uniform benignly dawdling around the front door of Willson's home before his car had come to a complete stop. His drive with Malter had been undeniably quiet, bordering on being awkward. He walked straight from the car, oblivious to whether Malter was following.

"Mr Willson. Bernardo. Whatever. My name is detective Nate Kelshaw…" Kelshaw called from the entry into the intercom. "I get that you're not mobile, but I'd like a word."

"No need to yell, detective. Upstairs," came the reply. "Follow the only sounds of life upstairs. James knows the way."

Kelshaw looked to Malter and then to likely locations for CCTV cameras before opening the door. "Why, in God's name, you'd need surveillance if you leave the door unlocked, Willson." He drifted off into a mutter, noisily traipsing up the stairs with Malter in tow.

On his arrival at the bedroom door, Kelshaw's eyes met Melanie's, seated close by an ageing man reclining in a hospital bed. He nodded to her and then directed his attention to the man. "You're Bernardo… or are you going by Willson today?"

"Hello, detective," Willson said. "I don't mind what you call me. You've already met Melanie, I hear."

"You're a rapist, and a murderer, and a good many of my colleagues had their careers and reputations destroyed by you," Kelshaw began. "There are many things I could call you, but in her presence, I'll keep it civil."

"At least now I understand your bias," Willson conceded with a measure of acceptance. "I'm sorry for what I've done. I won't labour the point, but there's also little to be gained by squabbling over it."

"So what happens now?" Melanie asked, sensing the need to say something.

"We have to assume he'll come after you and Tom," Malter replied.

"What with?" she asked.

"More like *who* with," Kelshaw mumbled before talking to all assembled. "If Melanie was a late inclusion to his plan, chances are that Nigel's only got limited people to work with, and the nurse said he didn't make any calls himself, but she let slip that she called some people on his behalf."

"And you've got the list of names?" Malter asked.

Kelshaw smiled. "Of course. They're all your patients, Malter."

"So this is good," Melanie said. "Hopefully, I can outlast some terminally ill people. The shock of last night aside, I'm reasonably fit and well." She expected to be reassured, but they met her in silence. "What's the problem?"

Malter and Kelshaw looked at each other, as if each wanting the other to share what they understood and that Melanie didn't.

"9/11, Melanie," Kelshaw said. "That's an example of what can happen when a person, or persons, commit to an outcome,"

"So, some of the patients are terrorists?" Melanie asked.

"No, Melanie," Malter began. "But my patients are terminal and, as such, they have nothing to lose. If a seed has been planted in their brains to do something, there's likely to be no stopping it."

"It's the same as with every jihadist," Kelshaw added.

"So, can't you lock them up as terrorists?" Melanie insisted.

"On what grounds? They aren't actually terrorists, and they don't even have any dubious affiliations. This I know because I already checked," Kelshaw began. "Trust me, if they were even remotely affiliated, I'd have a chance, but beyond our cultural xenophobia, we like to afford our citizens as much freedom as possible until they make a mistake. The trouble is that mistakes are born of trying to not get caught or in trying to survive the unsurvivable. Terminal patients are not likely to care either way."

"So who are they, your patients?" Melanie asked.

"The bad news, or good news, is you've got 11 surviving patients, Malter, but Nigel only met with 7 of them," Kelshaw said.

"But he only needs one," Malter said, immediately recognising the deflation on Melanie's face. "The saving grace may well be in who he's met with though, Melanie."

"If I may," detective Kelshaw interjected. "Nothing to lose tells me to rule out the ones with family." He scanned his list and tapped his pen twice. "Two names. One a retired ex-soldier, the other an ex-cop. Both outstanding candidates, if you ask me."

"Not really," Malter contributed. "Ben Thomas, the soldier, is now effectively blind. Brain tumour which as of yesterday is pressing on his optic nerve. Nigel more than likely wouldn't have known that until today, assuming they've spoken."

"And Farmer? The cop," Kelshaw said. "He'll have skills."

"Hamish? He's a chronic agoraphobic and biding his time until liver failure. He puts on a good show in the group sessions, but beyond the talk, he's just not capable of being outside enough to get anywhere to do anything to anyone."

"So this is good, right?" Melanie asked, upbeat. "I'm safe?"

"No Melanie. We've just discounted the detective's most obvious suggestions."

"Good suspects, both of them," Kelshaw said defensively. "If the Doc wants to rule them out, it's on his head or splendid news."

"So, who are the others?" Melanie asked, not trying to weigh into either option.

"No-ones," Kelshaw said. "All profiles suggest low likelihood. Varying ages and with tight-knit families, and none of them have any employment, skills or associations of any concern."

"Detective, we've already experienced driving a car and jumping out of a window to be skills of concern, so I'd be careful not to rule anyone out on that score."

"Point taken," Kelshaw conceded, "but they are no-ones."

Malter thought a while. "Detective, did you ever study what happened in 1914?"

"The Titanic or the start of World War I?"

"The Titanic was 1912, but yes, the start of World War I. Hundreds of thousands of young men with mundane lives joined for both sides."

"So?" Melanie asked. "I don't see where this is going, or if it's even constructive."

"Put differently," Malter continued. "All those no-ones thought it a good idea to come back a hero or die trying."

"I'm with Melanie, Malter," Kelshaw said. "I can't see the relevance."

"If you were a 'no-one' in 1914, just as now probably, beyond the lure of being a hero, how would you react to the suggestion to make good of your life, even in a small way? As if there's no downside."

"Perhaps I'd think bigger and concentrate on my legacy," Kelshaw suggested.

"Quite," Malter said. "What if you have nothing?"

"Family," Melanie offered. "Your legacy can be what you did or do for your family."

"And if you have no family?"

"Strangers?" Melanie asked with little conviction.

"And what could you do for them?" Malter asked to engage Melanie further. "If you have nothing to give. No time, no money, no assets. What then?"

"Service," Melanie said. She thought a beat before adding, "That's not a good thing for me, surely."

"No, Melanie," Malter exclaimed. "It's not."

37

Melanie was subdued. She looked to each of the men, hopeful for some consolation or assurance, but they met her with poker faces.

"OK, so Nigel," Kelshaw began, as much to break the silence as anything else. "Help me understand where his head is at. I know we're rehashing, but humour me."

"He's angry," Malter replied with a sigh. "Sure, many of my patients are angry and that's the crux of what's seen my program be so successful, and yes, sold a lot of books. I get them to confront their anger and ultimately to find peace. But that's not Nigel. He's too angry, and in that respect he's been a real challenge."

"We're beyond consideration whether he's going to feature on your list of successes, Malter," Kelshaw remarked.

"It's not, trust me. I'm not religiously aligned or inclined. I don't advocate any approach other than what will foster closure, and yet clearly he's not letting it go."

"So we let him die or I arrest him right now," Kelshaw said. "Closure."

"Except it won't help," Malter said. "You can't pin anything on him because he has done nothing himself, and based on that, you can't possibly have any belief that his death will stop whatever he's put in place."

"So protective custody," the detective began. "It might be an option. I'll need to first convince my higher that you aren't the problem, Malter."

"I'll take that as a positive, detective."

"I don't think they'll buy it, though," Kelshaw dismissed, smiling. "I might get them to come around, but that won't help Melanie in the immediate term."

"Or me," Willson said. "I'm not dead yet."

"Frankly, you're not a consideration," Malter said angrily. "You, I couldn't care less about."

"So I'm screwed," Melanie truncated a possible Malter tirade. She looked at each of Malter and Kelshaw, clearly hoping to be challenged. They met her with more silence. "Does it matter that Anthony isn't the father?" she asked.

"You mean *if* he's not the father?" Kelshaw quizzed. "You're assuming a paternity test would make a difference."

"But he's not. I only met Anthony after I fell pregnant."

The comment deflated Willson. "So I'm not going to die a grandparent?"

"You sure?" Kelshaw quizzed, ignoring Willson. "I mean, positive?"

"I was already pregnant when we met." She looked at Willson. "Sorry, Tom. I know I should probably have said something earlier, but I guess I didn't want that look on your face that I'm seeing now."

"Nice of Anthony to step into the role," Kelshaw said. "Rare too, so early in a relationship, unless he thought there was a chance."

Melanie sighed. "If you must know, it was me being pregnant that led to me agreeing to rehab. That's where we met."

"So who's the father?" Kelshaw asked insensitively.

"No-one," Melanie replied with a shrug. "I was using and I really have no idea." She thought a moment while caressing her bump, adding, "I treated the pregnancy as my lightbulb moment. It was my wake-up call to start anew, as if something good was to come of it. Life was actually looking up. I met Anthony, and it was as if things were starting to come together."

"Rehab relationships don't last, Melanie," Malter offered. "Surely they told you that."

"They did, but they didn't factor in the common ground beyond our addiction. Anthony felt abandoned, and so did I. Not that it's any of your business, but there was something between us. I guess that much is a moot point now, anyway."

"And I don't think it will make any difference," Malter said.

38

Malter's phone rang, and he fought his natural inclination to either decline or answer it. In his mind, no call was liable to be pleasant, and to even check the caller was to expose his hiding place. The phone kept ringing, and each ring escalated everyone's anxiety.

"Can I answer it?" Kelshaw asked. "Or smash it?"

Malter checked the screen and felt a guttural pit in his stomach on recognition of the number as being from the hospice again. "This will be about Nigel," he announced before answering the call. His glances at each of Melanie and Kelshaw and their respective responses only exacerbated their apprehensiveness. Malter stepped across the room to receive it in relative privacy.

"Bad news all," Malter said as he returned to the bedside. "That was Cindy, the nurse from the hospice. Nigel has passed."

"Why's that bad news?" Melanie asked. "We're deliberating what to do, but if he's dead…"

"Yes and no, Melanie. But only if Nigel himself was the concern," Malter replied. "Fact is, he wasn't up to doing anything himself and now we can't even negotiate with him."

"If that was even a remote possibility," Kelshaw interjected.

"Whatever he's set in motion is happening," Malter continued.

"So, what happens now?" she asked. "Is there any chance this could be the end of it? Are we potentially stressing for no reason?"

"I think that's unlikely, Melanie," Malter said. "Possible, sure, but unlikely."

"Careful, Malter. If you're so sure, maybe you could have prevented it and both a jury and review board will see it the same way."

"It's called retrospect, detective. In hindsight, perhaps I

underestimated his resolve, particularly when he wasn't very able-bodied himself. I didn't think he'd see to enlisting others."

"Still possibly also your dirty work," Kelshaw remarked. He held up his hand to prevent Malter from commenting. "I'm just calling it like others might see it."

"*His* dirty work, sure," Malter said. "To your question, Melanie, it seems crazy to suggest otherwise based on what we know."

"But you're an obvious benefactor," Kelshaw pressed. "Don't forget, you get as much from his revenge as him."

"By extension, you're saying that I'd be comfortable if something was to happen to Melanie here, and that's just not true," Malter said, a little incensed. "Regardless, you're overlooking the fact that poor Willson here is still alive. If Nigel's gone to this much effort, I think it's very unlikely that he wouldn't have made plans to see to finishing the job."

Melanie was the most uncomfortable at the crowded bedside, so much so that she took it upon herself to prepare some refreshments. She wasn't thirsty herself and judging by the lack of interest from Malter and the detective, they weren't either, but it got her out from the acrid mood of the room. On her return with two mugs for herself and Willson, the men were just as she'd left them. Malter just sat glaring at Willson. The detective sat fumbling with his phone, occasionally glancing at Malter and shaking his head.

"You got anything else to say?" Malter asked Willson.

"Nothing that I haven't already said. I'd only be repeating myself. You don't want to hear it, and it wouldn't change what's already done. What I did."

"I am interested, though," Malter pressed. "How *did* you live with yourself all these years? Knowing what you were capable of?"

"It helped that I was off my head at the time," Willson began. "Afterwards, I found it helped me separate me, what I was ordinarily, from what I was capable of. Gradually, my story went from the front page to somewhere in the middle of the paper, obscured by more interesting and current content. Once my notoriety dissipated, I tried to get on with my life. I found a job where I could be happy with anonymity. Of course it was easier before the internet and that Facebook thing. I found a nice girl after convincing her, and myself, that I was wrongly accused, guilty by association, bad choice of friends and whatever. It also helped that she was blinded by love, too, probably. We got married, had a family and I made good of a shaky back story."

"Until guilt got the better of you?" Malter asked. "I see a lot of suppressed guilt bubbling to the surface."

"I kept it together, kept it bottled pretty well," Willson said.

"Until they released Nigel, right?," Malter offered.

"Nigel was released, paroled, without too much fanfare, but I kept myself aware of that day for when it came and for what it might mean for me."

"Did you know he'd come for you?" Melanie asked.

"Not at first, but I was secretly apprehensive. For the first time, I shared my apprehension with my wife." Willson rubbed his eyes and jerked the nasal tube from his face. "I couldn't share without divulging my guilt. She didn't take it well."

"Did you expect her to?" Melanie asked.

"She said harsh words, that's for sure. I didn't blame her, but that didn't make it easier on either of us, all of us, my four kids included. There was stress in our home for the first time." Willson reached for his first sip of the mug prepared by Melanie. "Nigel left the prison at about 10am. I half expected him at my door by lunchtime, even though I didn't know if he knew my address. He made me wait until the next day."

"So he tracked you down?" Melanie pressed.

"He rang me. It was a Saturday morning and Sandra, Sandi, answered it. He announced himself and asked for me. I still remember the look on her face when she handed over the handset." Willson wriggled uncomfortably, but didn't continue. He closed his eyes and clenched them shut until a tear leaked from each eyelid.

"What did he say?" Melanie insisted.

"He said he'd come for me. He said I'd need to watch my back, sleep by all means, but to never close my eyes, because he'd come for me," Willson said. "But it was the way he said it."

"Must be a terrible thing to feel fear… much like my sister surely felt," Malter commented snidely.

"Sandi felt my fear, too, but from then on we weren't a couple, or a family. She didn't, probably couldn't, offer me any support. She was suddenly married to a criminal, and that person was also the father of her children. We didn't talk. I didn't try. Nigel called a few more times, just wanting to share that he knew where we lived, where my kids went to school, where Sandi and I worked. Eventually, I stopped answering the phone."

Willson paused for his own reminiscence. "By Monday morning I was ragged from a lack of sleep and called in sick. Sandi wasn't in any better shape after holding up in her, our, room for the best part of the weekend, away from me, but she still went to work. Anyway, I was home alone when the doorbell rang and I recall the hair on the back of my neck stood on end. It was just a parcel being delivered, but I couldn't bring myself to even answer the door. I retrieved it after the guy left. Inside the delivery, a box about the size of a shoebox, was a 'Good Luck' card. It was unsigned, but I knew it was from him. The postmark said he'd sent it within an hour of his leaving prison."

Melanie reached for Willson's hand in an unconscious act on feeling the stress of his recollection, but Malter intercepted her reach. "Remember what those hands did," he said. She returned her hand uncomfortably to her side.

"Anyway," Willson said, disappointed but understanding of being denied a comforting human touch. "I spent the next few hours thinking what to do, mindful that decisions needed to be made."

"You didn't think to go to the police?" Melanie asked, to which Malter scoffed, shaking his head.

"I thought about it," Willson remarked, ignoring Malter. "I knew they wouldn't do anything, even if they could. The police resented me for how I'd been acquitted on a technicality, they knew it and so did I. Perhaps Nigel could have been in breach of something, and maybe he'd go back inside, but the damage had been done. I recognised I was kidding myself if I thought I'd be able to get back to happy families."

Willson hid his face behind his mug before continuing. "My wife came home before the kids got back from school. She'd done her homework and found out all the history of Malter's sister, Jenny, what Nigel had done, and most importantly, what I'd done. All the things that blind love stopped her from doing when we first met. She was a lawyer herself, not criminal law, but she knew how to find out things. I greeted her at the door out of habit, a kind of loving instinct, but the way she withdrew told me she understood my culpability. I left and never went back."

"They were better off without you," Malter said.

"Clearly not, James. My leaving didn't help them, did it?"

"You never spoke with them again?" Melanie asked.

"By staying away, I figured I was giving them a chance to rebuild. I used to imagine what Sandi would have said to them to explain my disappearance. I know Anthony told you, Melanie, that I'd died, but it was tough not knowing whether she'd told them the truth or whether me being dead to them all was better or easier to swallow."

"So what did Nigel do then?" Melanie asked. "Anthony never mentioned him."

"Initially at least, Nigel did nothing. Absolutely nothing."

"You were never out of his thoughts," Malter said. "He spoke about you often."

"At first, I expected him to greet me at the door or at work or in the supermarket," Willson continued. "I slept with one eye open, just as he wanted, fully expectant of waking with him looming over me, but it never happened. I never saw him, heard from him, got any letters or parcels from him, but I never doubted he'd come, so I kept away from my family. It was the price I needed to pay for what I did."

"And that you didn't otherwise pay for," Kelshaw said.

"And they, your family, never contacted you?" Melanie coaxed Willson to ignore the interruptions. "Perhaps as they got older?"

"Time doesn't heal everything, Melanie," Malter said.

"Indeed, it does not, James. I hoped that I'd get a knock at the door from someone, Sandi or one of the kids, but no."

"Maybe your name change made it too difficult," Melanie offered.

"I've changed my name at irregular intervals ever since I left my family, just to try to extend my anonymity. Sandi changed her name too, last name anyway, and that of each of the kids to something different, probably so they could be free of their monster father. That said, if she or the kids wanted to find me, I was here to be found, but it never happened."

"I don't believe you never made contact," Malter doubted. "You couldn't help yourself with my sister..."

Willson resented the comment. "Her name is Sandi Lopez. She's the least likely looking person to have such a Hispanic surname, so you'll know it's her when you meet her to ask if she's ever seen or communicated with me in all those years. You ask her. She might even deny knowing me entirely, especially in light of the fact that her, our, children are all dead. I've tried calling her, but she may well have blocked my number."

"You said she was a lawyer?" Kelshaw asked, flitting through his notebook. "Where did she work?"

"Does, not did. She's still practicing. She's a named partner at a firm in the city," Willson replied.

"Was," Kelshaw insisted. "Another of Malter's patients this morning. Kelly Flintshire launched herself from a window onto her."

Malter, Melanie and Kelshaw all looked to Willson for his reaction, but there was nothing beyond frail hands clenching at his sheets. "I always knew this day would come."

39

"And you're sure that my patients are implicated?" Malter asked Kelshaw. "Or are involved?"

"Haven't we been through this?" the detective replied with a measure of frustration. "All of Willson's family, all at the hands of your patients. Cliff, Travis, Billy, Ken, and now Kelly. Seems definitive enough for me, and inevitably a jury. "

Malter considered the people listed. "Ken who?"

"Ken annoying," Kelshaw mumbled as he took out his notebook. He flipped back and forth through several pages before tracing his finger across some of his scrawled notes. "Swain, Ken Swain. You can't clear your tracks now, Malter."

"I'm not! He's not my patient."

"You know I can check, right?" Kelshaw grumbled as he produced his phone from his pocket. "I'm getting it looked into," he commentated while sending a message.

"So can I," Malter said, already reaching for his phone. "Tash. It's me. Ken Swain. Is he a patient or a pending patient?" The smile on Malter's face was immediate. He ended the call. "Not my patient, and I'm happy to be on record about it."

"So, who is he?" Melanie asked.

"Swain is allegedly the one responsible for the death of one of Willson's daughter, Jenny," the detective said as he flitted through his notebook. "Pisano, Jenny Pisano."

"You called your daughter 'Jenny'?" Malter asked incredulously. "You have no shame, Willson."

"Perhaps we can talk about that at another time," Willson said. "Moving on, maybe if we can make sense of who he is, it might change where we're at with Melanie here."

"If he's not, was not, a patient, does that mean that Nigel isn't, wasn't, involved?" Melanie asked.

"I doubt it. The detective's going to get more information, but it's unlikely to absolve Nigel entirely or put your mind at ease, whatever he says. I've known Nigel most of my life, and there's no way he's going to leave your friend Jack or Tom, or whatever he's calling himself, to get the last laugh."

"Even though he's now dead?" Melanie asked.

"Especially now he's dead," Willson added. "He visited me last night. The first time I'd seen him in years and I felt his anger."

"Do you blame him?" Melanie asked. "After what you did to his girlfriend."

"Did he mention the hammer?" Malter asked spitefully. "Did he tell you it was someone else's, or that he wasn't there?"

"No, James. I told her everything," said Tom with a sigh. He expected some disbelief, adding, "Every sordid detail. Melanie asked me to stop, but I needed to say it."

"Like you couldn't before a jury?"

"James, I am sorry. For that night, afterwards and ever since. I thought I could hide from what I did, but I couldn't. No matter what I did, the face looking back at me from the mirror saw to me never forgetting."

Kelshaw tended to his phone on receipt of a message before juggling his notepad and pen while returning his phone to his pocket. "OK. So Ken Swain wasn't a patient. Not even terminal. A vindictive arsehole, sure, but not likely to have done anything at your request, Doc."

"So why, then?" Malter enquired.

"I've got help looking into his history. Something will come up. Three from four of Willson here's kids are still linked to you, or Nigel, and the fourth is unlikely to be sheer coincidence."

"You're not still removing me from the equation?" Malter asked.

"Not until or unless I get a better theory. As of now, you're still the only verifiable link. To be honest, even if Nigel was still alive, you'd still be the only plausible link. I'll know more soon enough."

"So, what do we do until then?" Melanie asked. "Wait?"

"All we can do," Malter said.

The detective's phone rang. Expecting a gloat opportunity, he answered, enabling the speaker function to allow everyone to join the call. "I've got you on speaker, Piper. Speak freely. What have we got?"

"For starters, a correction," she began. "We made a mistake about Willson's daughter. The one who drowned in the car."

"Misidentification?" Willson asked excitedly. "Where is she?"

"No, she's still dead but the do-er, Ken. Definitely not a patient, of Malter's anyway." She paused to reflect, adding, "Willson's not within earshot, is he?"

"He'll live. Keep talking," Malter said. "So this Ken, he's not terminal?"

"I'm assuming that's Doctor Malter talking," she said. "He wasn't, but he's dead now, just the same. Issues, sure, but as good as we know at this stage, he wasn't terminally ill."

"What issues?" Malter asked.

"Marital, or he was married, but he's had some issues post-separation and divorce. Two kids that he only gets an hour a month of supervised visits for, in a public place, threats to kill, stalking… the full bit. The ex is in hiding from him, but now verified safe. Alcohol, not surprisingly, didn't help him, but he was getting help beyond what the courts mandated."

"From who?" Kelshaw asked.

"Counselling mainly," Piper replied. "Voluntarily."

"Doing as much good as the alcohol," Kelshaw muttered.

"Whoever this is," Malter asked. "Do we know who the facilitator of his sessions is?"

"Constable Piper Richards. I work with detective Kelshaw," she attempted to introduce herself clumsily without having someone to speak to directly. "To your question, I can send you details of the group coordinators. I've already got your number."

"As a professional, I can circumvent some privacy expectations," Malter said to the detective, anticipating a question. "Those same rules won't apply if it's all volunteer-based groups, so you might still like to try your luck, but I will most definitely be able to better gauge where he was at."

"He was also attending some ad hoc group sessions at a church, but to be fair, the church only provided the meeting venue," Piper explained. "The groups are purely voluntary, not for profit and not officially aligned to the hosting church, or any faith." She paused to allow any comments and questions, but ultimately continued without interruption. "And we've got another one. Not one of Malter's patients, though, Nate."

Malter couldn't help but breathe a little relief. "So another what?"

"Nate, detective Kelshaw, asked that I look into known people and anything current."

"I wanted to know about Malter's patients, but anyone else too," Kelshaw explained, primarily to Melanie. "Malter here was too quick to speculate as to coincidences of those involved. I don't do coincidences."

"So who?" Melanie asked, feeling a little left out of the discussion. "It's Melanie Nashman here."

"Hi, Melanie. Sorry about your partner," Piper empathised, but quickly moved on. "Mr Willson. Do you know an Amy Craven?"

Willson said nothing but breathed a long slow laboured breath.

"He's not saying anything," Kelshaw explained for Piper's benefit. "What about her?"

"Before either of you ask, no, she's not a patient," Malter said, pre-emptively.

"She terminal?" Kelshaw asked.

"No idea. I guess she could be, but that's not why she's interesting," Piper continued. "The woman pushed in front of the bus by the old guy, Barnes. Her name is, was, Amy Craven. Uniforms visiting her home in search of next of kin found letters from a Mr Tom Willson. It warranted a deeper look."

"Willson's still silent, Piper," Kelshaw said, adding, "but clearly the chance of this being a coincidence just took a significant dive."

"Oh, yes," she agreed. "Especially if you consider that Eric Barnes, the absconding geriatric from the nursing home you visited, Nate, was once the cellmate of one Nigel Newcott. A long time ago, but there it is."

"What was Nigel in jail for?" Melanie asked.

"Willson here might have omitted that detail," Malter said. "Nigel killed two of the three men responsible for the attack on my sister, his girlfriend. He was unsuccessful on the third." He glared at Willson.

"Great work, Piper. Yet another case for why I never accept coincidences," Kelshaw said, adding, "Keep going and keep us posted while I get more from Willson," as he ended the call.

"So who is she, then?" Malter asked as he leered at Willson, still labouring with slow breaths and his eyes closed.

"She's a warning," he replied. "That Nigel is a long way from being finished."

"How so?" Melanie asked.

"When Nigel visited me last night, he told me he knew of some journals of mine that I'd stored, or more correctly, hidden, in my garden shed. Not that I've checked recently, but I'm thinking if anyone was to look, they'd be able to confirm."

"So?" Kelshaw asked.

"I would have mentioned her in those journals," Willson said.

"And you think Nigel would have made someone harm her, because of what you wrote in a journal?" Malter asked.

"James, you're still not looking at this right. I get he's a friend and whatever he is to you professionally, whereas I'm just the devil incarnate to you both, but he's going to make me pay."

40

Willson and his bedside were quiet while everyone allowed themselves to be distracted in their own way. The detective was drawn to watching the CCTV monitors and the laps of the uniforms around the house, Willson gazed at Melanie, and Melanie stroked her belly as much as her limited show would permit, all of which could be done without communicating with others. Malter stared in Willson's direction without really looking at him, thinking.

"Who's Amy, Willson?" Malter asked critically. "Someone else's sister?"

"No-one," Willson said apprehensively.

"Bullshit," Malter barked.

"Careful, Malter," Kelshaw placated. "It's just as likely she's someone to you, not him."

"No doubt you'll check, detective, so there's little point in whatever I say about her, this Amy, whoever she is," Malter replied. "Tom here clearly knows who she is, though, and I'm guessing he also knows something about this Ken, too."

"Willson?" Kelshaw asked. "Time to cough up."

"I don't know this Ken person. Never met him, and never heard of him," Willson stated. "But Amy is a friend. We've corresponded for a long time."

"So when did you last see her?" Kelshaw pressed.

"Not for many years."

"But you still call her a friend?" Malter asked.

"You know, James, I have had a lonely life. Yes, I deserved it, but my point is my life has been far from perfect." Willson paused long enough for a breath, but not long enough for James to interject. "For what it's worth, I tried to make good as best as my circumstances would allow. I tried my hand at volunteering, for the homeless, reading groups, whatever, and I honestly tried my best to take part in the community and the world. I wasn't working, so I had the time and the best of intentions to be and do something positive."

"Why weren't you working?" Malter asked. "I see many people using work as a distraction from whatever else is going on in their life. Their deathbed is no easier for their labours, of course, which in most cases is unfortunate, but in your case, it's justified."

"James, whatever you think of me, I get it. Trust me," Willson insisted. "But you have to believe me when I say I tried."

"So why didn't you work?" Melanie asked. "Were you sick?"

"No, Melanie. I was fit and healthy, but so was Nigel. You know what it's like to look over your shoulder perpetually, knowing that he could be there? To second guess whether to answer the phone knowing that it could be him."

"It's called paranoia, Willson. You said he did nothing."

"Detective, it was more than paranoia. I started seeing him everywhere. Where I worked. Where I shopped. Where I volunteered. And everywhere I saw him, my welcome was retracted."

"It might not have been because of Nigel," Malter suggested. "I don't like you and it seems reasonable that others mightn't like you, no matter what kind of facade you front with."

"I know it was Nigel. He came to my place of work once while I was there, and I sat there sweating what he might say as he met my boss behind closed doors for the best part of an hour. I was later sacked because I'd lied in my application for employment. I did, but I'd been a competent employee with years of service until that time."

"Poor guy," Malter said sarcastically.

"I naively thought I'd be able to get another job, but mine was a localised niche and word got out. Whether it was by my now ex-employer or Nigel was irrelevant," Willson said with a sigh. "The fact is that I was jobless until I took a significant pay cut and went for the menial stuff that no one else wanted. I could scrub a toilet and those kinds of jobs didn't demand reference checks."

"That's so sad, Willson," Malter commented condescendingly.

"Nigel seemed content to have me taken down a peg, or so I thought, and the workplace visits stopped," Willson continued despite the interruption. "You have to remember that this was before social media and kids of today don't recognise that it was a very different time. I could disappear into obscurity reasonably easily, but not entirely, particularly if someone wanted to out me. It's not like he took out newspaper advertisements or wandered the streets of my neighbourhood with a sandwich board or anything."

"But he still made it hard?" Melanie asked.

"Hard, but not too hard, probably, Melanie. If he'd made it too hard, I would have been left with no choice but to move away, or perhaps end it," Willson said. "I considered it, ending it, but I didn't. I treated it as a measure of my reformation that I stuck it out. To neck myself would have been a cop-out."

"And you didn't want Nigel to 'win'..." Malter offered.

"Not at all, James. It was to honour your sister, and Nigel, that I kept going. Call it a penance, but I knew I couldn't do it at my hand."

"But you still thought Nigel would get to you?" Melanie asked.

"I always knew he'd come," Willson said pensively. "Occasionally, I'd sense his presence. That feeling when you know someone's behind you, but when you turn, there's no one there. I felt it every day. Every single day."

"Was he ever actually there?" Kelshaw asked doubtfully.

"Sometimes he was. In the distance or benignly going about his business. He'd wait until I saw him, then he'd sort of smile, and then he'd leave. I can't describe his smile, if you could call it that, in any way that you'd understand." Willson thought a little, adding, "It expressed confidence, anger and delight, all at once."

"And you never went to the police about it?" Kelshaw asked.

"For several reasons, no. For starters, he never overtly represented a threat. I could see that. It wasn't for a lack of witnesses, but they would not have seen anything worthy of approaching the police. I'd see him on the street while we both were doing shopping, so if the police were to ask anyone, there would be no verifiable threat. He never acted menacingly toward me or anyone else, in public, and then let's not forget that the police weren't exactly in my court. They knew I was guilty. It wasn't worth rubbing their noses in it. Bear in mind, I was still scared of going to jail if I gave them or anyone else justification to dust off the old case with fresh evidence."

"That would have been a real penance," Malter offered.

"Jail might have restored your faith in the system which failed you and Nigel, James, but it wouldn't have changed anything, really. I summoned the courage to approach the police at one point, but Nigel actually followed me into the station."

"Why would he do that?" Melanie asked.

"I think he just did it to remind me he was there. That he'd always be there. Had I gone to jail, I knew he would have found some means to join me there for sure."

"Get to the point, Willson," Kelshaw pushed. "Who's Amy?"

"I'm getting there. So I couldn't work, and inevitably Nigel interfered with even the banal act of shopping for food. Stores didn't need to serve me and they reserved the right to refuse my custom, which they did, typically after a visit from Nigel, I assumed. If I'd been disabled, there would have been laws against them refusing to serve me, but not if the manager had been briefed that I was a person better off not being associated with their store."

"You're breaking my heart, Willson," Malter said.

"I challenged them and got to speak with the manager of one of the supermarket chains near where I lived. He just flicked me a picture of me in front of his store, the chain logo so clearly visible it could have been an advertisement. People I bumped into in the street mightn't have known who I was, but if they did, they wouldn't want to be associated with anywhere, even a supermarket, so tolerant of me. The store, that entire chain, couldn't bear the prospect of me appearing on page one of the paper with their logo so visible, so they got the brief to refuse my entry. I ended up doing my shopping and whatever else only where Nigel was allowing me, particularly the smaller stores so pushed to the brink by those larger chains that appearing on the front page would have been a positive. He wanted me close."

Willson sighed with his recollection. "Forget anything recreational. Anywhere I went to more than once was liable to have a picture of me on their window, so eventually, I stopped trying. Not the library. Not the park. Not the movies. Nothing. I got the paper delivered and I watched TV. That was the extent of my participation in the world."

"So who's Amy?" Melanie asked, mindful of Malter and the detective's growing frustration.

"I tried going to church. It was a long-shot which could just as easily have ended up with me being blacklisted there too, but I gave it a go."

"You'd like to think they'd be tolerant," Melanie encouraged.

"Well, quite. I have no idea if Nigel tried to get to them or not, really, but regardless, I started going to church. I didn't find God. I didn't look for him. I just went, and Nigel allowed it. That's where I met Amy."

"Anything romantic?" Melanie asked.

"Nothing like that," Willson replied dismissively. "She and I just went to church. We got together over coffee after each service, and we just clicked. We became close, but initially only in so much as that after-service coffee. She was human contact, nothing more, but she meant everything to me. In the vacuum of family and friends, she was both. I'm saddened to say that I haven't actually seen her for a long time."

"For how long?" Kelshaw asked.

"If I had my diary, diaries, I could tell you to the day. Certainly years ago. She obviously knew of my history, because I told her, but our friendship continued regardless."

"Until?" Malter pressed.

"Until Nigel, of course. I was at her home having some afternoon tea when there was a knock at the door. It was him, brazenly appearing unannounced," Willson said, rolling his shoulders a little. "He told Amy how unfortunate it was for her she'd chosen her friends so poorly. The hair on the back of my neck stood on end."

"And?" Kelshaw urged for more.

"That's all he said. By this stage, Amy and I were close without being romantically so, and I was very fearful for her well-being, so much so that I knew I needed to stay away from her as well. I said goodbye, and I never saw her again. We still speak regularly, but we're both old school and appreciate the joy of receiving a handwritten letter, but we never saw each other again."

"Not even at church?" Melanie asked.

"I never went again. Or to the shops. Or anywhere. In retrospect, I'm surprised Nigel allowed even that much. Of course it helps that there's a posting box adjacent to my property "

"It doesn't pay to be your friend, does it?" Malter quipped.

"No, James, it does not. I thought by reducing my friend circle to zero I could remove the threat to others but…". Willson stopped mid-sentence.

"But Nigel has a long memory," Malter said.

41

Detective Kelshaw continued scribbling frenetically in his notebook long after Willson eased back into his pillows. The talking was draining on Willson's declining body, and he looked more fatigued by the minute; every measure of a dying man.

"So who else do you know?" Kelshaw asked as he wriggled his writing hand before re-engaging his pen. "Who else might be at risk, then?"

"Detective, I've not left my home in years, except to tend to my garden in my backyard and post a letter, but my health has deteriorated such that I can't even do that. I get my groceries delivered and I'm wholly dependent on paid carers and help."

"But you mentioned your shed and your journals," Melanie remarked. "How did you put them there?"

"Nigel knows about them, or so he says. I've needed to get my carer to add to the stash that I've buried out there. Some of the carers have been lazy, so it wouldn't surprise me if they just stacked them on a bench in the shed, knowing that I couldn't check or do anything about it."

"So why keep them at all?" Malter asked.

"I don't know," Willson sighed. "Nothing that makes sense now, but I guess it came down to my legacy and what I wanted to leave to my children. I made mistakes, and I wanted them to learn from what I'd done wrong. If anyone was to read them, they'd more than likely write them off as the ravings of a guilty man."

"Because they are," Malter sniped.

"What else would be in them?" Kelshaw asked. "Any more names?"

"Of people potentially at risk? No. Mention of my kids and Amy, sure, but no one else. I didn't want to risk getting them involved."

"Of karma coming back at you," Malter pushed.

"Quite," Willson accepted.

"And you're sure there's no-one else?" Kelshaw asked.

"I've kept to myself," Willson said, "except for Amy."

"She's accounted for, so that's a dead end."

"What about your carers?" Malter asked. "It seems like a fair bet that anyone you've been in contact with, at all, should be a little wary."

"Isn't that a little excessive?" Melanie asked. "I mean, they were just doing their jobs."

"That argument carried little favour at Nuremberg after the war," Malter said. "I doubt it will have been a big consideration from Nigel, either."

"So have you got a list of your carers or the provider who manages them?", Kelshaw asked. "I'm hoping their staff turnover is low."

"Top drawer, if you wouldn't mind, Melanie," Willson pointed to his bedside. "The number is there somewhere. To your question, detective, I've seen quite a handful of them over the last few months. Until then, I was independent and didn't need carers."

"If morning and late afternoon are different people, how many are we talking?" Kelshaw pressed.

"Perhaps five or ten, maybe more," Willson replied. "Most aren't that memorable, so I can't really say."

"Got it," Melanie said. "This business card says 'Call on me'. Domestic and nursing support services."

"That's the one. Call them and ask for Emily. I seldom need to call her because she routinely calls me, just to say hello and see if she can squeeze some more services and funds from me. Don't know her last name, sorry, unless it's on the card."

Kelshaw took the card from Melanie and rang Piper. "We need some digging on the providers of domestic help service for Willson here. Emily Jakeman." He told her the number and paused momentarily, as if she would magically have news to share pre-emptively at her fingertips. "We'll need a list of anyone who's been a provider for Willson. And we'll need it as a matter of urgency."

"On it," Piper said. "I was just about to call you anyway, Nate."

"What now?" Kelshaw sighed as he engaged the speaker function for everyone's benefit. "Who now?"

"Nothing, Nate. That's all I was going to say. It's been pretty quiet really, and nothing more than the usual stuff. Some prostitute was the victim of a hit and run last night, but I think she's the second or third this week."

"So nothing, really?" Kelshaw said.

"She's still someone's daughter, detective." Malter suggested, a little amazed at the lack of sensitivity. "She's got a name, and she's just as deserving of a future as Melanie here."

"What was her name?" Melanie asked.

"Not for disclosure pending notification of next of kin, probably, but in the circumstances and who cares, right?" Piper paused for comment. "Her name is Collette something. Her working name was 'Candace'. Of course, it would more likely be 'Candy'"

"What's her last name?" Willson asked. "Do you know her actual, real name?"

"What's it to you?" Kelshaw asked.

"I'd just like to know her name is all," Willson said casually. "Her real name."

"She can't tell you, Willson," Kelshaw commented. "In Piper's defence she's already broken protocols of disclosure, so you're going to need to fantasise as to her name."

"Picture a short, buxom young woman in her twenties," Piper said. "What last name do you think would work?"

"Blue eyes?" Willson asked.

"Sure," Piper said, playing along with Willson's interest. "Blue-eyed Candy the hooker. What surname works?"

Kelshaw was suddenly alert to Willson's interest. "Piper, I need a description of her. The name is irrelevant."

"The report says bleached blonde, short, 150cm, no idea what that is in feet. The obligatory butterfly tattoo on the small of her back and long scarred cigarette burns on her breasts that some big angel tattoos can't really obscure."

"Her father did them," Willson said. "She was a nice girl. Troubled, sure, but she was making good for herself, and no, I don't need your judgement. Consider it a function of my loneliness."

"Who did it, Piper?" Malter asked. "Concerned citizen didn't appreciate streetwalkers in his neighbourhood?"

"Just re-reading what we know, Nate," Piper said, accounting for a momentary delay. "OK. Witnesses got the licence plate of the vehicle registered to a guy. Uniforms picked him up, still sitting behind the wheel of his car with a Candace sized dent in the bonnet and windscreen."

"He say why he did it?" Kelshaw asked.

"Nothing to live for, he says," Piper said.

"So he upped and ran over a working girl. I don't buy it. There's always a reason," Kelshaw said. "Is he terminal?"

"Not that being terminal would account for behaving in a manner against a prostitute," Malter commented.

"A young woman, just the same," Willson said.

"He's not terminal, regardless," Piper said, adding, "according to what we know as of now."

"So what do we know?" Kelshaw asked.

"Newly separated. Father of two. History of anger issues for which he's getting support. We're investigating a theory that the victim, Candace, might have been in a relationship with the guy's ex," Piper serialised.

"Candace's partner's name is Lori," Willson contributed. "Does that help?"

Piper snorted a sigh. "So let's rack that theory up as confirmed. I'll let upstairs know."

"Can you get a list of the attendees of the support group he's attending?" Malter enquired. "I'd like to see if Nigel is in the picture there."

"You're thinking more candidates to attack Tom or Melanie here, Malter?" Kelshaw asked before redirecting. "Piper, when you get that list, you need to look back a while. 6 months should do it," he looked at Malter for his concurrence.

"I'd go longer," Malter commented. "Nigel will have been planning this for a long time, possibly years, so you'll need to see what balls he might have got rolling for years. And when you get the list, you might also like to cross-reference it against a list of recently aggrieved, bereaved, separated or divorced."

"Can I ask why?" Melanie asked. "Why would they be any more likely to hurt me?"

"Piper said this one claimed he's got nothing to live for. If Nigel's found a soft spot for others to be similarly plied…" Malter tapered off, hopeful he wouldn't need to labour the point, but elaborated on seeing an unconvinced look on Melanie's face. "Think of when you've felt at your lowest, and perhaps that little voice in the back of your head started a chorus that you had nothing to live for. Most people can silence those voices, most of the time, but there are many people who, for reasons of circumstance or genetics, just can't. Terminal illness, psychosis, relationship breakdowns or extreme loss; there are many things than can push someone to the edge. What if you had that voice in one ear, and a different voice, an outsider's voice, in your other ear suggesting a way to make good of your current predicament?"

"That's potentially a lot of people," Melanie offered.

Malter nodded subtly in acknowledgement.

42

"Willson, can you think of anyone else you might have interacted with?" Kelshaw asked. "Anyone at all?"

"I'm telling you, no," he replied. "Beyond talking with Amy and the occasional chat with my carers, no one. Even before I became bed-bound, I never ventured out of my house for fear of what Nigel might do."

"I don't believe you. Maybe you think you're telling the truth, but I think you're underestimating your circle of influence," Malter challenged.

"James, I get you don't like me, but Nigel killed me years ago. I'm just waiting for my body to get the memo."

"Willson, spare me a sob story," Kelshaw said. "Chronicle your day, your average day. It might help."

"My day is pretty much what you see. I get morning and late afternoon visits with whoever Emily coordinates. The rest of my time, I'm just alone with my thoughts."

"Neighbours? Anything online? Anyone at all?" Kelshaw pressed. "Pretend you care their lives might be in danger."

"No need to pretend, detective. I've locked myself away to protect others. You all being here is more company than I've enjoyed in many years. I honestly can't think of anyone," he maintained.

"Your kitchen," Melanie said. "There's a takeaway flyer on your refrigerator."

"So? Cholesterol isn't going to kill me now, so sometimes I have a pizza delivered. There are probably some leftovers if you're hungry. My appetite is not what it used to be."

Kelshaw instinctively made his way from the room to the kitchen.

He returned a minute later with the flyer in hand, "Piper's checking."

"What's to check?" Willson asked. "The pizza guy, Mickey, he comes, he delivers, he takes his tip and leaves. That's all. Not enough to warrant any mention in my diaries."

"Lucky him," Malter jibed. "I hope it's enough. It would be unfortunate for him if the simple act of delivering to you was enough for him to come to an untimely end."

"Well yes," Willson began. "Admittedly, I have said more than the obligatory small talk to him, and his pizzas are very good. My doctor introduced me to Mickey when he dialled a pizza after a consultation at his office. I was his last patient for the day and we got to talking and time got away from us and before we knew it..."

"So you've been in contact with your doctor, too," Kelshaw commented with a measure of frustration while simultaneously reaching for his phone and pen. "What's *his* name?"

"Abe Bounte. Spelled with an 'e', but pronounced like 'bounty'. Whatever, I just call him Abe. I didn't think to include or mention him. Nice guy. Very tall."

"And he's your doctor? How long for?" Malter asked.

"About a year ago, the local paper included a feature on local businesses, including a medical practice. I figured it was time I went for a checkup. I'd let that much slide, and not just because I'm old and male, but something didn't feel right."

"That will be the guilt, Willson," Malter said. "It's eaten away at you like it did Nigel."

"Well, yes. I got a referral from a GP to the oncologist, that's Abe, and our first meeting was his last for the day. His wife was working the evening shift as a nurse, so he offered me pizza instead of going home for a TV dinner. My visits ever since invariably included pizza, and always from Mickey, even if I'm too sick to eat. Of late, both Abe and Mickey visit me here. Getting a delivery to coincide with Abe's visits has become a bit of a tradition."

"Not that I really care, Willson, but I guess I'm interested," Malter began. "What have you got?"

"Some gastro-intestinal thing, that's certainly how it started. Abe could give you all the details. My ears heard the word cancer at its first mention and nothing else thereafter. Doesn't matter what kind it is. Abe pressed for me to do both chemo and radiotherapy. I honestly tried to tell him of my history so he wouldn't push, but he wouldn't take no for an answer. I put up with it for months, but you get to a point where you feel the treatment is worse than the illness. The headaches, burns and pain from head to foot. I quit and just accepted that my wait was nearly over."

"But you must be in pain if you're end-stage palliative. What meds are you on?" Malter asked, gravitating towards the foot of Willson's bed. "Where's your chart?"

"Forever the professional, James. That could almost be interpreted as caring for my wellbeing," Willson said, half smiling. "To your question, Abe sometimes takes it with him; he knows I don't and won't look at it. It's not like I'm liable to look for a second opinion. He says I'm dying, I feel like I'm dying, and many would say I'm overdue, so what do I care what's on my chart?"

"Well, yes," Malter conceded. "Care to give me the rundown of what would be on it?"

"I had vomiting for months, but that's stopped, thankfully. Now every bowel movement I have is just blood. Apologies for being so frank, Melanie, and I'm prescribed a diet of pills and potions to keep me comfortable. It doesn't change my prognosis."

"But you have carers, surely?" Malter asked. He looked at the mobile drug locker next to the foot of his bed. "Nurses? If there's scheduled drugs in that locker, you must have some clinically competent staff."

"As an ex-addict, I'm refusing most of the pain medication and it made little sense to have staff to prolong my wellbeing at the best of times, let alone now. I'm taking the pain as my penance. Emily sends someone a few times daily, but they're doing little more than changing my sheets and flushing my catheter now that I've largely stopped drinking fluids. The rest of the time, they just play on their phone. To be fair, I deliberately don't engage with them. Abe says I won't live much longer anyway, so I've said my goodbyes."

"That's a little cold," Melanie said. "I mean, to be left alone to die."

Malter made to speak, but Willson beat him to it. "On behalf of James and Nigel and others, dying alone after so many years is more than I deserve. I can't say I've had a good life, but it's been a long one, and I've spent most of it waiting for my life to catch up with what I did."

"I was going to say dying alone is most definitely what you deserve," Malter said angrily. "My sister bled out, alone. You're dying an old man on your own terms."

43

Malter and Kelshaw simultaneously received a message from Piper listing the attendees of the support group. Malter scanned down the list and then reviewed it a second time, more conscientiously. "There's no-one I know," he announced to the interested eyes watching.

"What church did you attend, Willson?" Kelshaw asked after reviewing the list himself.

"Some non-denominational, hands-in-the-air thing. Three blocks from here, but I can't recall the address. It's funny how the mundanity of addresses slip from memory because I never leave the house."

"So the same one that Nigel worked at," Kelshaw commented.

"No idea. I never saw him there," Willson said.

"I see where you're going with this, detective," Malter commented. "That was a long time ago, and incidentally, Nigel's not a listed group attendee either."

"Perhaps, but for a lack of other lines of enquiry, I think it warrants closer examination," Kelshaw said. "You might not care about Melanie here, but I certainly do."

Malter didn't bite. "It's got nothing to do with Melanie, but everything to do with a lack of plausibility."

"So?" Melanie asked. "It's just a church."

"In the absence of any other ideas, the detective is just exploring a possible link between Nigel and the church. Nigel used to work there, and so did the other party mentioned by Piper. It's nothing," Malter said.

"Nothing it may be, Malter, but I don't do coincidences," Kelshaw exclaimed. "For all we know, there could be a whole God-bothering flock intent on doing Melanie harm."

"I would think that's unlikely. Nigel mentioned no longstanding, let alone ongoing involvement with that church. I'd go as far as to suggest that his attitude would have been too antagonistic to people of faith, too," Malter said. "They might initially have tried to make him see the light or whatever, but that would have been futile."

"Is it possible he just played them along?" Kelshaw asked.

"Well, yes," Malter conceded. "Possibly, but I'm thinking it's very unlikely."

"While you hedge your bets, I'm looking into it," Kelshaw said. He started for the door until he noticed Melanie's attentiveness to his departure.

"So what are you saying, detective," Melanie asked. "If the church is a link and Nigel has managed to convince people of something, what's to say they'd do anything, anyway. I'm no-one to them."

"Fair point, Melanie," Kelshaw conceded. "I'm just going on what I know."

"Which is what, exactly?" Malter asked, flustered. He rose from his seat as if about to approach the detective. "I guess I should be happy in that you appear to be a little less interested in me, but come on, what have you got? Nigel worked at a church, a long time ago, that Willson and his friend also went to some time ago. That's not a theory."

"I can't sit by and wait for something to happen, Malter," Kelshaw said. "You told me Nigel's job with the church was all about influencing others. Considering the circumstances, it's a very reasonable concern he might have influenced others for this."

"Well, yes and no," Malter replied. "Yes, he could influence people, but I think the church is a waste of time. I'd almost agree with a concern, but I'd be more interested in the attendees of the support group which met at the church, not the congregation of the church itself. "

"Ruling out the larger group might be ok in your mind, but not in mine," Kelshaw said. He moved to the window to take a peek outside and took stock on the position of the uniforms dawdling in the afternoon shade. "For all I know, we could expect a human wave assault by the entire congregation."

"You're missing the point, still, detective," Malter persisted. "Nigel hasn't been in that capacity in the congregation for many years. He's possibly been involved with the support group much more recently."

"It's a reasonable assumption that he might have made friendships while there which outlived his employment. You work at someplace for long enough and anyone can make friends, let alone become part of the greater church assembly."

"You're not looking at this like Nigel," Malter began. He looked at Willson silently reclining in his bed, adding, "Nigel lost someone dear to him and he's angry."

"I get we don't even know if he's attended church since, but I'll put money on it he has," Kelshaw said. "He also has, had, no reason to go to a single Dads' support group, but it looks like he did. It's not like one of your *'I'm dying love-ins'*, Malter. He might have gone as a support to a friend."

"I wouldn't think so. Not that I know all his friends," Malter conceded. "But I'll guarantee there are several parallels between those groups and my group sessions."

"Other than terrible coffee and uncomfortable chairs?" Kelshaw teased.

"You're not getting it, detective," Malter sighed. "Those groups, theirs and mine. The attendees have nothing to lose."

The detective glanced at his watch. "For a want to do *something*, I'll check out the group at the church."

44

Detective Kelshaw arrived at the church and circled to the carpark at the rear. It was a huge open bituminised space with hundreds of spaces marked, but empty, except for a selection of vehicles beside a series of low-rise buildings on one side of the main building. He looked at his watch and theorised that the group would be in session in one of the lower buildings; fifteen cars meant at least fifteen in attendance.

"The group. Where is it?" Kelshaw asked the first person he saw in the building closest to the carpark, a slight middle-aged man with glasses and a tatty t-shirt seated in a corridor adorned with framed pictures of what appeared to be a concert. Only on giving the images a second look was it apparent that the concert was more than likely a standard Sunday performance.

"Which one? We got AA for the alcoholics, and NA for the addicts," the man replied as he stood. "No judgement, mind you, I've been to both at various times. My name's Warren 'C', and no, the 'C' isn't for Christ." He laughed a little to himself, "that normally gets at least a smile."

"Neither," Kelshaw replied.

"Got it. You'd have to be for the single parents. There are always grandparents in there too," Warren continued. "I should have picked it. Not that you can tell an addict 100% of the time. Second door on the right." He pointed in the general direction and smiled. "Find Christ. He helped me and he'll help you."

Kelshaw struggled with a confused smile. "Sure," he said, walking towards the designated door. He entered to a seated circle of attendees, some of whom glanced his way before returning their attention to a man standing, talking. Kelshaw thought about whether to join the circle or remain in the background. He listened briefly to someone pour their heart out, pausing periodically to shed or wipe a tear, occasionally to murmurs of understanding from the others. Kelshaw said nothing but made a bee-line to the coffee station in the middle of a wall covered with the same pictures as the corridor, but also some less grandiose photos of individuals, men and women, talking. He gave each of the faces on the pictures a once over and smiled when he recognised Malter in one of them; seated and looking engaged in a group.

He fixed himself a brewed coffee and scanned a handwritten list of names on the table, marvelling at the illegibility of some names. Curious, he thumbed through an adjacent stack of relevant self-help books in a basket under the table, presumably available for loan. He found what he expected without much effort; one of Malter's books; a signed copy. Kelshaw shook his head and took a mouthful of the coffee to wash what seemed like a bad taste from his mouth; the taste that came from being lied to. With that first jolt of caffeine, he recognised the fatigue of his long day and that he *could* have been in bed hours ago. He *should* have been in bed hours ago. He sculled his cup and helped himself to another and a biscuit and made his way to the circle as the standing talker took his seat.

One of the circle waved in greeting and gestured for Kelshaw to take the floor. "I'm Nate Kelshaw," he said, to which a chorus of "Hello Nate," began. "*Detective* Nate Kelshaw," he continued provocatively, silencing the chorus. "I want to talk about someone who might be a member of your group. Nigel Newcott. He looks like someone who's dying of cancer."

"Not the place, detective," the same man who'd ushered him to speak said. "Perhaps you're in the wrong room."

"Not in the wrong place," Kelshaw responded curtly. "Nigel Newcott. Is he a member or not?" He checked the faces around the circle and saw only a mix of shaking heads and shrugs. "It's not hard, people."

"I don't recall the name," the leader said. "And if he's in trouble, I'm not sure I'd be interested in helping. If he's a newly single dad with cancer, I'd say he's got enough on his plate than having to contend with a breach of our circle of honesty."

"He's dead," Kelshaw said. "So there's no breaching any bullshit circle."

"And there's no benefit in me or us talking about him," the leader replied. He glanced around the circle as if to reassure himself that he had the concurrence of the other attendees before adding, "if it's any consolation, the name doesn't ring any bells. Anyone else remember a 'Nigel'?" he asked of the floor. More shrugs abounded at the prompt.

"Of course, he could have used a different name." Kelshaw sighed before fidgeting with his phone. He found a picture of Nigel and held it up briefly for everyone to see and then handed it to the man on his right, suggesting it get passed around. "He looked thinner, more gaunt at his death. Anyone know him or seen him?"

They passed the phone around the circle as each person glanced or inspected the picture. Several took the time to zoom the image for a closer look, but ultimately they all seemed comfortable that the pictured man, this 'Nigel', was unfamiliar. Kelshaw took the phone from the man on his left as it completed its lap around the attendees. He stood and finished his coffee.

"Can we ask as to your interest?" the group leader asked. "Just because we don't know him doesn't mean we can't help."

"Doesn't matter, now," Kelshaw said. "I thought that someone would know him. If no-one knows him, there's nothing more to ask."

"Fact is, detective, even if we knew him, we might be reluctant to speak up if it meant a ride in your car," another man said. "We were talking about that video of you doing the rounds earlier." A few suppressed sniggers sounded, and Kelshaw suddenly appreciated his notoriety. He made his way from the circle and ultimately the room after leaving his mug on the coffee bench.

Once back in the corridor, Kelshaw leant back against the group room door. He reviewed the pictures on the walls and contrasted them with his childhood recollection of church.

"Not your bag?" Warren asked as soon as Kelshaw looked in his vicinity. "It's not for everyone. Just because you're a single parent doesn't magically make you inclined to appreciate talking with others. Some get it earlier than others, but don't be scared to give it another try later."

"I'm not a single parent, anyway," Kelshaw said as he gravitated towards Warren. "I was looking for anyone who might know someone from the group here." He flashed his police ID as he made to pass.

"Which group?" Warren queried. "I get you wanted the single dad's group, but which?" As he recognised the detective's puzzlement, he continued, "not everyone's available at 4pm on a Wednesday, so we have more groups. A lot of them."

Kelshaw presented the same picture of Nigel on his phone he'd earlier shown the group. "Nigel Newcott. Familiar?"

"Nigel? Sure," Warren offered at the mere mention of his name. He reached for the detective's phone and inspected the image. "That's him. Nigel. Nice guy, but he's sick. I haven't seen him in a bit and he looks worse in that photo than when I saw him last."

"He died earlier today," commented Kelshaw as he returned his phone to his pocket. "So you know him from a group here, a different group?"

"Sorry to hear that. Nigel's a regular. Was a regular." Warren allowed himself to smile openly, "but now he's with the Lord."

"I'm going to need a list of the attendees of that group," Kelshaw said with disinterest. "I need it now."

"Can't do that, sorry," Warren replied. "The groups are anonymous."

"But I saw a list of names. That's what I'm after. That's all I want."

"They're next to useless. Most of the lists just include first names and not even phone numbers," Warren said. "They're probably to justify the church's spend on infrastructure and coffee. I'm pretty sure they're not even collated, just filed away with a date and time."

"I still want it," persisted Kelshaw. "I'm sure it will be of help."

"Can't you just take my word for it, and that Nigel will be on lists?" Warren pleaded. "They're anonymous for a reason. The photocopier's broken, anyway."

"Help me out, Warren. Perhaps I could just look at the list and take a picture," Kelshaw appealed while he flaunted his phone.

Warren looked left and right and then at a ceiling-mounted camera. "Not without a warrant, detective," he said bravely, before looking at the camera again.

Kelshaw too looked at the camera. "It's one list, Warren."

"No, detective, it's not," Warren replied. He pointed to the corridor wall and a gap in the concert-like images filled with two rows of typed sheets set at eye height. "There are lots of groups, six days a week, except Sundays, obviously. Everything from purely social groups to support groups of all kinds of afflictions and challenges."

"I just want the one that Nigel went to," Kelshaw persisted. "With or without a warrant."

"You'll need the warrant then," Warren said with an air of finality. "And a photocopier."

"I don't need every sitting of that group," Kelshaw offered. "Any recent meeting would be fine for now, before I come back with the warrant."

"But which one?" Warren softened a little.

"Nigel attended more than one group?" Kelshaw asked. "He wasn't even a single parent."

Warren shrugged. "Groups don't vet attendees. Provided they aren't disruptive, anyone can attend. Numbers help and sometimes random participation encourages others to get involved."

"Which was Nigel? Simple attendee or participant?" Kelshaw asked. "Would you know?"

"Not really. I know they didn't ask me to remove him from any of the groups."

"But they were all a single parent group, right? Can you at least tell me that much?"

"No," Warren said.

"Come on. Even that much might help me, and others."

"I am helping. I'm answering your question, detective," Warren implored earnestly. "They weren't just single parent groups."

"Groups, plural?" Kelshaw asked. "So, not just the one group?"

"No," Warren replied. "And not just single parent groups."

45

Malter and Melanie sat on either side of Willson, watching him resting uneasily on his bed. They each knew they were waiting, but not what for. On the main, the wait was silent, with each person killing time in their own quiet way. Melanie had periodically offered small talk or some platitude to lighten the mood, but each time Malter would bring the conversation back to his disdain for Willson. She resigned herself to sit in an acrid silence.

Malter's phone rang. He answered but initially said nothing until he saw Melanie's interest and recognised detective Kelshaw as the caller. "We're here. You're on speaker."

"Nigel has been a regular here at many of the groups. No idea how many or in what capacity, but we need to assume his reach is, let's say, significant." Kelshaw waited for some kind of audible response, but no one said anything. "Did you hear me?"

Melanie broke the silence. "We're here."

"I've got Piper looking into what she can of the groups and if anyone recalled any particular actions by Nigel," Kelshaw continued. "I don't like her chances, especially if we need something now. It could take weeks or months to identify everyone from the CCTV at the church, and that will only give us a list of names, nothing more. I didn't see any cameras in the actual meeting rooms, so we're going to need to vet every attendee. And that's the simple part. I've got no idea how we dance around the topic of asking them if Nigel asked them to kill anyone."

"Are you still only interested in me, detective?" Malter enquired.

"So glad you asked, Malter. It might have been nice for you to have mentioned that you'd been to those groups in what looks to have been a professional capacity," Kelshaw said. "Before you deny it, your photo was on the wall and there was at least one of your books on offer, presumably to be borrowed."

"It didn't seem relevant, detective," Malter said, digging deep to present himself without guilt. Especially in retrospect, he recognised how the detective would interpret his oversight. "Your suspicion aside, I speak widely and I gift my books to a lot of groups and organisations."

"Sure," Kelshaw said arrogantly. "You're in luck that Nigel is so well known. His involvement seems increasingly likely."

"As well as me, or instead of me?" Malter insisted. "It might not be important to you, but it is to me."

Melanie took a breath to speak, but ended up saying nothing. A tear strayed down her cheek. She half sobbed another breath and said, "James, can we please move on…". Malter reached for her hand across Willson in bed, but she withdrew both hands to her lap.

"Ok, we can table that question for later," Malter began. "Can we revisit the possibility of ongoing security for Melanie, detective?"

"For how long? That costs money and requires approval, neither of which will be easy in the circumstances, to say nothing of the delay. I'm not even entirely satisfied that she's at risk, so why don't you use book-selling bullshit to think about a more realistic option?"

"You still questioning the need to do anything, detective?" Malter asked, the question raising the eyebrows of Willson and making Melanie look up from her hands. "Using my book selling bullshit, your words, but I prefer to call it a brain. If you think we need to do anything, you must accept that Melanie here is at risk. What if she was your Peaches?"

"Go on," Kelshaw commented noncommittally. "I'm listening."

"OK, so let's think this through," Malter began condescendingly. "Would locking me up or arresting me solve your problem and, or, reduce Melanie's current level of risk to zero?"

"Not completely," Kelshaw conceded. "A good start, sure, but then what?"

"Would me smothering Willson right here, right now, or taking him out into the street to be set upon by whatever Nigel had planned be enough to give Melanie some assurance as to her wellbeing?" Willson looked at Malter incredulously and opened his mouth, but said nothing as Malter raised his hand placatively.

"I don't think that's going to be enough either, Malter," Kelshaw said. "Willson could die now for as much as I care, but I don't think that will allow Melanie to sleep at night."

"We agree on something, detective," Malter sneered at Willson. "So we need to get and keep Melanie safe. Can you at least get that ball rolling?"

"I can make some calls, sure, but I don't like your chances. There are only a few avenues for that kind of protection, and Melanie here won't meet any of the criteria. She's no one important, she's just one person, there's no explicitly identifiable threat and there's no finite timeline for when the threat will subside. I can't realistically expect ongoing round-the-clock protection for a single woman who may or may not be awaiting some imminent assault at the hands of whatever percentage of the population has attended support groups at that church."

"Or groups at other venues, or that he met while in jail," Malter added.

"Malter, that just makes it even more unlikely. Whether it's two or ninety per cent of the population with a death wish for Willson or Melanie, you won't get funding for ongoing protection for one person. And for that point, we don't know whether to anticipate an attack by individuals or groups, hammer, gun, bomb or vehicle, each of which demands a different counter approach."

"So she needs to be in a bunker," Willson suggested, finally breaking his silence.

"Sure, Willson," Kelshaw placated. "A cost-free bunker able to withstand anything, probably barring a nuke, that she can stay in until she dies or until everyone that Nigel may have influenced, or their children, dies."

"Satisfied, Willson?" Malter asked as he looked at the fading old man on the bed. "It looks like Melanie's going to inherit your guilt."

"But she could stay here," Willson offered.

"And then what? This is unlikely to end when you die, Willson," Malter said.

"I've already instructed my solicitor to transfer the title to this place to her after I die, so she could stay here indefinitely."

"Not ideal, sure," Willson said. He looked at Melanie, adding, "You'll be safe here. This place is a product of my fears over the years. I knew he'd come eventually and for a long time that encouraged an element of self-preservation."

"You've just been hiding out, Willson, nothing more," Malter chided.

"Yes, and hardening this place," Willson answered with some accomplishment. "My home became my fortress. It's reinforced external walls, reinforced doors, the glass is bulletproof, intrusion alarms, video… you'll be safe here, trust me. Even the landscaping is to thwart a ram-raid type attack. No one's getting in unless I allow it." He looked to gauge Melanie's interest, adding, "When I got sick, I was thinking it was a waste. I'd spent time, effort and a lot of money looking to protect myself from someone, but it didn't stop my cancer. Now it seems fortuitous."

"Karma's like that," Malter said.

"Well, yes, James. Perhaps my paranoia might end up being of value to you. For your benefit, Melanie."

"But Nigel visited you last night," Kelshaw noted. "If the place is so impregnable, how did he get in?"

"I let him in. It's not like he challenged my security, but I figured there was nothing to gain by denying myself the chance to say 'sorry' and nothing to lose in having the confrontation, particularly as I'm nearly dead, anyway. I knew he'd come. I thought he'd allow me to say my piece."

"How did you fund it all?" Kelshaw asked. "If you haven't worked in years and keeping a house like this costs money, to say nothing of your security and ongoing home care."

Willson looked at his watch. "It doesn't matter now, but I got an out of court settlement."

"For what?" Melanie asked.

"The travesty that was my case," Willson said with a sigh. "That I was so marginalised despite my acquittal. Some ambulance chaser law firm thought it was worth a try and it got legs without making the news. More than a little embarrassing since I've come to terms with my guilt, but at the time, I was comfortable with the myth of my innocence. They didn't make the dollar figures public, suffice to say I've been comfortable, financially at least. I'd give it all back for what I've lost."

"And there's Nigel who died alone and penniless…" Malter added.

"I'm not proud of it," Willson lamented. "For a good while, I rationalised it by saying that whatever pain I caused Nigel didn't give him the right to get back at me. So says the law."

"Can I go out on a limb and say that staying here is not an option," Kelshaw said.

"I'd agree," Malter agreed. "Even after Willson dies."

46

Melanie struggled with her composure but felt the weight of Malter and Willson's efforts to keep her grounded. Several times Willson attempted to distract her with talk of his home security, but each attempt descended into white noise. He even tried to encourage her to track the detective's return on several screens and facilitate his entry, but she wasn't interested. First losing her Anthony, now this.

"Malter, I've been thinking about Nigel. What was his state of mind when last you spoke to him?" Kelshaw asked the moment he entered Willson's bedroom. "Could we be overreacting?"

"Do you want to answer that, Willson?" Malter redirected. He watched as the guy floundered, so he continued. "This guy raped and killed Nigel's girlfriend. You're wondering if Nigel's up to do anything about it. I think that's more than a little possible."

"I get that," Kelshaw accepted. "But now that he's dead, is it at all possible that this will end when Willson eventually passes? Will Melanie be off the hook then?"

"When I was attacked, when Anthony was killed, mention was made of a 'bloodline'," Melanie offered. "I don't know whether or not those words were from Nigel, but that has me at least concerned for my child."

"I know," Kelshaw said. "I was naively hopeful the Doc was going to share some contradictory wisdom, maybe something from his bestsellers..."

"I just don't see it ending with Willson dying or the subsequent dancing in the street," Malter said.

"If I'd known Melanie was going to be implicated, or if any of my children were going to be harmed, I would have done what I could to prevent it. Let him kill me if necessary."

"I wish he'd killed you, too," Malter sighed. "All your pity play and apparent remorse and you didn't let him."

"Funnily enough, I actually don't think he came to kill me," Willson recalled. "I let him in and said my piece. Then he asked me to ring Anthony, which I did, and then to call my other children, but before I could, he collapsed. Had I been able to do anything about it myself, like get out of my bed, I possibly could have done something other than call the ambulance. They saw his hospice admission bracelet and the rest you know. It wasn't how I thought our last meeting would go. The only real upside is that his collapse gave me a chance to ring my other children, not that it helped. David hung up on me, and Jenny and Chris didn't answer."

"Jenny and Chris were probably already dead," Kelshaw said. "Time of death was about the same time as that of Anthony."

"Does it even matter now?" Melanie asked. "It doesn't even seem to make any difference. Whether he did or didn't, it doesn't improve my situation."

"Humour me, Melanie," Malter interrupted. He looked inquisitively at Willson. "Why don't you think he came to kill you? His time was running out, and he knew it. Surely he would have accepted that as being his last chance, his only chance. So why wouldn't he have done it?"

"Unless he saved that job for someone else," Kelshaw said. "That might at least explain it."

"But the other people, the groups, your patients, James?" Melanie asked. "Not long ago, you were convinced he could have enlisted many people to help him. Now you don't think so?"

"I know, Melanie, but it just seems too unlikely that he'd have passed up the opportunity to kill Willson himself if he was able."

"OK, so he was covering all bases," Melanie offered.

"Possibly," Malter thought aloud. "He wanted to make Willson suffer, sure, but he expected to witness that for each of Willson's children during his visit. So if Willson here thinks Nigel wasn't prepared to do the deed last night, that suggests he wasn't interested in doing it himself."

"So we're back to being at risk of anyone that Nigel met," Melanie said.

"No, we're not," Kelshaw disagreed. "I think I see where the doctor is going with this. Nigel wasn't going to allow just anyone to finish the job. That was a gift for someone."

"Nigel talked about a gift," Malter said. "Beyond the ring, he talked about giving me a gift." He sat in silent recollection. "He said '*the gift we're giving you*'."

"We?" Melanie asked. "You're sure he said 'we'?"

"Definitely," Malter declared confidently.

"We still need to consider that he could have been referring to the people from the groups," Kelshaw said. "Just putting it out there."

"Noted, but I don't think so," Malter said. "I've known Nigel for a long time and he's never once referred to others sharing his anger, not even me. Until today. It should have roused my attention, but I was a little distracted."

"Does *that* help me?" Melanie asked. "I mean, does it change my situation?"

"It might," Malter began. "Your position was, is, hopeless if Nigel set something in motion that can't be stopped, particularly after he died. Now at least we've got a chance. Far from having to contend with you looking over your shoulder forever, now we just might need to identify who that person is."

"And of course, if they're alive, we can try to defuse their zeal or the otherwise curtail their actions," Kelshaw contributed. "Not only is it 'something', but we can protect you from a single person, Melanie."

Melanie wiped her eyes with a tissue from her cuff. "So, does that mean you can find him? Or her?"

"We'll try, Melanie," Kelshaw said to take control. "Malter? Thoughts?"

"Why would you say, 'her', Melanie?" Malter asked. "I'd suggest detective Kelshaw here would think of a male, and not that it's my domain, but I would have thought a man, not a woman."

"Gender equality?" Melanie mocked with a smirk. "I don't know. I'm just thinking if I was angry enough, would I be capable even without a 'Y' chromosome? Could I? Possibly."

"But we're not talking about you," Malter said. "Most people, no matter how angry, would struggle with taking that next step into revenge. No matter how loud those voices are in your head, it's a big step to do something about it."

"Nigel managed," Kelshaw noted.

"Actually, he didn't," Malter said, thinking. "Nigel's smart, but it's not like he employed Jedi mind tricks to overpower ordinary people into zealots."

"People will do amazing things for a friend. I see it all the time, Malter," Kelshaw explained. "They will lie, destroy evidence, bury a body. You'd be surprised."

"But few would kill, on their own, for a friend. Participation is one thing, but to do something completely for someone else is different. For a friend, for love, whatever, there would need to be something shared," Malter explained. "It's almost plausible if Nigel found people who hated Willson enough to get revenge to the same extent."

"So Nigel scoured the population to find someone who hated my ex-wife, my children, Amy and whoever else enough to kill them?" Willson asked, incredulous. He shook his head, slowly at first, then more animatedly. "I have done terrible things, but not them. I kept tabs on their comings and goings and they've done nothing to warrant that."

"You're right. That's why I said it was *almost* plausible," Malter countered. "People do the wrong thing every day, sometimes things as bad as you, but I can't see each of your family having done that. I'd call it statistically impossible. Whatever proportion of the population is capable of killing, I think it's unlikely that there's one who attends a support group, willing to target each of Willson's loved ones."

"Don't discount the psychos," Kelshaw added.

"Yes, but they would be a lot less susceptible to the suggestion from Nigel, and if sociopaths wanted to do it, they would have done it, not wait for him to ask or suggest it," Malter replied.

"So we're back to what exactly?" Kelshaw asked as he sat down in his chair once more. "We're still looking for a single person?"

"Come back to what we know, detective, not what we think," Malter replied. "And please don't dwell on that thought that I'm implicated."

Kelshaw sighed before producing his notebook and pen, more out of habit than need. He flicked through several of the most recent pages. "Ok, we've got dead relatives and friends of Willson, all done by people at this point assumed to be known by Nigel."

"And why would they?" Malter asked. "I've been involved with many terminal patients and amazingly few spend their remaining time fixated on revenge, let alone revenge for the benefit of someone else. Even if Nigel had courted those friendships for years, as if he knew who was going to die before they age to the point of uselessness, why would ordinary people do that, even if they have nothing to lose?"

"He might have some control over them, like a cult," Melanie offered.

"OK, Melanie. Plausible, sure, but Nigel just doesn't fit the profile. I've never seen him with any adoring throngs of... anyone. That I saw him in the hospice this morning with visitors at all was more than a surprise."

"He might still surprise you, Malter," Kelshaw offered. "You don't know everything about your patients."

"I never profess to know everything about them, just enough to guide them," Malter explained. "So, what else have you got?"

"They might owe him. Settling a debt to prevent a family member from paying it is a pretty common motivator into crime," Kelshaw reasoned.

"It would need to be quite a debt, and more correctly, some people would need to have racked up that debt concurrently, to be payable one particular day." Malter put his head back and rolled his shoulders into a shrug. "Fact is, I don't know. He might have had his fun, proved he could have the last laugh, and that's all."

"So it could be over, but we have to assume he had more friends?" Melanie asked. "Does that summarise matters?"

"Yes and no," Malter said cryptically. "They might not be his friends."

"Associates from the groups, Malter, whatever," Kelshaw argued with a measure of frustration. "Help her out."

"I'm just saying that it's unlikely he found enough people to keep this going and have you look over your shoulder forever, Melanie. I'd say when the detective does his homework as to the background of those who attacked Willson's children, none of them will have a vendetta against Willson's children. They might not have even met."

"So now you're suggesting Nigel found people willing to attack and kill people they'd never met?" Kelshaw asked. "I thought you were saying those kinds of people are rare."

"Like hen's teeth. I think you need to focus not on who Willson's children are, or were, and their associations, but rather, look at the backgrounds of the attackers. I'm guessing they'll all have issues, long-standing issues. Get someone damaged enough and while they might not be willing or capable of harming just anyone, suggestibility will most definitely be possible if they thought they were getting back for themselves." Malter took a breath to check for some understanding from the others. "A woman who's been raped given the opportunity to get back at her assailant would, most definitely, and without too much encouragement."

"I still don't buy it," Kelshaw disagreed. "You're saying that all of Willson's children are, what, rapists, and Nigel tracked down their victims to suggest now was the time?". He shook his head in disbelief. "All of Willson's children's backgrounds came back clear, no red flags of any description. Piper's checking their attackers, but even if they were victims of someone else doesn't make them inclined to attack just anyone else."

"I'm not saying that being a victim predisposes anyone to harm just anyone, even if they were dying," Malter began. "But, assuming they are dying, if the opportunity avails, I think many would." He stopped talking to no one and turned to face the detective. "They did the attacks at night, right? What if Nigel tipped off victims of someone else's crimes and gave them Willson's children? All he'd need to do was give them an address and tell them what they'd want to hear. Without sharing too much about Cliff's history, I think that's a very plausible explanation for what he did to Anthony and probably what happened to the others."

Kelshaw nodded. "In the dark, it would be easy to see an innocent person as the one you'd love to get even with."

"And I'm guessing the support groups he visited gave him a ready pool of people wanting to get even with someone," Melanie added.

"And Nigel's certainly smart enough to have groomed them," Malter remarked.

47

Melanie took it upon herself to get some space. She wasn't so much nervous as anxious, but the difference was beguiling and the perpetual sniping between the men was irritating. She left the room under the guise of a need for a fresh cuppa, but everyone appreciated it was for space.

She peeked into each room, increasingly aware of the cameras and their motion detecting lights. Each room was empty but for floor coverings and curtains, which failed to obscure security grills on each window. Tom wasn't lying about both his isolation and his fortress.

Room by room was the same except for a smaller room next to the stairs, which in any other home it might have served as a storage room. Unlike the others, it was locked, but Melanie heard the lock release almost on cue, again with the flashing of lights on an overseeing camera. "Habit has that one locked," Willson announced from his room by intercom. "Be my guest."

The room was largely the same as the others, except for a bookshelf with a single book lying flat on the shelf. Melanie inspected it and, on the realisation it was a photo album, took it back to Willson's room. "Look at what I found," she said excitedly.

"You've found a stick of hay in a stack of needles, Melanie," Willson explained. "It's perhaps my only possession."

"So why not keep it by your side?" Malter asked. "Now's the time to embrace such keepsakes."

"Careful, James. Some could interpret that comment as concern for me," Willson said light-heartedly. "It was, until recently, right here," he said as he struggled a tap on his bedside table as if to illustrate its usual position. "After Nigel's visit last night, it seemed too provocative to keep it beside me. I asked the paramedics to place it in that room before they left. Out of the way."

Melanie flitted from the first to the second page, expectant for the distraction, but it was blank. The next page was the same, and the next. Only then did she discover that the entire album had just one photograph on the very centre page. "I think someone's taken all the photos, Tom," she said. "There's only one left."

Willson shook his head. "It only ever had one photograph."

"Of what?" Malter asked. He felt drawn to reach for the album, but Melanie placed it on the bed. She moved marginally to one side, as if to allow Malter to see at the same time.

"Who are all the people, Tom?" Melanie asked as she looked. She scanned three rows of adolescent faces in school uniform with a stern-looking matriarch of a teacher seated in the middle of the front row. In front of the teacher's knees was a class nameplate doubling as a modesty board labelling the assembled students as being 'Class 12M, 1977'. "What school is this? There's a tall boy in the back row obscuring the school name."

"James?" Willson invited. "Look familiar?"

Malter edged himself closer to inspect the photo. He glossed over the faces to concentrate on the school insignia and immediately recognised the significance. "My school, but in 1977, I was still in primary school."

"But your sister wasn't," Willson said. "Can you pick her?"

Malter accepted the challenge after first doing some mental arithmetic. In 1977, he was eight years old, his sister would have been 18. He closed his eyes to picture her, his last memory of her, then stripped back several years to morph that memory into a perfectly nubile young woman, still at school with the world at her feet and her head in the clouds. His older sister. The one who was always the big loving sister, except for when he, as the younger sibling, wanted to rush her from the bathroom. The one who was a constant in his world until she wasn't. She was standing in the second row to the right of and behind the teacher, who could only be Mrs Moginie, who he remembered as his own teacher some years later. "Please don't tell me it's a coincidence that Jenny's in this picture, Willson."

"No, it's not, James," he replied. "You'll see Nigel there, too. They were close, even then."

"So, why do you have it?" Malter asked while trying to identify Nigel; there he was, beside Jenny, possibly surreptitiously holding hands.

"When I first saw your sister, she was about the same age as in that photo. Same uniform, same sexuality dripping from her."

"Time doesn't make me comfortable in hearing that kind of talk from anyone, you especially. She's my sister," Malter exclaimed angrily. He drifted off into silence before adding, "*Was* my sister."

"I wasn't at school," Willson explained. "It was the seventies and jobs were plentiful, and I drifted from job to job as I pleased. I mixed with people of my age, but testosterone being what it is, was, I noticed a beautiful girl."

"She must have been, what, five years younger than you, Willson," Malter commented.

"Closer to ten. I first saw her walking a younger boy home, holding his hand. Only now I think of it does it occur to me it was probably you, James," Willson said. "She wasn't like others I'd pass on the street. After that first sighting, she was all I dreamt of."

"I don't think I need or want to hear this, Willson," Malter cautioned.

"It was innocent, I can assure you. I only lusted after her from afar. You might not know or recall, but we used to live close by, and so I used to see her around regularly, walking to and from school, with friends, with Nigel, with you."

"Innocent is not an appropriate word for you to use, Willson, ever. You can't honestly tell me it was a crime of opportunity after sharing that," Malter said. "Some would describe your actions as premeditation."

"Like I would have had a chance with her anyway," Willson continued, unperturbed. "Sure, I fantasised about being with her, probably much like any man would have, but she was always going to be with Nigel. There was just something about the way they looked together. That look of an inevitable pairing."

Willson drifted off, remembering. "Nowadays they'd call it depression, but back then I didn't know what it was. I had friends and family, jobs, enough money in my pocket and life was by any measure good, but I felt incomplete just the same," he explained. "To be clear, that much is nothing to do with Jenny. It's just how I was."

Malter looked again at the photograph. "1977. That photo was years before you killed her."

"At first I just withdrew," Willson recalled after taking a small sip of water from his bedside. "I stayed in my room and stared at the ceiling until moving the TV from the family room into my room so I could withdraw completely. My parents were less than impressed by my selfishness. Now that I'm older, I see their point, but at the time it enraged me and I grew violent with their confrontations, their persistent encouraging me to get help. Eventually, I moved out on my terms, but it was much to my parents' relief to be sure."

Willson took a deep breath and paused before continuing. "I stayed with friends and as I wore out my friendship with one, I'd move on to another, gradually churning through good friends and onto acquaintances until I ended up on the couches of friends of friends. By this stage I was drinking heavily, numbing myself, and being in that state, I was susceptible to being influenced by others, good and bad, but at the time, I was only subject to bad influences. I took to heroin easily. It was the late seventies and everything was plentiful and cheap. I could work cash jobs for just enough to keep going as the epitome of a working addict. Moving out of home meant that I never saw Jenny, either."

"But you did," Malter clarified. "Please don't let this airing of your conscience degrade into you denying any involvement in what happened to her."

"I honestly didn't see her for a long time, and gradually I didn't think to dwell on her either," Willson said, shaking his head. "Between the drugs and my new acquaintances, life went on, until my using hit some threshold and almost overnight I went from being a functional addict to just an addict. I needed more than I could buy with my earnings from the few jobs I could perform, and inevitably the more I used, the less capable I was of doing any proper job. And then I met some people willing to pay, in drugs, for jobs I could perform between scores, in that finite window between getting high and being fixated on where my next high was coming from."

"Robberies," Kelshaw reasoned. "Usual story."

"Robberies, sure, but anything requiring not too much thought or conscience. I can't account for everything I did. I honestly can't remember. Sometimes I still get dreams, nightmares, that I know are just gently clouded, drug-addled recollections. They're not pretty."

"But you remember Jenny, don't you?" Malter asked.

"Most definitely," Willson replied. "I can't recall if I was on my way to or from a job; I was a bit blurry. I know we were well and truly loaded up, that's for sure, and we decided it was time for a party and then there she was by the road, walking home. I remember being beside myself at the opportunity, it being Jenny and all, but at that moment I couldn't grasp whether it was an opportunity for good or for bad. We offered her a lift. The rest you know."

"So it's Jenny's fault!" Malter exclaimed, infuriated.

"No, James," Willson confessed defensively. "The fault is mine, all mine, and I own everything that happened thereafter, but that acceptance doesn't absolve me or give you back your sister. I just felt you needed to understand."

"All I understand is that you deserve to die," Malter vented.

"James, perhaps you need a little fresh air," Melanie suggested. "Tom's trying for forgiveness."

"Forgiveness?" Malter mocked, incensed. "I'd pity Hitler before him, but you're right, I do need some fresh air. I'm going to visit your doctor, Willson."

"Uniforms have already checked on him. He's fine," Kelshaw reported. "Probably best left to the police, anyway, Malter."

"He might share things with me that might help, like how much pain you're liable to be in while you die," Malter said. "Whatever. I need a break from the sorry rantings of a guilty man."

48

Malter arrived at doctor Abe's rooms following rudimentary directions from Willson. It was a set of specialist oncology consulting suites with Abe as a named partner, an adjacent general practice, and a spare room used by various alternative therapists. It was a cleansing stroll and had relaxed him, but it had taken time. He looked at his watch, hopeful, but on scanning the posted surgery hours, he accepted that the doctor was unlikely to be present. He made to enter the offices anyway, thinking that there might be someone willing to share his whereabouts after hours under the guise of something professional, but a tall, gangly man exiting with keys in hand met him at the door.

"Abe? Doctor Abe… Bounte?" Malter asked presumptively, struggling with the pronunciation.

The man stopped and looked at Malter. He smiled. "I know how it's written, but it's pronounced, '*Bounty*'. Hi James," he said, offering his hand. "I'm assuming you're here about Willson."

"I am," Malter replied, a little aloof to being recognised. "How'd you know who I was?"

"I figured you'd come eventually, probably if Willson ever mentioned me. He's certainly mentioned you," Abe confirmed, locking the door behind him. He pointed to the small off-street carpark and gestured for Malter to follow as he walked. "You don't remember me, do you, James?"

"No, I don't think we've ever met," Malter said. "I meet so many people through my books that, sadly, I can't remember everyone."

Abe smiled. "I read your books, sure, but I thought you might remember me," he said, adding, "… or from Jenny. She used to call me 'Lurch'."

"You knew my sister?"

"And loved her," Abe said heavily. "Of course, she only had eyes for Nigel ever since primary school, but that's not to say that others couldn't love her."

"And here you are years later, the doctor of the man who took her from us," Malter jibed. "Tell me, is that a challenge?"

"Sure," Abe offered. "Not so much confronting my demons, but confronting the demon."

"And you're ok with it?" Malter asked. "You're a better man than me."

"I'm heading back to see him now. If you'd waited long enough, we could have met there."

"Willson never suggested you were coming," Malter said. "I actually came to check on you."

"I'm fine. Why would you even ask?"

"Many people involved with Willson have..." Malter began, struggling to compose words to explain. "They...".

"I'm fine," Abe said. "Nigel and I still talk. I know what's going on."

"He died earlier today," Malter declared.

Abe shrugged. "Decades of anger unvented. Anyone who says inner turmoil doesn't affect your physical health need only have taken one look at him."

"Sad but true. I see it a lot," Malter said.

"I'm fine, though," Abe repeated. "What else do you need?"

"I guess I could ask about Willson. What's he's got?"

"Doesn't matter," Abe said. "He'll be dead soon."

The comment silenced Malter for a moment. "As much as I'll be happy to see him gone, that sounds more than a little unprofessional, Abe," he said. "*Doctor* Abe."

"Ethics aside, I'm still human," Abe replied. "What he did to your sister. Whatever happens to him, he deserves."

"So how long's he got?" Malter asked. "I wanted to look at his chart, but you've got it."

"His chart won't change his future," Abe said.

"But his symptoms?" Malter challenged. "Just talking with him suggests he's gone downhill quickly. I just figured he might warrant a second opinion. Just saying."

"He doesn't need a second opinion, and anything prolonging his life is a waste," Abe declared curtly. "You, of all people, should understand that much."

"But his treatment?" Malter asked. "Did you even explore a surgical option or just launch straight into chemo and radiotherapy?"

"Not your concern, James. I get this might be at odds with your bookselling agenda, but especially because you're not even a medical doctor, let it go."

"But…" Malter pressed.

"James, get back to Willson and Melanie. Spend some time watching him die and think of your sister."

"Melanie?" Malter asked. "I didn't think you'd met."

Abe ignored the question. He rummaged in his pocket for keys and clicked to unlock an adjacent Mercedes. "I'll even give you a ride."

49

Malter settled into the passenger seat beside Abe. The car was immaculate but smelled strongly of fuel. "Excuse the smell," Abe said as soon as they were both seated. He wound down all the windows as soon as the engine started. "There's a fuel can in the back and it might have toppled over," he explained.

Appreciative of the drive, Malter tried not to focus on the fumes and instead looked to some small talk until he saw Abe, crooked to allow his lanky frame to assume something resembling a driving position. "Is this your car?" he asked, incredulous. "You can't possibly be comfortable."

Abe smiled, shaking his head. "No, it's my wife's. Someone rear-ended me, nothing too nasty, but it's in getting fixed just the same, and Cindy's lent me hers."

"When was this?"

"A few days ago," Abe replied. "I wasn't even in the car. Whatever, it's not a big deal. It's just a car and I see enough sick people every day to put the inconvenience of a bingle into perspective. You'd understand that."

"You didn't think to get a replacement car?"

"I did, but I only need to drive as far as her work, then she can take over," Abe explained. "It's not far."

Malter watched Abe struggle until they both burst into tears of laughter. The lightened mood remained long after the first intersection, and neither felt obligated to interfere with small talk thereafter. Gradually, the streets became familiar as they approached Malter's office. He felt inclined to pop in, but he recognised there was little point in doing so. Only when they drove to the rear carpark of the hospice did Malter think to speak.

"Cindy the nurse. She's your wife?" Malter asked with realisation. "I speak to her nearly every day and I never even knew she was married."

"Nurses can have a life outside of work, too," Abe chuckled. "Married nearly 35 years."

"Cindy's one of the better ones," Malter said, smiling at his own ignorance. "I'm happy for you. A great professional match, you and her."

Abe struggled a cramped wave as soon as he saw his wife at the entry doors and wound down the window to acknowledge her more overtly as she approached. He grabbed his door handle but didn't open the door, watching her walk excitedly to the car instead. "She wasn't my first choice, but we've been happy together."

"A bit harsh," Malter insisted, adding, "She's great."

"Indeed, she is," Abe said. "But she's not your sister."

Malter looked to Abe, thinking. "You went to school together," he said, remembering the school photograph with the tall boy in the back row. "Does Cindy know?"

"Sure," Abe said. "She was Jenny's best friend. Her passing brought us together. The three of us grieved together."

"Three?" Malter queried.

"Cindy and I," Abe said. "And Nigel."

Malter was about to say something until Cindy tapped on the windscreen. Abe opened the door and unfolded himself out of the vehicle to a warm hug and a kiss. He closed the driver's side door behind Cindy. Malter made to release his seatbelt to move to the back seat before she grabbed his arm to stop him. "It's ok. There's more room in the back."

She waited for her husband to do his best to get comfortable. It took a while. Eventually, the movement settled. "Are you done yet, Abe?" She started the car when she saw a nod in the rearview mirror.

"I'm guessing you know where we're going and who he is. Are you planning to sit and wait in the car, Cindy?" Malter asked.

"No," she replied, looking at her watch. "I want to watch him die."

"You make it sound like he's got a timetable to die to," Malter contended. "I've made a career of dying people and as bad as he looks, he's not there just yet. You know this, Cindy. "

"I do," she said. "But he's a special case."

"As much as you, and I, may want him dead, and no matter how special a case he is, his death is still a function of his body giving out," Malter said. "Based on what I saw of him today, I'd say he's still a way off, even if I'm not privy to the detail of his chart."

"Would you swear to that in an enquiry?" Abe asked from the back seat.

50

Malter pondered the question while Cindy drove and Abe wriggled uncomfortably in the back seat. No one spoke, but Malter felt an exuberance, almost excitement in the air.

"Is Willson even dying?" Malter asked. "And no, it's not a philosophical question."

"He is," Abe replied. "Massive organ degradation all over. He is most definitely dying."

"Was that from before or after he started therapy?" Malter asked provocatively.

Abe smiled at the question. "Chemo and radio are a tightrope at the best of times, but you know this, James," he offered. "The drugs are effectively poison, and the radiation is just as likely to cause cancer as kill it. Let's just say I tried everything and my records will show I actively treated intestinal masses which turned out to only be the secondaries."

"An investigation could reveal there were never any masses," Malter provoked. "It could almost be something in his diet could have precipitated your treatment and malpractice did the rest."

"Perhaps," Abe said with a shrug. "Of course, I could just as easily defend such egregious allegations as proof of my treatment against the initially identified growths. I did my best until Willson stopped the treatment. Who's to say that had my treatment continued, I wouldn't have completely cured him?"

"But instead, I'm guessing an autopsy *could* reveal that he glows in the dark and his body is so poisoned that it would pollute the soil and water table if they ever buried him. Radiation and chemo poisoning will leave a trace."

"He won't be in any position to argue either way," Abe went on. "He's going to be cremated. And if it makes you feel any better, he already had cancer before he came to me, so it's not like his conscience tracked me down. He was going to die. I just might have expedited his demise a little. Perhaps."

"Does he even know who you are, and that you knew Jenny?" Malter asked.

"He even had that picture of Jenny at school at his bedside," Abe began. "If he was less fixated on her and spared a glance at anyone else in the photo, he would have recognised me in the back row. If he does know, he certainly hasn't let on."

"I'm in it, too," Cindy offered. "No-one ever noticed me when she was in the room."

Abe reached forward to touch Cindy lovingly on the shoulder as she drove. "Moving on doesn't mean turning your back on what's happened," he said. "Jenny's passing ultimately brought us together."

"So what happens now?" Malter asked, while Abe resumed his sprawled position with a contented look on his face. "What are you wanting to achieve in seeing him?"

"His death is imminent," Abe declared.

"And you're ok with that?" Malter asked. "Both of you?"

"And you're not?" Cindy asked with some surprise. "It's for Jenny."

Malter allowed himself to be distracted with the journey. No-one spoke again.

51

"Are you ready?" Abe asked as soon as the car was stationary outside Willson's house, already reaching for the handle with his hand while preparing to push the door open with his foot. Malter thought to answer before appreciating the question was not for him.

His wife nodded into the rear view mirror with a wry smile. She exited the car and met with Abe, reaching for his hand. Looking back at Malter still seated, she asked, "You coming?". Malter accepted the prompt and joined them at the curb.

They all stood looking at the front door, Abe and Cindy hand in hand, with Malter in the background. Abe checked his watch and Cindy checked her phone. "No messages," she said.

Abe acknowledged the comment with a nod, saying, "it's time." They headed for the front door, initially oblivious to whether Malter was following. They stopped when they reached the doorstep, and only then did Cindy look over her shoulder to check on Malter. "Last chance, James. It's time to say goodbye."

They assembled at the front door. "What a surprise, Abe," Willson said through the door intercom, to which Abe looked up and smiled at the camera. "And this could only be the Cindy you've told me so much about." Abe edged to one side and coaxed her to look at the camera. She smiled and made to find the microphone to speak, but Willson announced, "please come upstairs, Cindy, rather than struggle with that thing," adding, "and I see you found James as well. Lovely."

Abe held the door open chivalrously for Cindy and Malter to enter. "I'll meet you upstairs," he said. "James will show you where to go, Cindy." He watched as Malter led the way.

* * *

"You look worse than you did an hour ago," Malter said on seeing Willson. He hovered in the doorway, looking at the fading old man sinking into his bed until he felt Cindy by his side, trying to peek a look.

"I hope it makes you happy when I say 'I feel it', James," Willson conceded. "I understand you're a hospice nurse, Cindy," he said, looking past Malter. "It's lovely to meet you, finally."

Cindy stepped forward marginally at the prompt but still kept her distance, opting to wave a subtle greeting directed more at Melanie than Willson.

Willson waited a while in the hope of Cindy saying something, but she stayed silent. "Do you and James work together?" he asked benignly.

"We do often," she said, finding a voice. "Sometimes patients prefer to die away from people they love…"

"And sometimes they have it thrust upon them, don't they?" Malter added. He watched the deflation in Willson with some accomplishment. "But to Cindy's point, if they must die away from their loved ones, nurses like her provide the best of care."

"I think I'm settled here and now, all the same," Willson said.

Abe joined the group at Willson's bedside, saying, "I didn't think you'd mind some extra company, Tom."

A smile appeared from behind Willson's gaunt eyes. "Thank you. All those years of being alone and to finally have some companionship is special, particularly now."

"You know, James, I have read all of your books," Willson said on looking at Malter. "I even considered lining up to get one signed, but I didn't know how you'd react."

"I don't know how I would have reacted either," Malter remarked.

"But anyway, I'm wondering if this is the release that you write about and that I've been waiting for before I die. I've said my piece, my peace. I'm ready."

"Does it strike you as being more than a little karmic that I'm here? We're here, Willson?" Malter asked.

"Now's not the time, James," Abe said. "The man is dying. Let him have his peace while it lasts."

"He doesn't deserve peace or release," Malter challenged.

Abe made to say something more until Willson struggled with a gesture with his hand to stop him. "It's ok, Abe. I understand his pain and to challenge it is to undermine my regret and guilt. I'm oddly appreciative that he's here, just as I'm glad both you and Cindy are too."

"You're under my care, Tom. Why wouldn't I be here?" Abe challenged.

"But it's more than that, isn't it?" Willson asked. "You and the lovely Cindy. The tall boy in the rear and I'm guessing Cindy is the girl on the far left, second row." He looked at the photo album, now back on his bedside. "Am I right?"

"How long have you known?" Abe asked with some disbelief.

"Perhaps I always knew, but on one of my habitual re-scans of that photograph, my eyes strayed. I wondered what each of those young men and women grew into, and ultimately what impact the death of Jenny would have had. You were easy to place, Abe. I figured a lanky adolescent could only grow into a lanky adult. It occurred to me you were possibly the same tall young man walking Jenny home now and then, sometimes with Nigel, sometimes not. I remembered you offering her special attention occasionally too when Nigel wasn't there, presumably to console her after their periodic tempestuous teenage blips."

"I was just a friend," Abe said shyly. "To them both."

"There's no judgement, Abe, not from me anyway. I saw how they used to be together and who am I to say whether their relationship might have withstood the test of time," Willson dared. "Regardless, it seemed like the universe was telling me something that you would end up treating me."

"You found me, remember?" Abe recounted defensively. "It's not like I tracked you down. You appeared in my waiting room with your referral and a half-hearted interest in your health."

"And as to my care, whether you did all you could or, in fact, made it worse, it doesn't matter now," Willson suggested. "I get how much it must have challenged you, particularly in your profession. Regardless, here I am in my final hours and I have more company than I've enjoyed since… I don't know when."

"She was my best friend, Tom," Cindy bleated angrily, finding a voice. "Jenny and I were inseparable, and you took her from me."

"I will say to you what I said to James, that I am sorry," Willson conceded. "If I must, as seems likely, I will plead for your forgiveness, yours and Abe's and James', until I die."

"It doesn't bring her back though, does it, Tom?" Abe badgered.

"No, it does not. Nothing I can say will change that, and nothing you can say will absolve me of my guilt. My actions have cost me everything and everyone I have loved, as well as my own life."

An uneasy silence descended on the room. Malter, Abe and Cindy seethed at the dilemma of wanting to say more, but at the futility of doing so. They could repeat themselves over and over, but it wouldn't change any outcome. Jenny was still gone, outlived by the man who killed her, the man who was now before them declining rapidly. Melanie, too, felt the tension, but she appreciated that nothing she could say or do was going to ease any stress.

"So what happens now?" Willson asked.

"Anyone got a hammer?" Malter asked flippantly.

"Not funny," Melanie noted. "Everyone's going to relax and allow Tom to just be. Aren't we?" She looked around, expecting to see supportive consolatory faces.

"Melanie, I fear if you weren't here, I would already have been set upon," Willson suggested with a grin. "James I've known might have harboured long-suppressed animosity towards me, and looking at him tells me that's true. Abe and Cindy here, I didn't think were up to it. Admittedly, I wasn't expecting any of you to be with me now, but such is life."

Willson did as good a job at trying to gauge the intent of the others as his dwindling lucidity would allow. Long seconds passed.

52

The air at Willson's bedside was heavy with an angry mix of resentment and anticipation. Despite Willson struggling to maintain his alertness, Malter, Abe and Cindy held their ground and kept their distance, more interested in what the detective was thinking and liable to do next.

"Just as you mightn't have expected my company, Willson, this is *not* where I thought I was going to be when I woke up this morning," Malter said.

"I am interested in what's going through your head now though, James," Willson asked. "Despite your books, here you are, and I'm not capable of any resistance. What are you going to do?"

Malter said nothing.

"What about you, Abe," Willson turned his attention from the smouldering Malter. "You probably had a chance with Jenny, ready to step in the next time Nigel made a mess of things and you got the balls to prove your mettle, but I put that dream to rest, didn't I?"

"And you, Cindy. How does it feel to have lived your life in her shadow? It must be exquisite to spend each day married to a man who must openly describe you as the runner-up."

"I know what you're doing, Willson," Malter offered, hoping his words would soothe a seething Abe and distraught Cindy. "You think you're going to make us hate you enough to put you out of your misery? We've been there for forty years."

"Yes, but were you prepared to do anything about it for any of that time, James?" Willson asked. "You've spent many of those years advocating for '*closure*' and '*moving on*'," he said with struggled air quotes, "but behind those bestsellers is the same little boy still living in denial."

"Perhaps," Malter breathed, digging deep to keep his composure. "Perhaps I wish Nigel had finished what he started, and not now after so long. Maybe I wish he'd done to you what you did to Jenny. The hammer. The rape."

"And the rest," Kelshaw blurted, losing his abstraction.

Willson coughed a little before his eyes snapped shut. Abe stepped forward to check his breathing and pulse. "He's liable to drift in and out," he said. "He'll probably come around soon."

"What else was he referring to?" Malter asked, not willing to be interrupted by Willson's lapse into unconsciousness. "Abe?"

"It wasn't all made public, detective," Abe said. "I only know about some of it from talking with Nigel."

"What else?" Malter pressed, suddenly aware that he was not privy to all details.

"You were a child and didn't need to know," Cindy added. "Your parents asked that you be protected."

"It won't help, James," Abe said.

"He told me," Melanie piped in. "I nearly threw up."

"I deserve to know," Malter pushed.

"No, James," Abe disagreed. "You deserve to get on with your life and not let it be marred by him," he said, pointing viciously at the sleeping Willson. "Don't give him the satisfaction. Just because he's finding it too confronting for us to be here doesn't mean we should give him what he wants."

"Actually," Kelshaw spoke, thinking, "what you wanted has almost already been done."

"I'm sorry?" Malter queried.

"Whether or not it was intentional, Nigel has almost reciprocated what Willson did, just not to Willson himself. His sons were killed by a hammer, gun and run over, respectively, which is what happened to your sister. His daughter technically drowned in a car, but we're still waiting for the forensics to confirm whether there was any rape. They recovered her from a submerged vehicle partially clothed but without underwear, so the safe money is on assuming she was also subject to at least some form of sexual assault."

Malter's eyes glazed over as he processed this new information. "Not that I really want to know, but which killed her."

"The investigation pieced together what happened as best they could. They'd do a better job now than they could back in the day,"

Kelshaw began. He looked at Malter and the others before deciding to continue. "She had both offensive and defensive wounds, and also ligature marks from being tied up, which provided a decent timeline of events. Best guess is that she was shared around in that state for at least the first 24 hours before they struck her unconscious with the hammer, probably to facilitate simpler rape."

"I didn't think it was for that long," Malter choked in disbelief.

"Up there with a record, sure. They raped her, fed her, doped her up and then started over again. They untied her once she was unconscious, no idea why. Far be it for me to get into the mind of a smack-head. Some time later she came to and escaped. It was dark, so they panicked and one of them, probably not Willson, set off on foot after her with a shotgun while the others got in the car. At least six shots were fired, but the barrel was sawn off so short that they were effectively un-aimed shots. Still, they got lucky with one. That shot in the back as she ran pierced her lung and knocked her to the ground. Thereafter, she was easy pickings to be run down."

"Please tell me that's everything," Malter queried, his mouth agape.

"You wanted to know," Kelshaw commented. "Of course, what's been heard can't be unheard."

"He's not finished, James," Abe cautioned apologetically. "You now know this much, so you might as well know the rest. Her body was also burned. Isn't that right, detective?"

"Yes and no," Kelshaw noted. "Partially, sure. Not public knowledge, but the post mortem showed some scorching in the lungs."

"So she wasn't quite dead when she was burnt?" Malter asked, incredulous.

"Afraid so," Kelshaw apologised. "I'm sorry to be the one to tell you."

Malter composed himself momentarily before making a lunged effort to smother Willson with a pillow as he slept. Abe and Cindy struggled to restrain him while the detective looked on.

Kelshaw smiled. "I was going to turn my head," he smirked as everyone settled each other away from Willson's bed. "I still am, mind you, but now I guess I'm interested in why you two would want to stop Malter."

Abe and Cindy looked at each other, then back at the detective. "Maybe we don't want James to do anything in the heat of the moment he might later regret," Abe said. "James still needs to live with himself."

"The heat of the moment was years ago," Kelshaw explained. "Malter's actions are forty years in the making."

"I wish you'd let me kill him," Malter argued, still trying to de-escalate himself. "Any fallout would be worth it, for my sister and for Nigel."

"So, doctor Abe, why'd you stop him?" Kelshaw persisted.

"They did it for me," Malter said, curious to understand the detective's interest. "I don't know whether I'm appreciative, but I know they did it for the right reasons."

"Abe?" Kelshaw pressed. "Or should I ask Cindy?"

"What's the problem?" Malter asked. "I feel like they're getting the third degree for what was probably the right thing to do."

"Malter, I just heard Willson imply that his treatment might have made him worse, to which Abe said nothing. I would have thought that the implication of malpractice would have prompted some kind of reply, but no. The point is, Willson made an accusation and Abe did nothing. He could have smothered Willson himself for the slight, but he didn't, and he could have left you to it, but he didn't," Kelshaw explained. "I want to know why?"

Abe maintained his silence. He kept hold of his wife's hand and leant down to give her a gentle kiss on the cheek while he kept his eyes on the detective. He glanced at his phone, his actions prompting Cindy to do the same with hers.

"Got somewhere to be?" Kelshaw asked Abe. "You're checking the time a lot."

"He's probably mindful of the time for Willson's obs. No matter what he thinks of the guy, it's hard to completely suppress that clinical urge to care," Malter offered. "Right, Abe?"

"Sure," Abe replied.

Willson stirred violently, waking with a deep breath. He opened his eyes and took stock of those around him. He paused a long blink and when he reopened his eyes, he sighed with acceptance. "Am I in hell?" he asked.

"Not yet," Malter seethed.

Willson sighed. "How long have I got?" he asked. "I've had years of waiting and frankly, I don't think I can do much more, especially with you all here."

"If your condition changes noticeably by the day, you have days, by the hour, you've got hours," Cindy offered. "That's what I tell families."

Willson looked to his doctor for his concurrence. "She sees a lot more families than me," Abe offered. "What she says is sound, but James could offer more insight with someone like you."

"Like me?" Willson asked.

"With regrets and a burdened soul," Malter declared. "My program tells me you're more likely to last longer. You need peace to pass, and while being without it won't sustain you indefinitely, it could prolong your life for at least a while."

"Could?" Willson asked with some concern.

"Peace doesn't always come from just *saying* you're sorry," Malter explained. "I know it might have made you feel better, but the universe thinks there's more to be done."

"It didn't give me the satisfaction I expected," Willson conceded. "I meant what I said, but…"

"Rape and murder perhaps warrant more than a 'sorry', Willson," Malter dismissed. "To what Cindy said, I've seen a marked change in you over the last few hours. I'd say you're looking at hours, tops." Cindy looked up from her nervous flitting with the lock on the medicine locker and nodded in agreement.

"So I need to wait for some magical peace to descend on me, but until then I need to wait?" Willson asked mockingly. "I expect this is going to be like trying to urinate with others watching."

"You'll die when your body is ready, Tom," Malter said. "I wouldn't be hanging too much hope on the prospect of that being dependent on anything."

"So what do we do until then?" Melanie asked. "I can stay. I'd like to."

"Thank you, Melanie," Willson replied appreciatively. "It means a lot to me." He reached for her hand, reassured that she didn't baulk at the contact.

"I'll stay too," Malter echoed. "Different reasons."

Willson nodded acceptingly. He looked to Abe and Cindy, "Are you staying to watch me die, too?"

"We'll stay. I'm almost inclined to ring for Mickey's pizza, too. It's almost a tradition," Abe said, lightening the mood marginally, which almost brought a smile to Willson's hollow-eyed face.

"What about Melanie?" Kelshaw asked. "Have we forgotten your concern for her wellbeing?"

Malter recognised the puzzled look on Abe's face and explained. "In case you weren't aware, Nigel may well have coerced some people, including my patients, to inflict harm on Willson's family. Whoever or whatever, Willson's family is now all dead, but as Melanie's pregnant, there's some concern that he mightn't be finished."

"She'll be fine," Cindy insisted with an air of authority. "Nigel knew about her, and that her child couldn't be related to Willson."

"So you knew what he was doing?" Malter asked. "And you let it happen?"

Cindy said "Nigel and I, Abe and I, have maintained a friendship for many years and I don't need to share everything we've spoken about over that time. When he and I last spoke about Melanie, he emphasised she was never in danger." She looked at Melanie and commented, unapologetically, "You'll be fine."

"I don't feel like it, Cindy," Melanie noted.

"If Nigel was here, he'd possibly even apologise. Not for what happened to your Anthony, but for your stress," Cindy continued. "Let's just say Cliff might have overstepped beyond what Nigel would have encouraged."

"When was this?" Kelshaw asked.

"A few hours ago," Cindy replied.

"And you'd swear to that?" Kelshaw pressed.

"For James' benefit, sure," Cindy said. "Melanie will be fine whether she stays or goes."

"Can I suggest those staying need to lighten up," Melanie commanded. "Whatever the past, it's done."

"In all seriousness, Melanie, I don't think it's your place to suggest the rest of us let bygones be bygones," Malter said.

"My loss is just as real as yours, James," Melanie remarked. "And my pain is, what, forty years more recent." She stroked Willson's frail hand and addressed him. "I lost the love of my life less than 24 hours ago and you're telling me I have no place?"

The comment silenced Malter. "My point is we don't need to be preached to about it, Melanie. Can I be civil? Sure."

"For the one who's made a fortune selling books advocating for peace and forgiveness and closure, I didn't think you'd find it a challenge to be asked to consider the now, not the past," Melanie challenged. She eased her tone marginally, adding, "I'm just saying that Tom here is dying, what's done is done and perhaps, just perhaps, he's entitled to die in peace."

"She's got a point, Malter," endorsed detective Kelshaw. "I don't necessarily like the guy either, but look at him, he's dying. I'm no expert, but surely he hasn't got long."

"Really, detective?" Malter primed. "What have you got against the guy?"

"Maybe not as raw as yours or Melanie's, but my mentor on the force lost his job after the craziness of Willson's trial cum circus," Kelshaw confided. When he saw Malter about to comment, he added, "it mightn't sound like much, but when he lost his career, he lost his way. He took his own life several months later."

"So if the detective can be big about this from history, and I can accept now, doesn't that make you seem positively hypocritical, James?" Melanie proclaimed. She looked at Abe and Cindy, and then back at Malter. "Let him know some peace."

Malter felt the weight of her argument. He sighed and agreed, "Fine," eventually adding, "I'll still keep my indifference."

"So what happens now?" asked detective Kelshaw. "How long's he going to be in and out for?"

"Clinically," Abe said, "he's probably got a few hours." He looked at his watch and reached for Cindy's hand. "We're staying."

"There you go again, Doctor Abe," Kelshaw remarked. "Are you sure we're not keeping you?"

"All part of the service," Abe replied with a smile.

"Perhaps we could take it in turns to sit with Tom," Melanie suggested. "You don't need to say anything or hold his hand. Just be with him." She glanced at the others before coming to rest her look on Malter. "If I'd written some books on the matter, I might have the insight to understand how much it might help."

"Best intentions or not, Melanie, it's a bit much to expect us to just sit in silence," Malter mocked. "It would only be worse if you were to suggest sharing a story and a laugh."

Melanie conceded the point as Willson opened his eyes and looked around before fading out again. "Tom told me about his diaries, boxes of them in his shed. Perhaps we could browse them."

Malter looked at Abe and Cindy and shrugged. "They might make for a good read."

"And it will get us out of the house," Cindy said in support. "It might make all the difference to everyone's mood, too." She smiled at looks of concurrence from all.

"So who's getting them?" Kelshaw asked. "I'm not offering, mind you, and I can't leave any of you here, with the exception of Melanie, for fear you might expedite Willson's demise."

"This is easy, everyone," Melanie insisted with a huff. "Tom said five boxes. That's one each. We go together, we bring back one box each together." She led the way from the room, expecting the others to follow.

53

An odd dynamic accompanied the group as they descended the stairs. No one was really walking at the front, or the back, or setting the pace or lagging, such that they moved like a school of fish. No one said anything, as if they each accepted a purpose and role and resigned themselves to completing that task.

Suddenly aware of the home's security, Melanie expected a struggle with the back door as she approached, but she found the door unlocked. "So much for security," she mocked as she held it open for her entourage.

"He disabled it," Kelshaw explained. "It's been offline all the time I've been here as much as I can tell, but the cameras are on." Prompted at their mention, he made a quick check of the visible cameras, adding, "were on. They look to be off now."

"That was me," Abe offered. "It seemed little point keeping them on while we were all here."

"How noble of you," Kelshaw lampooned. "Nothing to do with the possibility of recording some dirty secret for posterity?"

Abe walked unflinchingly out the door, still holding Cindy's hand. "Your arrogance astounds me," Kelshaw continued to otherwise deaf ears.

They walked single file on concrete pavers across an overgrown lawn to the small cement sheet shed. It was unlocked, but only big enough to allow one person to enter, so Malter peeked inside. "Five boxes," he reported. "One each," he said as he passed the non-descript cardboard archive boxes to waiting hands.

They reversed their journey back to the house with Kelshaw in the lead. He struggled to open the door while still holding his box before placing it on the ground to afford the use of both hands. The door still wouldn't open, much to his frustration, as he re-cradled his cargo.

"It's locked," Kelshaw said. "Who was last out?"

"I was," Melanie accepted, "but I kept it open, just a little."

"Well, it's not open now," Kelshaw said. He pulled and pushed the door a little as if to emphasise the point, but no actual movement ensued despite some motion detecting cameras being activated. "And the security is now on."

"It can't be," Malter said. "In his state, I think it's amazingly unlikely he would have come to enough to think to re-enable it."

"So, how do we get back in?" Melanie asked. "We're this close to giving him some comfort. It doesn't seem fair that we can't be with him."

Malter scoffed. "You're right about not being fair," he mocked.

"OK, ideas, people?" Kelshaw asked authoritatively. "How do we get back in?"

"His phone is still on," Malter noted, "if anyone has his number, we could try that and maybe rouse him." He watched Abe and Cindy, seemingly disinterested in what he was saying, return to the centre of the yard and place their respective boxes on the ground. They stood hand in hand with their boxes at their feet, looking at the upstairs windows. "Surely you can't see Willson in his bed from there?" he queried.

"And you can forget throwing rocks at the window to attract his attention if he's even awake," Kelshaw offered. "If it's bulletproof, as he claimed, then rocks won't even make a sound."

Melanie too took an interest in Abe and Cindy standing motionless, gazing up at the window. She gravitated to join the couple, asking, "What can you see?"

54

Regardless of whether the windows in Willson's home were bulletproof, the glass was still transparent. Malter, Kelshaw, Melanie, Abe and Cindy all stood in the centre of the yard, gazing up at the upper storey, watchful for anything that might be visible. Now was not the time to appraise the aesthetics of the security screens.

"He can't be moving around," Malter suggested as he took stock of each of the windows, settling on the same window that Cindy and Abe seemed to be focussed on. "And that's not even Willson's bedroom."

"He's right," Kelshaw agreed. "His room looks out at the street, not the backyard." His comments didn't distract Abe and Cindy, still fixated.

"I had a look around," Melanie said. "All the rooms are empty. Identical and empty."

"Ladies and gentlemen, what are you watching for?" Kelshaw asked, somewhere between anxious and frustrated. "I would have thought he's not capable of getting around."

"He's not," Malter said, looking at the others. His lack of understanding was shared by Melanie and Kelshaw, evidenced in their incredulous glances, but not Abe and Cindy. "Is it possible there's someone else in there?". The comment attracted a momentary look from Cindy, but she returned her attention to the window.

A uniformed police officer appeared from the side gate, cigarette in hand and more than a little surprised to see people until he recognised the detective. "Nate," he said in greeting. "I've been doing laps of the house for hours. I wasn't expecting to see anyone."

"I don't suppose the front door is open or unlocked," Kelshaw asked. "We can't get in."

"Couldn't say for sure, but I wouldn't think so," the uniform said. "The security was just activated after the last visitor arrived. I heard the lock engage not long after he entered."

"What other visitor?" Malter asked.

"Phil, the other member out front signed him in," the uniform replied. "He's still there if you want me to get him." He baulked at walking off as if to suggest his preparedness to return with his colleague.

Kelshaw sighed. "Constable, what are you supposed to be doing here?"

"The brief was a little light on, so just presence, I'm guessing," the uniform said defensively.

"You don't think your brief might have been to prevent strangers accessing the home under that brief?" Kelshaw teased.

The uniform shrugged. "He looked harmless enough. He looked like my uncle not long before he died. The guy's obviously sick. I watched him struggle between the taxi and the door, so much so that I offered him a piggyback up the stairs. He said it wasn't necessary and that he'd manage. Hardly a threat."

"Another of your patients, Malter?" Kelshaw asked, holding up his hand to keep the constable from disappearing.

"Can you describe him?" Malter asked the constable.

"He said he was just visiting to say goodbye. He had a present, wrapped…" the uniform continued.

"So we're assuming the guy's not just a legitimate well-wisher, a friend," Melanie said. "Is that fair? He really might just be a friend."

"Based on what Willson shared today and what we know, I'd say there's less than zero chance of that," Kelshaw stated.

"What did he look like, constable?" Malter coaxed.

"Male. Slight build. Fair hair. I'd be guessing at his age, somewhere between 50 and 80. I know my uncle looked ancient…"

"Who are you thinking, Malter?" Kelshaw asked, truncating the uniform's word picture.

"It doesn't match any of my patients," Malter said. "And to be honest, I don't know whether I'm thrilled about that. If I knew who it was, it might help."

"Could he be looking for me?" Melanie asked.

"If he is," Malter said flippantly, "he's now locked inside and you're safely outside."

"I don't like this," Kelshaw noted. "Constable, you may very well have let the fox into the henhouse."

"I'll get Phil to confirm the guy's name," the uniform reported, briskly heading off towards the side gate.

"So how do we get in to check?" Malter asked. He looked at the others, expecting ideas.

"You don't," Abe said. "You aren't getting into that home fast enough to do anything."

"And you're basing that comment on what, your extensive home security experience?" Kelshaw mocked. "You've seen the plans for his entire system and you're satisfied that there are no simple, fast means of access?" he continued condescendingly.

"No, I know there's nothing you can do," Abe said, looking lovingly at his wife. "Because I know who's in the house."

55

"So you saw someone?" Kelshaw asked Abe, still fixated on the upstairs windows, but when no reply came, he redirected his attention. "Cindy, help us out. Who did you see?"

"There!" exclaimed Malter. "I saw movement." He pointed to the window. "The curtain. I saw it move."

"Who was it, Malter?" Kelshaw pressed while looking for himself.

"I didn't see a face, only the curtain," Malter replied.

"It could have been the wind," Melanie suggested.

"If the place has been secured, there won't be any wind," Kelshaw disagreed, more than a little agitated. He grabbed his phone to make a call but instead looked at Malter. "And you have no idea who it could be?"

"Based on what the uniform said, no," Malter confessed. "Of course, it could have described Nigel as general as the description was, but not now that he's dead. Not unless his ghost is making haste to haunt Willson."

"I thought the same thing," Kelshaw remarked. "And you're sure he's dead?"

"As much as I know," Malter conceded. "Cindy here was the one who told me."

Kelshaw looked sternly at Cindy and the way she was squeezing Abe's hand until she felt the weight of the detective's stare. She took her eyes off the window to look first to Malter, then to Kelshaw. "It was the last thing I could do for him."

"So he's still alive?" Malter asked in disbelief.

"For now," Cindy reported. "But not for much longer."

A different uniform appeared at the side gate and headed directly to confront detective Kelshaw. "Nate, the visitor gave his name as 'Nigel Newcott'. He had ID and yes, I checked it."

"Thanks, Constable. We've just worked that out," Kelshaw accepted.

"So what's the problem?" the uniform asked. "Spence said you had issues with me letting him in."

"Time and place, constable, now might not be the time to have this discussion. Right now, we need to focus on how we might gain entry to that house," Kelshaw remarked. "For future reference, if you're on a basic security detail, you don't let people in without approval."

"The owner of the house, the guy inside in bed, invited him in," the uniform said, pointing at Malter, "so what's the problem with this Nigel guy?"

"The owner of the home did not explicitly let Nigel in though, did he, and don't tell me he did," Kelshaw argued with disinterest while looking up at the window. "The guy inside is comatose."

"Yeah, I get that, but I assumed you were all together," the uniform continued. "Nigel even grabbed something from the car. Not your car, Nate, the car they all arrived in. The tall guy and the woman." He pointed at Malter, Cindy and Abe. "I figured it was a present. It was wrapped, sure, but not much of a gift. It smelled of petrol. I did ask, but he said a fuel can toppled and spilt over his present and he didn't have time to get a new one. He wasn't too perturbed, so neither was I."

Malter looked to Abe, still fixated on the window, and recalled his explanation of the petrol fumes in the car. He looked back to the uniform and asked, "this present, was it about the size of a fuel can?", approximating the size with his hands.

The uniform thought for a moment. "Sure", he shrugged.

"This mention of petrol and I swear I can smell it myself," Melanie said. "And smoke."

"I smell it too, Melanie," Malter added as a realisation came over him. He made to say something as he replayed his discussions with Nigel over and over in his head. '*Expect more from me*'. It seemed so obvious in his recollection. It seemed so relevant now. He looked to Abe and Cindy, whose fixation on the upper storey windows had now turned to excitement.

"Detective, I think Nigel is going to set fire to the place," Malter announced. "I should have picked it earlier. I'll try to call him."

"Burn on earth before you burn in hell…" Abe muttered.

Kelshaw was already on the phone. He acknowledged Malter with a simple nod, as if to say he understood the immediacy required while watching for something at any of the windows.

"So, what are we waiting for?" Melanie asked. "I can't just stand here waiting to see smoke."

"Melanie, I'm sure the detective is doing his best," Malter said, half-heartedly placative. He looked to Kelshaw, still talking on the phone while fruitlessly re-trying the rear door and several reachable windows. Kelshaw ended his call and kicked loose an edging rock from the garden before raising it above his head to thrust it into the closest window. The rock did little more than to make a deep vibration, as if the pane was a glass dungeon door.

Kelshaw was deflated and disappointed at the lack of achievement despite his exertion. He dusted off his hands and looked at Malter for more ideas. Before the reverberation from the impact of the rock on the glass had even stopped, the security screens lowered to cover all the windows.

56

"Piper's escalating things at her end," Kelshaw said to Malter. "Of course, if you've got ideas or suggestions, now's the time." He edged backwards away from the house to afford a better view of thickening wisps of smoke emerging from the heights of the roofline. "We need access."

"How far off is the fire brigade?" Melanie asked. "I can't see any fire, but I can smell it."

"Malter?" Kelshaw asked. "Do you think you can talk Nigel down or out?"

"Not before he's finished," Malter replied. "I'll try, but he's not answering his phone."

"Neither's Tom," Melanie said. She stopped pacing the yard to confront Abe and Cindy. "I hope you're happy with yourselves. Being burnt to death would be a terrible way to die." They said nothing in reply.

"Perhaps the only blessing is that Tom might be unconscious and oblivious to what's happening around him," Malter remarked. "I feel sorry for Nigel who won't be so fortunate."

Kelshaw answered his phone and engaged the speaker. "We need an ETA on the firies, Piper. We've got increasing amounts of smoke and no means of access."

"No ETA, yet. Something is going on at the fire station," Piper said. "All the vehicles are locked in."

"If they don't get here fast, there'll be little point in them getting here at all," Kelshaw declared. "Tell them to just drive over whatever's blocking them in."

"They would if they could, but they can't," Piper sighed. "It's not a vehicle, but people."

"Protesters?" Kelshaw asked. "Set one of *their* homes alight. That will disperse them."

"Whatever, Nate. They're doing their best to keep the station locked down," Piper said. "I'm assuming that takes the immediacy from those other checks you wanted."

"Probably," Kelshaw offered. "It seems like I'm set to watch this thing end now. The speed of the fire brigade's arrival will just dictate whether we're rescuing people or dusting the ash from their bodies."

"Whose bodies?" Piper asked. "Willson, and who else?"

"Nigel Newcott," Kelshaw declared. "He seems intent on having his last hurrah burning to death with Willson."

"So, do you want to save him or stop him?"

"Undecided, Piper," Kelshaw said. "Malter might offer a more definitive perspective. Willson's getting what's coming to him and that's been long overdue. Nigel is possibly doing what he's wanted to do for years."

Malter considered the question. "Detective, if Nigel can't be saved, where does that leave me?"

"Ah yes, Malter," Kelshaw began. "Self-interest is the best kind of interest in your patient, right?"

"I don't know whether it's self-interest, just whether you're going to continue to hound me."

"Nate," Piper interrupted. "That other thing you wanted to be checked. I'm just looking at the screen while you bait doctor Malter."

"Where are they?" Kelshaw asked. He looked at Malter's puzzled expression and offered an explanation. "I thought I'd triangulate your patient's mobile phones just to see where they are. I didn't trust your belief that your patients were all so incapable, in case they were coming to meet us here."

"At the fire station, all of them," Piper declared. "I'd say they're what's holding up your chance at extinguishing the fire." She ended the call, and Kelshaw returned his phone to his pocket.

Abe and Cindy looked at Malter with an air of accomplishment. "Nigel didn't want good intentions to interfere with justice," Abe explained. He pointed to a window now opaque with swirling clouds of smoke.

"Cindy," Malter asked, "is it possible Nigel brought any meds with him?"

"What kind of question is that, Malter?" Kelshaw asked. "For himself or Willson?"

"For himself," Malter said. "Perhaps if he gets enough on board, he might save himself the pain of burning to death."

"He's not interested," Cindy sobbed. "I even offered him extra, but he's too fixated on watching Willson burn to dull any of his senses with even a paracetamol."

Malter looked at each of the windows. "But Willson is already unconscious," he said. "The only one who's going to feel it is Nigel." He thought, noticing the snide look on Abe's face. "That drug locker next to his bed. I'm guessing it's a standard palliative stocking?"

"What's the problem?" Kelshaw asked. "What's the problem with it?"

"With adrenaline, if that's your question, sure," Abe replied with a smile. "Willson won't miss a thing. All of his senses are going to be heightened."

57

Nigel braced himself against the door frame to Willson's room and watched him sleep, primarily to assure himself that he was only asleep. The guy was largely still except for his breathing, but every few seconds he twitched in his semi lucid state enough to show he was still alive, perhaps only just, but that was enough. In much the same way, Nigel took stock of his own state. Climbing the stairs had been a stretch, particularly with his cargo, but his innate tenacity was enough to overcome his body's desire to just let go. He was so close now.

He looked over his shoulder towards the stairs to admire his handiwork, content that the house and its contents were now burning, not just the fuel he'd brought with him to start the blaze. By his estimation, his timing was perfect. Even if the fire brigade arrived now, their best efforts would not change the outcome. He shook the contents of the fuel can to confirm he had just enough left and leaned against the wall while he closed the door behind himself and prepared for the long four steps to the bed.

He faltered a little. A painful trip followed his ambitious first step and then a lunged fall to the drug locker beside Willson's bed frame. Neil Armstrong had achieved less.

Abe and Cindy had done well. The locker was unlocked, just as planned and just as well. While he knew the combination, he appreciated his limited focus would make that task even more difficult, doable but difficult, and he didn't want that kind of stress to undermine what was a glorious moment.

Nigel flipped the locker cover open noisily, straying a look at Willson, but the guy didn't stir, much to Nigel's disappointment. He rifled through the meds intended to keep the patient alive, comfortable or pain-free until he found what he was looking for; three labelled syringes, all drawn up and ready for immediate use. In a clinical setting, they probably had many uses that Abe and Cindy would have well understood when they explained it to him, but Nigel was only interested in one use, and how much to administer relatively safely to not make it a lethal dose. Longer term, too much would not be good for Willson's health, but that was the least of his concerns. For now, Willson needed to be alive, awake and alert. Very alert.

Continuing his rummaging, Nigel found the scalpel; apparently not a standard item in such a cabinet, but Abe had left one inside to be found. Now he was ready. He lifted the sheet and cotton blanket covering Willson's legs and stabbed the blade into the sole of his foot; soft and without calluses from his being bed bound for so long. That Willson didn't move prompted Nigel to re-thrust the scalpel a few more times until a small puddle of blood pooled under his heel. He now knew the size of the dose required. He removed the protective cap from each of the needles with his teeth and administered them in quick succession. Cindy would surely have faulted his technique and choice of injection site, but it did the job. The first roused Willson marginally. The second woke him fully with a gasp. The third opened his eyes wide like saucers. Nigel cast the needles to the ground and looked at Willson, his face flushed while he hyperventilated and his heart beat mercilessly with the adrenaline.

Nigel waited until he saw he had Wilson's complete attention. "You're now primed for 'fight or flight'," he said with a grin, "but I sincerely doubt you're capable of either."

Willson darted looks around the room and did his best to quickly appraise his situation. It didn't take him long. "Where are the others?"

"Locked outside," beamed Nigel. "It wasn't right that you'd have companionship in your final moments."

"Nigel, I'm sorry. Perhaps I never said it enough for you to believe me," Willson pleaded, desperate to impart sincerity with eye contact. "Without friends, family, work or social interaction, thanks to you, has allowed me a lot of time to consider. All these years alone with my thoughts and not a moment has gone by when I haven't dwelled on my regret, shame and remorse."

Nigel was fixated on the pulsing veins in Willson's neck. He grabbed the scalpel again and looked up when the noise of Willson's talking stopped. "You were saying?"

Willson had the look of a scared rabbit on seeing the blade. He closed his eyes momentarily before continuing unabated. "Only that you gave me time to understand my culpability. I don't know if that was your intention, but regardless, you succeeded."

"Not a day went past when I didn't think about what and who you took from me. I couldn't allow you to be distracted with any manner of busyness. I wasn't going to let you hide from what you'd done by burying yourself in work or family or anything else."

"So why didn't you just kill me?"

"And let you get off lighter than me?" Nigel laughed. "You gave me a life sentence. That's what I gave you."

"So, did you need to take my children? They'd done nothing to you, and I'd already abandoned them in an effort to protect them."

"Can you hear your own hypocrisy?" Nigel replied angrily. "You think I overstepped because they were innocent? Jenny was innocent, too. You think just because you were trying to do the right thing for them, that I should deny you some loss? I'm just sharing how it feels to lose someone, and you weren't even close to any of them. Consider yourself lucky I didn't do it sooner, so you'd have years of wallowing in your loss and not just guilt."

"I don't think there was any luck involved."

"True," Nigel began. "I couldn't run the risk of being in jail, again, and miss taking your last breath from you."

Willson waited for Nigel to say more, until his phone vibrated on his bedside. He let it ring, not allowing himself to break eye contact with Nigel. "Should I answer it?"

"What do you think?", Nigel teased. "What would you say?"

"Maybe to tell them you're here?" Willson offered. He waited for a response, but all he got was a blank grin.

Nigel looked at his watch. "They'll know by now."

"Abe and his wife?"

"They want to see you dead, too, just not as much as me. Melanie played a part as well, passively of course."

"She was in love with my son, nothing more, Nigel."

"Yes, but I didn't want you to take your own life when you heard of what happened to your kids. I knew her pregnancy would give you that glimmer of hope to keep you alive for this. For me."

"So what happens now?" Willson asked calmly. "I never imagined I'd leave this room alive, but now I'm guessing that's going to come sooner than the cancer will dictate."

"Good guess."

"So what is this? Do I get to choose whether I die slowly or quickly?"

"You get to share your guilt once and for all," Nigel replied.

"And then?"

"And then you'll get to understand Jenny's last moments first hand. She died alone, in pain and in fear, as will you." Nigel started fossicking in the drug locker and presented several ampoules. "You have more than enough meds here to drift off painlessly. I dare say it's going to be a nicer passing than you gave Jenny."

"Or?"

"Or nothing. That's your option."

"There's no upside for me," Willson conceded. "Not trying to be provocative, especially as it would undermine my remorse, but what happens if I keep my mouth shut?"

Nigel shrugged. "Sure. I guess you could. You're banking on some things, though, particularly that I won't do my best, or worst, to coerce you. While you ponder that, look at me and think if there's anything I wouldn't do to you."

"Noted," Willson replied curtly.

"And I'm prepared to channel all of my remaining strength into seeing you suffer," Nigel declared as he edged around the bed to sit on the armchair. "You're also taking a chance that I *need* to hear your confession, just like Abe tells me you've shared with Melanie and everyone else, for *your* closure. Fact is, I don't need it, I want it, sure, but I'm getting my closure, regardless. Cindy was the one who wanted to hear your final words preserved for posterity, and Abe thought it necessary to absolve Malter. You already took his sister. It doesn't seem right that he'd be implicated for what I'm going to do to you. Kelshaw's not going to let it go without some pretty compelling explanation and evidence to the contrary."

Nigel leaned back in his chair and struggled to raise his leg. He slid his foot under Willson's mattress before sliding his hands along his legs past his foot, reversing the movement a second later with a handgun. Willson looked mortified. "You mentioned it in one of your journals," Nigel explained. "I'm paraphrasing, but I believe you said it was there for your protection if ever your fortress was breached." Nigel made a performance of looking over his shoulder. "You given up on protection?"

"In context, I think I later went on to say that my protection was over-rated," Willson offered after a deep, calming breath. "I think I described it as an ill-gotten souvenir of the myth of my persecution. Once I came to terms with my guilt, really came to terms with it and not just with what's happened over the last 24 hours, I saw it as yet another reminder of what I'd done."

Nigel worked the action on the weapon and flicked off the safety. He casually aimed the gun at Willson's feet and then moved his aim along the length of Willson's body, stopping at his throat. "My suggestion would be to take the offer of drugs before I kill you."

Willson sighed. "I've been more sorry than you could imagine, Nigel. If it will make a difference, turn on the camera on your phone and I'll say anything you want."

"Nothing imparts sincerity like a tear, Willson. It was a nice touch," Nigel said mockingly as he balanced his phone securely against the drug locker and checked the image. Content that the video framed Willson reclining on the bed, he smiled into the camera.

Willson wiped the tear and sniffed. "I meant it. I'd been preparing what I said in one form or another for many years. Fact is, I would have said it under duress or not had I been given the chance."

"But you didn't. You've kept your mouth shut until now."

"What difference would it have made, to me or you?" Willson asked. "It wouldn't give you back your Jenny or the decades I lost of my family. And to say it now doesn't change the fact that you've seen to the death of anyone who meant anything to me."

"How's your conscience?"

"Not clear enough to make a difference to where I'm going." Willson sighed. "Whatever you give me, just bear in mind that being an ex addict my body might still have some memory of narcotics. I don't know if that means I'll need more or less."

Nigel was silent and still while he considered Willson's last. "Did you know if Jenny was still alive or conscious when you burnt her?"

"Didn't I just explain this for all to hear?" Willson asked, a little exasperated. "Please let it go and just let me die with my guilt."

"I'm interested, though," Nigel pressed. "Did you know she was alive when you burnt her?"

"I can't remember."

"Bullshit. You've had years to recap and relive that night and you've kept it to yourself. I'll bet you could account for every minute of the time you had with her." Nigel stared Willson down, waiting, until he realised he would need to press. "I *know* you remember every single moment. I'm interested in the details you haven't shared."

"This doesn't help you, Nigel," Willson said calmly, sensing Nigel's escalation.

"Tell me who first suggested picking her up; was it you or one of your degenerate friends?"

"I've long since taken ownership for everything that happened," replied Willson. "Now especially, it doesn't matter if it was me or them. I'm before you now."

"Tell me about the fear in her eyes when your offer of a lift turned nasty. Her screams the first time you raped her…"

"Please, Nigel. I can't do this any more than I have already."

"Her horror at being violated by more than one of you," Nigel continued. "Her pleading for her freedom while you and your buddies rested before giving her another go."

"Nigel, I'm sorry…"

"How many times did she beg you to stop, Willson? Did you roll her over to violate another orifice because you got sick of seeing the pain in her face, or did you just want to humiliate her just that little bit more?"

"Stop!" Willson yelled as his red, swollen eyes suddenly released a torrent. He cupped his face in his hands before wiping away a sheet of tears with his forearm. "I didn't know if she was still alive. Yes, I could have checked, but I didn't. In all my reminiscing, I've wondered what would have changed had I checked. Fact is, when she ran, the party was suddenly over and my high disappeared with a crash. I've spent days since then, doped up on nothing more than coffee, stressing over what might have been different if my conscience surfaced at that moment rather than years later."

"So why didn't you?" Nigel asked, enraged.

"I guess I fell into self-preservation mode," Willson sighed. "It quickly became a question of how to limit the fallout of what we'd done. She'd been with us for days. They didn't have DNA evidence back then, but rapes still got prosecuted with a fraction of the evidence that we'd left behind, on her, in her." He bit his lip while he pondered what else to say. "My high was gone, and I really saw what I'd done to that beautiful young woman, and I was repulsed. Bruised, bleeding, a gunshot wound and broken bones from being run down. She was a terrible sight."

"So you just burned her body and hoped for the best? You are scum, but I don't believe you."

Willson looked furtively towards the ceiling with closed eyes and cautious heavy breaths. "I gave her one last hit, my last hit. My accomplices, friends, whatever you'd call them, were freaking out and trying to tell me I needed it more than her." Willson pinched his eyes shut before opening them to face a seething Nigel.

"Tell me, why would you inject a dead, abused, body?" Nigel demanded. He watched as Willson pressed his head back into a pillow and stared at the ceiling. "Look at me, you bastard."

"She cried," Willson confessed with penitent eyes. "She moaned a little when I dumped her on the ground back at our makeshift campsite, and then she started to cry. I couldn't handle it, so I gave her my last H." He uttered an exasperated sigh. "Now that's said, can I *please* have something for my pain and then can do what you want with me," he pleaded.

Nigel was dumbstruck. His eyes opened and closed rhythmically with his panted breathing. He stood and reached into the drug locker, propping himself up with his other arm. He grabbed several vials and inspected their labels before casting a long look over a pained and deflated Willson. His face turned to a scowl as he threw each of the drugs at the wall, the smash spilling their limited contents into tiny splatters. Exhausted by the exertion, he emptied the entire locker contents onto the floor at his feet before stomping between deep breaths to crush everything to the sound of broken glass and plastic.

"You promised," Willson exclaimed. "You got my confession. I deserve to have some measure of relief."

"You and I have vastly different opinions of what you deserve," Nigel said as he stood. "In fact, I offered for you to enjoy Jenny's last moments first hand. Based on what you said you did to her, I hope your heart, if indeed you have one, is *really* racing about now."

"Nigel, please!" Willson began. His tears dry, he began sweating profusely. "I'm so, so sorry."

"Relax. You raped her for days, and frankly, I don't have the strength or the time to have you experience that facet of reciprocation. I also can't offer you the pleasure of being run over, either," Nigel offered placatively. He took his time to compose a struggled breathing pattern, before smiling noncommittally. "But that's where the differences between your passing and hers end." He quickly took aim at Willson's knee and fired two shots. The immediate wincing and shriek of pain on Willson's face told him he'd found his target at least once. He then fired another two shots into Willson's abdomen. Willson silenced his own cries and looked at Nigel with pained acceptance.

Without another word, Nigel grabbed the fuel can at his feet and splashed Willson liberally until the container was empty. He grabbed his phone and momentarily checked that the video was still recording and zoomed in on Willson's panic-stricken face. He presented a disposable lighter from his pocket and stood smiling. Gloating. Waiting.

"Please, Nigel," Willson pleaded while his hands clutched at his bullet wounds under the covers until blood seeped through the sheets. "I'm sorry," he said with a reduced zeal.

"And I miss my Jenny and everything my life would have been had you not taken her from me." Nigel dwelled on the look in Willson's eyes and then lit the nearest corner of the fuel soaked bedsheet. He stepped back to lean against the bedroom door and watched and filmed. And cried.

58

Malter felt a challenge of conscience and the stares of detective Kelshaw. "I had nothing to do with this, detective. Believe me."

Kelshaw struggled with his impotency to do anything about the fire and the prospect of witnessing what was coming. He produced a single set of cuffs from his belt and held them dangling, looking at each of Malter, Abe, and Cindy. "I'm trying to work out how many sets I need."

Abe took a deep breath after what seemed a last glance at the window. He kissed his wife before offering his wrists to the detective. "I'm happy to join you for a chat at the station, detective. Back seat or front is fine."

Kelshaw only shrugged, which incensed Malter. "You're baulking at implicating Abe? Please tell me the cuffs aren't still for me?"

"No," Abe said, grinning at the detective. "He just knows he's got nothing on me or Cindy, and I bet that brain is working overtime to reappraise the fact that he's got nothing tangible on you either, James. Far from being perpetrators or accomplices, we're witnesses to your complete lack of involvement."

"I'll find something," Kelshaw declared. "I don't need to decide right here and now and there will be better minds than mine, or yours, that will implicate at least one of you."

Malter retrieved his phone. "I'm ringing Nigel, again."

"To stop him or clear yourself, Malter?" Kelshaw asked. "Anything he says will be admissible."

"He won't answer," Cindy offered. "He has nothing more to say to anyone but Willson."

"But if he said it to me, or the detective ..." Malter said, drifting into a mutter. "Beyond getting the police off my back, I'd love to hear what he'd say to him."

"A vicarious confession," Kelshaw mocked. "There's a book in that for sure," he said cynically.

The screens on one of the upper windows raised slowly as Cindy suddenly reached for her phone, as if she was awaiting a cue. She looked at her screen, then gave a thumbs up to a pained but smiling face appearing at the window of a less smoke-filled room. The prompt encouraged everyone to acknowledge Nigel, responding with his own laboured thumbs up.

"It's done," Abe explained. "Willson's gone."

"Hand your phone over, Cindy," Kelshaw demanded. "I want to see what he sent you."

"You've been sent it too," she replied. "We all have." She ignored the others clambering to verify their own message receipt to press play on the video she'd been sent. "James, this message has also been sent to the media, and the video has been posted on all socials," she said.

Malter glanced at his phone but opted to look at Cindy's screen as she oriented it for all to see. They watched as Nigel's face offered a preamble of what would follow before Willson, fully alert, with eyes beaming, took his turn on camera. Willson offered his confession, his apology and his acceptance of what was pending. Cindy paused the video as soon as she saw Nigel briefly direct the camera to capture his face. There were still five minutes of video left. "The rest is likely to be a little dark and probably best muted." She returned her phone to her purse. "I'll watch it later."

"Is there a happy ending?" Kelshaw asked flippantly.

"That depends on your perspective," Abe said. "For Willson, not so much. That's a given."

Everyone looked at Nigel upstairs at the window, his face and splayed palms pressed against the glass, periodically glancing over his shoulder at what was likely to be flames licking at the door to the room.

"Is he coming out?" Melanie asked. "If Tom's dead, what's he got left to prove?"

"Nothing, but nothing outside that house, either," Cindy replied.

"Justice awaits," Kelshaw mumbled. He held up the cuffs to which Nigel only smiled, despite periodic coughing outbursts attributed to the smoke.

"You saw the video, detective," Abe said. "There's no jury anywhere that will do anything to Nigel, even if he miraculously left that house alive. As we speak, I'll bet everyone from prosecutors and government to the police commissioner is working to prevent that video making the news, not just to prevent prejudicing a jury, but more likely to snuff out renewed backwash that Willson kept his freedom to the last."

Kelshaw re-pocketed his cuffs and walked off, just as Nigel fell away from the window.

59

The security shutters on all remaining windows rose, first on the top storey, then on the ground floor, revealing a swirling tumult of smoke enclosed behind glass. Flames were now visible in the upstairs rooms. In a wave of adrenaline, Malter raced to the back door, hopeful that it too might be unlocked, but it remained secure and impregnable. The reality of his failed heroism hit him hard.

"Nigel's not coming out," Cindy announced. "That would never happen. The shutters are probably just pre-programmed to open in the event of fire, but the top floor is already toast."

A distant siren drew nearer and louder until the rumble of a heavy diesel engine accompanied it. There was a commotion beyond the side gate and Melanie was first to investigate, as if happy about the distraction. She stopped at the gate and retreated with a firefighter in tow.

"Many inside?" he asked. "I need to know how many people are in the building."

"Two," Malter replied. He looked to Abe and Cindy for their input before adding, "but I doubt they'll be alive."

The firefighter passed on the message to a radio handset attached to his collar and nodded in response to another muffled voice. "You can thank the idiots who blockaded our station for that," he said with frustration. "Still, we'll do our best." He looked over the rear of the building and again passed on a summary of the windows and the door to his headset. "Has anyone bothered to check if that door's locked?"

"Yes, we checked and yes, it's locked," Malter confirmed. "For what it's worth."

"What's that supposed to mean?" the firefighter challenged. "Are there people in there or not?"

"They won't be alive," Malter conceded.

The firefighter nodded. "The police will want a word," he said before walking away, talking into his headset. "Rescue unlikely. Let's contain it then switch to recovery."

"The police already know," Malter mumbled to no one in particular.

Cindy, with Abe in tow, offered Malter a conciliatory hug. She wiped a tear from her eye, saying, "I said I wouldn't, but we've known each other a long time. The hug is from me."

Malter floundered at the embrace. "To be honest, I can't describe what I'm feeling."

"Welcome to the real world, James. It's a crucible of empathy, anger, forgiveness, revenge and disbelief, all confronting your long denial," Abe said. "You'll be fine."

"But Nigel. His death," Malter struggled.

"He'd been on borrowed time for months," Abe said. "This kept him going, but now it's done."

"It's just," Malter began, but he couldn't continue.

"It's ok, James," Cindy said. "He's done what he always wanted."

"To burn to death?" Malter asked. "I doubt that."

"No, but he's got the closure he wanted. That he needed," Abe explained. "It's not what you expected or what you wanted for him, but then again, you thought you could just ignore your shared past."

Malter struggled to contain himself to the affront. He made to say something, but Cindy offered a reconciliatory perspective. "Your time together wasn't without merit. I know this because he told me." She looked at Malter, expecting to be challenged. "You made him think."

"Not enough, though," Malter replied. "As much as I hate the man, I would never have advocated for doing what he did."

"His death is an act of love for your sister," Cindy said. "More than anyone else, you understand that death is intimate. His death is even more so."

"But this doesn't bring Jenny back," Malter challenged.

"Look in your heart, James," Abe suggested. "Tell me you now don't have a measure of closure. That was Nigel's gift."

With the backdrop of an inferno, Malter breathed and smiled.

Epilogue

Malter stretched his arms above his head and rolled his shoulders before flexing and shaking his fingers to restore some blood flow to his writing hand. He wriggled in his seat and craned his neck to get a better look at the queue of people waiting to get their copy of his latest book signed. He felt his publicist's hand encouragingly on his back but didn't bother looking at her; she just wanted to make sure that the line kept moving.

"I'm no longer in remission," a mature woman said, leaning forward across Malter's table, "but your books have me ready."

"Thank you," Malter affirmed. Too fatigued to say anything further in reply, he simply smiled and placed his hand on hers while he fought the inclination to check the time. He knew the honesty of a human touch and didn't feel compelled to say anything more.

"Can you please sign it for 'Casey'," she asked. "Casey with a 'C'."

Malter put his pen to the page and the same words flowed, this time with the name Casey inserted, as he'd already done many times today and the days before and was liable to do again in a different city tomorrow. The publicist patted him on the back; a silent gloat that she'd done her job marketing this book for the families, rather than for the patients, as with his prior books.

Malter saw the appreciation in the eyes of this latest purchaser as she checked what he had written and smiled. She shuffled past to the cashier, ably supported by a gentleman, presumably her husband, probably Casey. "I hope it gives you comfort," Malter commented and smiled at his nod of acknowledgement.

"In loving memory of 'Peaches'," the next in line said. "That's what I want written, Malter."

"Yours is a freebie, detective," Malter declared before even looking up. He ignored the tap on his shoulder from the publicist; she always resented anything that wasn't a paid sale. He wrote the message he'd planned for this very opportunity, if it ever arose.

"I don't even know why I'm here," Kelshaw said gruffly. "But Piper said I might get something out of it."

"Detective, it's not often you get a guarantee in this life, but without going out on a limb, I guarantee you in particular will get something from this book," Malter declared as he slid the book across the table. "If you take the time to read it, that is."

"Well, I have time on my hands now," Kelshaw grumbled.

"I heard you'd retired," Malter said. "I hope it was on your terms and that our time together didn't interfere with your plans."

"Retired or pushed, it doesn't really matter," Kelshaw commented. "Fact is, my plans all disappeared when Peaches died. I was just hiding in my work and it was time I left."

Malter sighed and put his hand up in the air. "So was I," he accepted. "I didn't realise I was in denial, and it wasn't until Nigel's passing that I recognised how inconceivable it was that I'd neglected the families and those left behind."

Kelshaw choked on a cough. "I don't even know what the book's about."

"It's a collection of case studies," Malter explained. "Jess the lawyer, you might remember her. She was dead against it, but I was insistent."

"My experience tells me only a fool goes against their lawyer's advice, Malter," Kelshaw cautioned. "What was her problem?"

"She said I was liable to open up a can of worms, but I saw that as the real reason those stories needed to be told," Malter began. "I realised I'd been so focused on the patients, that I'd completely overlooked the need for their loved ones to get their closure."

"Quite, but I tend to agree with your lawyer."

"Well, yes, so we compromised," Malter admitted. "It turns out the issue wasn't so much about sharing stories, but the breach of confidentiality implicit in their telling. It also turns out the confidentiality is with the now deceased, so who's to say what was really a breach. Arguably a legal grey area and Jess is ready for when or if it's challenged, but so far no-one's complained."

Kelshaw baulked before picking up the book offered. "Not my cup of tea, but I'll give it a go."

"Sure," Malter said noncommittally. "I recognised how much I would have loved to have spoken to Jenny just once more, to understand her, her life and her loves, and I imagined that she would have the same regret, but of course, the way she died made that impossible. But terminally ill patients are different, and in my time with them, I get to understand what their family and friends meant to them. It needed to be shared, and it was wrong of me to have kept those loves and memories to myself."

Kelshaw said nothing in reply. He took the book and flipped it open to read the inscription Malter had written. 'Peaches loved you. Chapter 1.' He looked at Malter and smiled.

The End.

Author note

Thankyou for reading my book, 'Closure'. I've loved writing it, editing it, rewriting it, and ultimately watching the way the story has evolved from a blank page to a finished story. I sincerely hope you enjoyed it!

Regardless, I'd really appreciate you taking the time leave a review online. No obligation, but those little ratings and reviews really help authors out and maybe even help them get noticed by more readers.

Of course you could also put in nice word with your friends, too…

Thanks, again.

Garrett

Also by Garrett Addison...

The Traveller.

Enter the world of an unnamed family man struggling in his pursuit of a work/life balance. Too much travel at the whims of his tyrannical boss, known variously as Stalin and 'the Anti-Christ', has left him failing at work and at home, but after his wife prophetically warns that his next trip will be different, he is suddenly a world apart from his usual self. Confident, capable and unafraid of his manager, opportunities abound as he embraces his altered state away from home.

What begins as a quest to reclaim his career and satisfy his ego soon descends into the pursuit for revenge on his boss. With nothing but success in his wake and seemingly limitless potential at his disposal, it's only fitting when he is coerced to work with his nemesis in a remote corner of the world. It's more than just a chance to get even after years of abuse, more than the opportunity for a confrontation; a final solution to what he sees as the bane of his life is on offer. What could possibly go wrong when he's in his prime? Succeed or fail, either way this trip will be the making of him or the end of him.

Sometimes to get the measure of your life, you just need a break from being yourself... ***because nothing lasts forever.***

Also by Garrett Addison...

Minions.

Devlin Bennett's life is no longer in free-fall, but only because he's hit the bottom. What's worse, his notoriety is such that opportunities and friends are few and far between. Until a new job lands in his lap.

Benign and well-paid, the role and his new peers are unfazed with his history. It's the chance he's desperate for and his life is surely on the improve. But when he is warned anonymously to not join a list of deceased past employees, the job loses some of its lustre. Unable to walk away or ignore the warnings, he needs to understand whether he's been handed a lifeline or a death-sentence.

His concerns are shared by an ageing detective investigating the death of the latest employee. Together, they just might unravel the truth that lies amongst a newly bereaved woman, a Balkan sociopath, a battered performance artist, an elusive ex-employee and his enigmatic employer's reference to a 'greater good'. What they learn might benefit them both, and others.

Guilt is just a matter of how much you understand the bigger picture.

Printed in Dunstable, United Kingdom

91219636R00131